"I wish you wouldn't do that."

"Do what?"

"Rush around treating me like I'm helpless."

She was so close that nothing but an inch of air separated the front of her lacy blouse from his hard chest.

He stared into her face as his hand wrapped around hers. "I'm not a child."

"I know."

His hand squeezed hers. His gaze lowered to her lips. "I'm a man."

Yes. Yes, he was. A half-naked man with big, sweaty muscles and smoldering eyes.

Suddenly, she felt kind of hot and light-headed.

Probably from all the testosterone she was inhaling.

By Rachel Gibson

RACHEL GIBSON

Nothing But Trouble

AVON

An Imprint of HarperCollins*Publishers*

AVON BOOKS
An Imprint of HarperCollins*Publishers*
10 East 53rd Street
New York, New York 10022-5299

Copyright © 2010 by Rachel Gibson
Excerpts from Untitled, *True Confessions, Not Another Bad Date, Tangled Up In You, True Love and Other Disasters* copyright © 2011, 2001, 2008, 2007, 2009 by Rachel Gibson
ISBN-13: 978-1-61664-419-2

Chapter One

Just because a man was lucky to be alive, didn't mean he had to be happy about it.

"Last night, your hockey team won the Stanley Cup without you, how do you feel about that?"

Former NHL superstar and all-around badass Mark Bressler looked beyond the bank of microphones and wall of cameras to the dozen or so reporters filling the media room inside the Key Arena. He'd played for Seattle the past eight years, been the captain for the last six years. He'd worked for most of his life to hold the Stanley Cup over his head and feel the cold silver in his hands. He'd lived and breathed hockey since he'd laced up his first pair of skates. He'd left his blood on the ice and broken more bones than he could recall. Professional hockey was all he knew. All that he was, but last night his team won without him. He'd watched from his living room as the rotten bastards skated around with *his* cup. How in the hell did everyone think he felt? "Of course I wish I could have been there with the boys, but I'm thrilled for them. One-hundred-percent thrilled."

"After your accident six months ago, the man sitting next to you was hired to fill your shoes," a reporter said, referring to the veteran hockey player, Ty Savage, who'd replaced Mark as the Chinooks' captain. "At the time, it was a controversial decision. What were your thoughts when you heard that Savage would take over?"

It was no secret that he and Savage didn't like each other. The last time Mark remembered being this close to the man, he'd faced off with him during the regular season. He'd called Savage an over-rated prima donna asshole. Savage had called him a second-rate wannabe pussy. Just another day at the office. "I was in a coma when Savage was signed. I don't believe I had 'thoughts' about anything. At least none that I recall."

"What are your thoughts now?"

That Savage is an overrated prima donna asshole. "That management put together a winning team.

All the guys worked hard and did what they had to do to bring the cup to Seattle. Heading into the playoffs we were fifty-eight and twenty-four. I don't have to tell you that those are impressive numbers." He paused and carefully thought out his next sentence. "It goes without saying that the Chinooks were *fortunate* that Savage was available and open to the trade." He wasn't about to say he was grateful or the team was lucky.

The overrated prima donna asshole next to him laughed, and Mark almost liked the guy. Almost.

The reporters turned their attention to Ty. As they asked about Savage's sudden announcement to retire the night before and his plans for the future, Mark looked down at his hand on the table before him. He'd removed the splint for the press conference, but his right middle finger was as stiff as the stainless-steel rods and pins fusing it into a permanent fuck-you.

Appropriate, that.

The reporters asked questions of the other Chinooks seated at the long press table before the questions turned back to Mark. "Bressler, are you planning a comeback?" a reporter asked.

Mark glanced up and smiled as if the question didn't poke at his deepest wound. He looked into the man's face and reminded himself that Jim was an okay guy—for a reporter—and he'd always been fair. For that reason, Mark didn't hold up his right hand and show his contempt. "The docs tell me no." Although he didn't need doctors to confirm what he'd known the moment he'd opened his eyes in the ICU. The accident that had broken half the bones in his body had shattered his life. A comeback was out of the question. Even if he'd been twenty-eight instead of thirty-eight.

General manager Darby Hogue stepped forward. "There will always be a place in the Chinooks' organization for Mark."

As what? He couldn't even drive the Zamboni. Not that it mattered. If Mark couldn't play hockey, he didn't want to be anywhere near the ice.

The questions turned to last night's game, and he settled back in his chair. He wrapped his good hand around the top of the cane resting against his thigh and brushed the smooth walnut handle with his thumb. On a good day, Mark hated press conferences. This wasn't a good day but he was here, in the belly of the Key Arena, because he didn't want to look like a poor sport. Like a jerk who couldn't handle seeing his team win the most coveted prize in hockey without him. Too, the owner of the team, Faith Duffy, had called him that morning and asked him to come. It was hard to say no to the woman who still paid the bills.

For the next half hour, Mark answered questions and even managed to chuckle at a few lame jokes. He waited until the last reporter filed out of the room before he tightened his grasp around his cane and pushed himself to his feet. Savage moved a chair out of his way, and Mark muttered his thanks. He even managed to sound sincere as he put one foot in front of the other and headed across the room. He picked up his usual methodical pace and made it as far as the door before the first twinge settled in his right hip. He hadn't taken any medication that morning. He hadn't wanted anything to dull his senses; as a result there was nothing in his system to take the edge off the pain.

His teammates slapped him on the back and told him that it was great to see him. They might have meant it. He didn't care. He had to get out of there before he stumbled. Or worse, fell on his ass.

"It's good to see you." Forward Daniel Holstrom caught up with him in the hall.

His thigh started to cramp and sweat broke out on his forehead. "You too." He'd spent the past six years on the front line with Daniel. He'd initiated Daniel his rookie season. The last thing he wanted was to collapse in front of the Stromster or anyone else.

"Some of us are headed to Floyd's. Join us."

"Another time."

"We'll probably go out tonight. I'll call you."

Of course they were going out. They'd won the cup the night before. "I have plans," he lied. "But I'll meet up with you soon."

Daniel stopped. "I'm going to hold you to that," he called after Mark.

Mark nodded and took a deep breath. God, just let him get to the car before his body gave out.

He was beginning to think God was actually listening until a short woman with dark hair caught up with him at the exit.

"Mr. Bressler," she began, keeping pace with him. "I'm Bo from the PR department."

His senses might be dulled by the pain, but he knew who she was. The guys on the team called her the Mini Pit Bull, Mini Pit for short, and for good reason.

"I'd like to speak with you. Do you have a few moments?"

"No." He kept walking. One foot in front of the other. With his bad hand, he reached out for the door. Bo pushed it open for him, and he could have kissed Mini Pit. Instead he mumbled a thanks.

"Human resources is sending a new home care worker to your house. She's stopping by today."

What did a home health care worker have to do with PR?

"I think you'll like this one," Bo continued as she followed him outside.

A June breeze cooled the sweat on Mark's brow, but the fresh air did nothing to relieve the pounding in his head and the aches in his body. A black Lincoln waited for him at the curb, and his pace slowed.

"I personally recommended her."

The driver got out and opened the back passenger door. Mark eased himself inside and clenched his jaw against the pain knotting his leg.

"If you could give her a chance, I'd appreciate it," Bo called out as the driver shut the door and returned to the front of the car.

Mark reached into his pants pocket and pulled out a bottle of painkillers. He popped the top, dumped six into his mouth, and chewed. Like a shot of Jose Cuervo, Vicodin straight up was an acquired taste.

Bo yelled something as the car pulled away from the curb and headed for the 520. He didn't know why human resources kept sending home health care workers to his door. He knew it had something to do with the organization's aftercare program, but

Mark didn't need anyone to take care of him. He hated being dependent on anyone. Hell, he hated being dependent on the car service that hauled him around.

He leaned his head back and took a steady breath. He'd fired the first three health care workers within moments of their arrival. He'd told them to get the hell out of his house and had slammed the door on their behinds. After that, the Chinooks' organization had let him know that the nurses worked for them. They paid the nurses' salaries as well as his medical expenses not covered by insurance. Which were enormous. In short, he couldn't fire anyone. But of course that didn't mean that he couldn't help them to quit. The last two health care workers the organization had sent over had stayed less than an hour. He bet he could get this next one out of his house in half that time.

His eyes drifted closed and he dozed the twenty minutes to Medina. In his dream, images flashed across his weary mind. Images of him playing hockey, the cool air hitting his cheeks and whipping the ends of his jersey. He could smell the ice. Taste the adrenaline on his tongue; he was once again the man he'd been before the accident. Whole.

The Lincoln smoothly merging into the exit lane roused him, and, as always, he woke in pain and disappointment. His eyes opened and he gazed out the window at tree-lined streets that reeked of money and pretension. He was almost home. Home to an empty house and a life he didn't recognize, and hated.

Teams of landscapers mowed and edged immaculate lawns in the small Seattle suburb. Some of the wealthiest people in the world lived in Medina, but wealth alone did not open doors and guarantee entrée into the exclusive community. Much to his former wife's dismay. Christine had wanted so desperately to belong to the exclusive group of women who lunched at the country club in their St. John and Chanel suits. The older women with their perfect hair, and the younger wives of Microsoft millionaires who reveled and basked in their snobbery. No matter how much of his money Chrissy donated to their causes, they never let her forget that she'd been born to working-class parents from Kent. Even that might have been overlooked if her husband had made his millions from business and finance, but Mark was an athlete. And not an athlete of an acceptable sport like water polo. He played hockey.

He might as well have been a drug dealer, as far as the people in Medina were concerned. Personally, he'd never cared what people thought of him. Still didn't, but it had driven Chrissy crazy. She'd been so consumed with money and so sure that money could buy her anything, and when it hadn't bought her the one thing she desperately wanted, she'd blamed him. Sure, there were some things he'd done wrong in his marriage or could have done better, but he wasn't going to take the blame for not getting invited to neighborhood cocktail parties or for getting snubbed at the county club.

On his fifth wedding anniversary, he'd come home after five days on the road to find his wife gone. She'd taken all her things but had thought enough to leave behind their wedding album, waiting for him on the granite island in the middle of the kitchen. She'd left it open to a picture of the two of them, Chrissy smiling, looking happy and gorgeous in her Vera Wang gown. Him in his Armani tux. The butcher knife stuck through his head in the album had kind of ruined the picture of wedded bliss. At least it had for him.

Call him a romantic.

He still wasn't sure what she'd been so angry about. It wasn't as if he'd ever been home enough to really piss her off. She was the one who'd left him because he and his money hadn't been enough for her. She'd wanted more, and she'd found it down the street with a sugar daddy nearly twice her age. The ink on their divorce papers had barely dried when she'd moved a few streets away, where she was currently living on the lakefront not far from Bill Gates. But even with the pricier address and the acceptable husband, Mark didn't imagine the girls at the country club were any nicer to her now than they'd ever been. More polite, yes. Nicer, no. Not that he thought Chrissy would mind all that much. As long as they air-kissed her cheek and complimented her designer clothes, she'd be happy.

The divorce had been finalized a year ago, and Mark had put "get the hell out of Medina" on his to-do list. Right after winning the Stanley Cup. Mark was not a multitasker. He liked to do one thing at a time and do it right. Finding a new home was still number two on the list, but these days it took second place after walking ten feet without pain.

The Lincoln pulled into his circular driveway and stopped behind a beat-up CR-V with California plates. The health care worker, Mark presumed. He wrapped his hand around his cane and looked out the window at the woman sitting on his front steps. She wore big sunglasses and a bright orange jacket.

The driver came around to the back of the passenger door and opened it. "Can I help you out, Mr. Bressler?"

"I'm fine." He rose from the car, and his hip cramped and the muscles burned. "Thanks." He tipped the driver and turned his attention to the brick sidewalk leading to his porch and the double mahogany doors. His progress was slow and steady, the Vicodin finally kicking in to take the edge off the pain. The girl in the orange jacket stood and watched him approach from behind her big sunglasses. Beneath the orange jacket, she wore a dress of every imaginable color, but the color nightmare didn't stop with her clothing. The top of her hair was blond, with an unnatural shade of reddish-pink beneath. She looked to be in her late twenties or early thirties and was younger than the other workers had been. Prettier too, despite the hair. The top of her head barely reached his shoulder, and she was kind of skinny.

"Hello, Mr. Bressler," she said as he moved up the steps past her. She held out her hand. "I'm Chelsea Ross. I'm your new home care worker."

The woman's jacket did not improve on closer inspection. It was leather and looked like she'd chewed it herself. He ignored her hand and dug around in his pocket for his keys. "I don't need a home health care worker."

"I heard you're trouble." She pushed her glasses to the top of her head and laughed. "You aren't really going to give me a hard time, are you?"

He stuck the key into the lock, then looked over

his shoulder into her bright blue eyes. He didn't know much about women's fashion, but even he knew that no one should wear that many bright colors together. It was like staring at the sun too long, and he feared getting a blind spot. "Just trying to save you time."

"I appreciate it." She followed him into the house and shut the door behind them. "Actually, my job doesn't officially start until tomorrow. I just wanted to come today and introduce myself. You know, just say hey."

He tossed his keys on the entry table. They skidded across the top and stopped next to a crystal vase that hadn't had a passing acquaintance with real flowers in years. "Fine. Now you can leave," he said, and continued across the marble floor, past the spiral staircase to the kitchen. He was starting to feel kind of queasy from all that pain medication he'd downed on an empty stomach.

"This is a beautiful house. I've worked in some really nice places, so I know what I'm talking about." She followed behind him as if she was in no hurry to get the hell out. "Hockey was good to you."

"It paid the bills."

"Do you live here alone?"

"I had a dog." *And a wife.*

"What happened?"

"It died," he answered, and got a weird feeling that he might have met her before, but he was fairly sure he'd remember that hair. Although even if her hair was different, he doubted he'd hooked up with her. She wasn't his type.

"Have you eaten lunch?"

He moved across the marble floor to the stainless-steel refrigerator. He opened it up and pulled out a bottle of water. "No." Short and perky had never been his type. "Have I met you before?"

"Do you watch *The Bold and the Beautiful*?"

"The what?"

She laughed. "If you're hungry, I could make you a sandwich."

"No."

"Even though I don't officially start until tomorrow, I could manage soup."

"I said no." He tilted the water to his lips and looked at her over the end of the clear plastic. The bottom of her hair really was a weird shade. Not quite red and not quite pink, and he had to wonder if she'd dyed the carpet to match the curtains. A few years ago, a Chinooks' fan had dyed her pubes blue and green to show her support. Mark hadn't seen the woman up close and personal, but he had seen the photos.

"Well, you just turned down a once-in-a-lifetime

offer. I never cook for my employer. It sets a bad precedent, and to be totally honest, I suck in the kitchen," she said through a big grin, which might have been cute if it wasn't so annoying.

God, he hated cheerful people. Time to piss her off and get her to leave. "You don't sound Russian."

"I'm not."

He lowered the bottle as he lowered his gaze to her orange leather jacket. "So why are you dressed like you're just off the boat?"

She glanced down at her dress and pointed out, "It's my Pucci."

Mark was pretty sure she hadn't said "pussy," but it had sure sounded like it. "I'm going to go blind looking at you."

She glanced up and the corners of her blue eyes narrowed. He couldn't tell if she was about to laugh or yell. "That's not very nice."

"I'm not very nice."

"Not very politically correct either."

"Now there's something that keeps me awake at night." He took another drink. He was tired and hungry and wanted to sit down before he fell down. Maybe nod off during a court TV show. In fact, he was missing *Judge Joe Brown*. He pointed toward the front of the house. "The door's that way. Don't let it hit your ass on your way out."

She laughed again as if she was a few bricks short. "I like you. I think we're going to get along great."

She was more than a *few* bricks short. "Are you . . ." He shook his head as if he was searching for the right word. "What is the politically correct term for 'retarded'?"

"I think the words you're fishing for are 'mentally disabled.' And no. I'm not mentally disabled."

He pointed the bottle at her jacket. "You sure?"

"Reasonably." She shrugged and pushed away from the counter. "Although there was that time in college when I fell doing a keg stand. Knocked myself right out. I might have lost a few brain cells that night."

"Without question."

She reached into the pocket of her ugly jacket and pulled out a set of keys with a little heart fob. "I'll be here tomorrow at nine."

"I'll be asleep."

"Oh, that's okay," she said, all cheery. "I'll ring the doorbell until you wake up."

"I have a shotgun loaded with buckshot," he lied.

Her laughter followed her out of the room. "I look forward to seeing you again, Mr. Bressler."

If she wasn't "mentally disabled," she was nuttier than squirrel shit. Or worse, one of those perpetually cheerful women.

* * *

What a serious asshole. Chelsea shrugged out of her leather jacket and opened the door to her Honda CR-V. A bead of sweat slid between her cleavage and wet the underwire of her bra as she tossed the jacket into the back and slid into her car. She shut the door and dug inside the hobo bag sitting on the passenger seat. She grabbed her cell phone, punched the seven numbers, and got sent straight to voice mail. "Thanks a lot, Bo." She spoke into the phone as she pushed the key into the ignition. "When you said this guy could be difficult, you might have mentioned that he's a straight-up tool!" She shoved the phone between her ear and shoulder, started the car with one hand, and rolled down the window with the other. "A little more forewarning might have been nice. He called me retarded and insulted my Pucci!" She flipped the phone shut and tossed it on the passenger seat. She'd saved for two months to buy her Pucci dress. What did he know about fashion? He was a hockey player.

She pulled the car out onto the street and drove past the homes of the rich and the snobby. A strong breeze blew through the window, and Chelsea pulled her dress away from her chest and let the cool air dry her skin. She was probably going to get a boob rash and it was all Mark Bressler's fault. No, he hadn't made her wear a leather jacket on a hot June day, but she felt like blaming him anyway. He was a jock. That was reason enough.

God, she hated people like Mark Bressler. Rude people who thought they were better than everybody else. For the past ten years, she'd been surrounded by people like him. She'd booked their appointments, walked their dogs, and planned their events. She'd been the personal assistant to movie stars and moguls. Celebrities from A to D list until she'd finally had enough.

"Enough" had come last week in the guesthouse of a B-list actor who'd suddenly hit it big with a leading role in an HBO series. She'd worked for him for five months, lived in the guesthouse, made sure he was ready for his appointments, and ran his errands. Everything had been fine until the night he'd come into the guesthouse and told her to get on her knees and give him oral sex, or get another job.

Ten years of pent-up anger and impotence had curled her hand into a fist. Ten years of crappy jobs and disappointment, of working her ass off. Ten years of watching other pretentious, talentless, *nasty* people succeed, while she waited for *her* big break. Ten years of sleazy sexual propositions and thankless jobs swung her arm back, and she'd punched him in the eye. Then she'd packed up the CR-V and called her second-rate agent to tell her she'd had enough. She'd moved a thousand miles from Hollywood, away from the egos and arrogance, only to land smack-dab employed by one of the biggest a-holes on the planet. Although technically, she supposed, Mark Bressler wasn't her employer. The Seattle Chinooks paid her salary—and the big fat bonus.

"Three months," she muttered. If she stuck it out for three months, the Chinooks' organization had promised a ten-thousand-dollar bonus. After meeting Mr. Bressler, she knew the bonus for what it was.

A bribe.

She could do it. She was an actress. She'd put up with worse for far less. She pulled onto the 520 and headed to Bellevue and her sister's condo. She wanted that ten grand. Not for any noble reasons like helping the sick or donating to a local church or food bank. She wasn't going to please her family and finally get that degree in nursing, drafting, or graphic design. She wasn't going to put a down payment on a home or a newer car. She wasn't going to do any of those things that might secure a future or improve her mind.

At the end of three months, she was going to use that ten grand to improve *herself*. Until a few days ago, she hadn't had a plan of action. Now she did, and she had it all figured out. She knew what to do and how to go about it, and nothing and no one was going to stand in her way. Not the risk involved to her health or the disapproval of her family was going to keep her from her goal.

Especially not one cranky, oversized, overbearing hockey player with a mean streak and a huge chip on his equally huge shoulder.

Chapter Two

"This is great, Chels. Thanks."

Chelsea glanced up from her plate of spaghetti and looked across the table at her sister Bo. The meal wasn't great. It was Prego. "I'm a gourmet cooker."

"It's better than Mom's."

The sisters shuddered. "She never drains the grease off anything."

"Flavors the sauce," Bo quoted their mother as she lifted her merlot. "Cheers."

"What are we toasting?" Chelsea reached for her glass. "My skills at opening a jar?"

"That and your new job."

Except for the hair color, looking at Bo was like looking into a mirror. Same blue eyes, small nose, and full mouth. Same small bones and big boobs. It was as if the Olsen twins had gone out and bought sets of matching stripper boobs. Only the reality of being built like their mother wasn't quite so glamorous. The reality was that they'd been born to suffer backaches and shoulder pain. By forty, they were doomed to start saggin' and draggin'.

Bo touched her glass to Chelsea's. "Here's to lasting longer than the other home care workers."

Chelsea was the older of the two, by five minutes, but Bo was the more mature. Or so everyone always pointed out. "I'll last longer." She wanted that ten grand, but she didn't want to tell her sister what she planned to do with the money. The last time she'd brought up the subject of breast reduction, the whole family had flipped out. They'd accused her of being impulsive, and while that was occasionally true, she'd been thinking about getting a reduction for years. "He may have questioned my intelligence and disrespected my Pucci, but I've worked for a lot of jerks and I know how to win him over with my charming personality. I'll just smile and kill him with kindness. I'm an actress. No sweat." She took a drink, then set the glass on the table. "Although he must have a few brain cells out of whack, because who doesn't love Pucci?"

Bo raised her hand.

"You don't count." Chelsea twirled spaghetti on the tines of her fork. "You're afraid of color, and Mark Bressler doesn't count because he's too big a jerk to appreciate the artistry of designer clothes." Bo's apartment was a lot like Bo. Stark and minimalist. There were a few ink sketches above the black-and-white-striped sofa. She had a few dusty silk ferns, but no real splashes of color anywhere.

"He's a hockey player." Bo shrugged and took a bite. "Elite hockey players are arrogant and rude." After she chewed, she added, "Although whenever I worked with Mark, he wasn't bad. At least not like some of them can be. Before his accident, we were doing a big media push using him and some of the other players, and he was relatively nice. Sure we locked horns, but he eventually listened to reason. He didn't balk at taking his shirt off." She smiled and held up one hand. "The guy had an eight-pack. I. Swear. To. God."

Chelsea thought of the man walking slowly up the sidewalk toward her, leaning on his cane, looking anything but weak. Everything about him radiated strength and darkness. Eyes, hair, energy. A dangerous archetype. Like Hugh Jackman in *X-Men*, minus the claws, facial hair, and superpowers. *Not* to be confused with the Hugh Jackman who'd hosted the

Oscars and sang and danced. She just could not picture Mark Bressler busting out in song. "How bad was his accident?"

"No one in aftercare told you?"

"Some." Chelsea shrugged and took a bite of garlic bread. "They gave me a folder with his schedule and some info in it."

"And you didn't read it?"

"Glanced at it."

Bo's eyes rounded. "Chelsea!"

"What? I saw that he has a physical therapist come to the house twice a week, and I was going to read the rest tomorrow. I never read everything till the night before. It keeps it fresh in my head."

"That was always your excuse in high school. It was a wonder you even graduated."

She pointed her bread at her sister. "What happened to Bressler?"

"Last January he hit some black ice on the 520 bridge. His Hummer rolled three times." Bo took a drink of her wine. "It was horrible. The big SUV looked like it had been compacted. No one thought he was going to live."

"Is he . . ." Chelsea tapped her finger to her temple. ". . . a few fries short of a Happy Meal?" That might explain his rude behavior and dislike of her Pucci.

"I'm not sure how he is mentally."

"I knew a makeup artist who worked on the set of *The Young and the Restless*. After she took a header off a balcony, she was never the same. It was like she didn't have a filter anymore and everything that ran through her head spilled out of her mouth. She told one of the directors that he had shit for brains." Chelsea finished her bread and added, "It was pretty much true, but she got fired anyway."

"I thought you were an extra on *The Bold and the Beautiful*."

"That was last month. I worked on *The Young and the Restless* about three years ago." She shrugged. "I played a bar hag and I wore a tank top and a pair of Daisy Dukes. My line was, 'Wanna buy a girl a drink?'" She'd hoped that that one brilliantly delivered sentence would evolve into a permanent role, but of course it hadn't happened.

"I have *Slasher Camp*," Bo said through a smile. "We can fast-forward to your scene and watch it over and over."

Chelsea laughed. She'd been the first slut to get axed, literally, in the B-movie. "I think that was my best scream ever."

"I thought your best scream was in *Killer Valentine*."

"That was a good one too." Again, she'd been the first slut to get killed off. That time with a dagger in her heart.

"Mom hates the horror movies."

Chelsea reached for her wine and looked across at the good, successful twin. "Mom hates most things about me."

"No, she doesn't. She hates seeing you seminude and covered in blood. She just worries about you."

This was yet another conversation that Chelsea didn't want to have. Mostly because it always ended the same. Bo feeling bad because everyone thought Chelsea was a fuckup. Impulsive and rash, but in a family full of aggressive overachievers, someone had to be the bottom bear on the totem pole. "Tell me more about Bressler," she said, purposely changing the subject.

Bo stood and grabbed her empty plate and glass. "He's divorced."

Chelsea probably could have guessed that one. She stood and drained her wine. "Kids?"

"No."

She reached for her plate and followed her sister into the kitchen. "He was the captain. Right?"

"For about the past six years." Bo set her dishes in the sink and looked over her shoulder at Chelsea. "He had some of the highest stats in the NHL, and if he'd played in the winning game last night, he would have won MVP." She turned on the water and rinsed her plate. "The day after the accident, the whole organization was in turmoil. Absolute chaos. Everyone was worried about Mark, but they were also worried about the team and what the loss of the captain meant to the Chinooks' chances at winning the cup. The late Mr. Duffy moved quickly and signed Ty Savage. Everyone was shocked at how well it all worked out. Savage stepped in and did an awesome job of filling Mark's shoes. Or skates, rather. Mark didn't have to worry about anything but getting better."

Chelsea had been at the winning game the night before with Bo and Jules Garcia, Mrs. Duffy's assistant and a dead ringer for Mario Lopez. The Mario when he guest-starred on *Nip/Tuck*. Not the Mario of *Saved by the Bell*.

Chelsea wasn't much of a hockey fan, but she had to admit that she'd gotten caught up in the fever and had watched from the edge of her seat. The three of them had stayed during the cup presentation ceremony and watched all the players skate around with it held over their heads like conquering heroes. "Was Bressler at the arena last night?" She opened the dishwasher and loaded it as her sister rinsed.

Bo shook her head. "We sent a car for him, but he

never showed. I think he has good nights and bad nights. He must have been having a bad night."

Chelsea pulled out the top rack and loaded glasses. "It must be a huge load off his mind to know that his accident didn't cost his team the cup."

"I would imagine. He almost died and had bigger things to think about." Bo handed her a plate.

"And I imagine that waking up after an accident like that, a person must feel so lucky to be alive. I knew a stunt double who fell from a burning building and hit the air bag wrong. After he woke from his coma, he went back to school and is now an injury lawyer. It changed his whole life and put it right into perspective."

"Yep. Sometimes something unforeseen happens and can change your life." Bo turned off the water and dried her hands. "What are you going to do with the ten-thousand bonus?"

Chelsea shut the dishwasher and turned her face away. If there was one person on the planet who could read her, even when she didn't want to be read, it was her twin. "I haven't decided."

"What about school?"

"Maybe." She walked into the living room and ran her finger over a fake fern that needed dusting.

"What about investing? I could hook you up with my broker."

She could lie, but her sister would know. Evasion was her best option. "I have a while. I'll think about it."

"You can't just blow it on designer clothes."

"I like blowing money on clothes." When she had the money to blow. "Especially designer clothes."

"Well, I'm sorry to be the one to tell you this, but Mark Bressler is right. You're a collision of discordant color."

Chelsea turned and looked at her sister standing in the doorway to the kitchen, dressed in black and white with her short dark hair pulled back in a stubby ponytail. She almost smiled at her sister's description of her.

"The bonus you get from the aftercare program won't go far if you spend it on clothes. If you sign up for classes now, you can go to school this fall."

They hadn't talked about Chelsea leaving, but now was as good a time as any. "I won't be here this fall. I'm going back to L.A." She expected her sister to protest, to try and convince her to stay so they could live close to each other. She didn't expect her sister's next words to feel like a punch in the chest.

"You're thirty and it's time to be responsible, Chelsea. You tried the whole actress thing. You need to set more realistic goals."

She'd known the rest of the family felt that pursuing her acting dream was silly. She knew that they rolled their eyes and said she was unrealistic, but she hadn't known Bo felt that way too. The punch turned to a little pinch in a corner of her heart. "If I suddenly get responsible, what would everyone talk about when I leave the room?" The rest of the family could say what they wanted about Chelsea and it never hurt near as badly as when Bo said it.

Bo sighed. "You can't act in slasher movies for the rest of your life. And do you really want to be someone's assistant forever?"

She pushed her hair behind her ears. No, she didn't want to be someone's assistant forever, and she knew better than anyone that she couldn't be in slasher movies for the rest of her life. She was getting too old, but she had a plan. When she'd run from L.A., she really hadn't had much of a plan. Other than getting out of town before she killed someone. Thanks to the Chinooks' organization, she had one now.

"Don't get all hurt and sad. All I'm saying is that maybe it's time to grow up."

"Why? You're grown up enough for both of us," she said, and managed to keep the hurt she felt inside from leaking into her voice.

"I've had to be. You were always the fun twin. The one that everyone wanted to be around." Bo folded her arms beneath her breasts. "The one who threw parties when Mom and Dad went out of town, and I was the one who ran around with coasters so your friends' beer cans wouldn't leave rings on Mom's coffee table. I'm the one who cleaned up afterward so you wouldn't get into trouble."

The pinch moved from her heart to the backs of her eyes. "You ran around with coasters because you always wanted everyone to think you were the good twin. The smart twin. The responsible twin." She pointed across the room at her sister. "And you never had to clean up after me."

"I'm still cleaning up after you."

"No. You're not."

"Then why are you here?"

"Because I needed my sister." Her hand fell to her stomach as if she'd just been punched, but she didn't cry. She was a better actress than she'd ever been given credit for. "I was going to move out of your apartment after I got my first paycheck, but I don't have to wait. I have enough money for first month's rent plus a deposit." She looked into her sister's blue eyes. They were so different, yet so alike in more ways than just their looks, and they knew exactly what to say to hurt each other. "I know the rest of the family thinks I'm a fuckup, but I never knew you felt that way too."

Bo dropped her arms. "Now you do."

"Yeah." Chelsea turned toward the spare bedroom. "Now I do." She walked down the hall before her emotions over took her ability to control them. She quietly shut the door behind her and sat on the edge of the bed. Bo was the other half of her soul. The one person in the world who could truly hurt her.

Chelsea stretched out on the bed and stared at the wall. The only time she ever felt like a loser was around her own family. Her mother was a successful promoter in Vegas. Before his death three years ago, her father had been a cardiologist. Her brother was a lawyer in Maryland. Her older sister lived in Florida, and was a CPA who had a handful of clients and raked in millions. Bo worked in the promotional department for a Stanley Cup–winning hockey team. And Chelsea . . . was an out-of-work actress.

The only time she was unhappy about her life was when she was around her family. She'd love to please her family by being a household name and having the cachet that brought with it. She'd love to land major movie and TV roles. She'd kill to have more in her portfolio than slasher films, bit parts on TV, and television commercials. She certainly wished her résumé wasn't filled up with so much background work that it was kind of embarrassing. But that didn't mean she was an unhappy person.

She wasn't. Sure, she'd gotten fed up with her life in Hollywood. She'd needed a break. Maybe her decision to leave was a little rash, but she was going to go back, and when she did, she'd be better than ever. Her body would be more in proportion. No more backaches. No more shoulder pain. No more slutty bimbo roles.

The door behind her opened, and she felt the weight of her sister on the bed. "I don't want you to move out."

Chelsea wiped the tears from her face. "I think it would be best."

"No." Bo spooned her like they were kids again and wrapped an arm around her shoulder. "I like having you here, and I want you to stay as long as you want. I'm sorry I said those things. I don't think you're a fuckup. I think you're impulsive and I worry so much about you."

Chelsea turned and looked into her sister's blue eyes. "I know, but you shouldn't. I've been taking care of myself for a long time. It might not be in the profession that you or Mom likes, but I've never starved." Except for the few weeks in the beginning when she'd lived in her car, but her family didn't know that.

"I'm sorry I got mad and said those things to you. I just want you to stay. I've missed you."

"I've missed you and I'm sorry too." Her sister was the yin to her yang. The dark to her light. One could not exist without the other. "I love you, Boo."

"Love you too, Chels. Sorry I said that about your clothes. I know what you wear is important to you." Bo gave her a little squeeze, and she could hear the smile in her sister's voice. "They're not all *that* discordant."

"Thanks. And your clothes aren't all *that* boring." Chelsea laughed. "At least we've never had to fight about clothes, like some sisters."

"True. Or boys."

Dating had always been tricky. For some reason, if either she or Bo turned a guy down, he'd ask out the other twin. But the sisters never fought over boys because they were attracted to opposite sorts of men. So it had never been a problem. "That's because you've always dated geeky mama's boys, and I've always dated smooth-talking losers. We should both start dating out of our type."

Bo held up one hand in front of Chelsea and they high-fived. "I don't want to think about you leaving. So let's not talk about it for at least three months."

"Okay."

"What are you going to wear to work your first day?"

Chelsea thought of the man who'd insulted her

intelligence and her clothes. "I have a Gaultier tunic that I wear with a belt and skinny jeans." If Mark didn't like Pucci, he was going to hate her feather-print Gaultier.

"Take it easy on the poor guy, Chels," Bo said through a big yawn. "He's only been out of the rehab hospital for a month. I don't know if his body can take the shock."

Light from the sixty-inch television screen bounced and shifted across Mark's bare chest. His right hand squeezed a stress ball as he watched highlights from last night's game. He sat on a leather sofa in his master bedroom, a black outline in the darkness. The sports coverage changed from the Stanley Cup highlights to that morning's interview inside the Key. He watched himself and wondered how he could look so normal, sound so normal. The accident that had broken his bones had ripped out his soul. He was empty inside, and into the void had leaked a black rage. It was something he couldn't get over. Had never tried to get over. Without his anger he was hollow.

With his free hand, he lifted the remote and pointed at the TV. His thumb slid across the up arrow and he skimmed past reality shows and cable reruns. He paused on a porno on Cinemax. On the screen, two women went at it like cats, cleaning each other with their tongues. They had nice tits, shaved coochies, and stripper heels. Normally, it was the sort of high-class entertainment he would have enjoyed. One of the women stuck her face between the other's legs, and Mark watched for a few moments . . . waiting.

Nothing lifted his boxer briefs and he hit the off button, plunging the room into darkness. He tossed the gel-filled ball on the couch beside him and pushed himself off the couch. He hadn't had a decent erection since before the accident, he thought as he walked across the room to his bed. It was probably the drugs. Or perhaps his dick just didn't work anymore. Surprising that it didn't bother him as much as it should.

Given his sex life before, not getting it up should freak him out. He'd always been able to get it up. Day or night, didn't matter. He'd always been ready to go. It had never taken much to get him in the mood. Now, not even hot lesbian porn interested him.

Mark shoved back the thick covers on his bed and crawled inside. He was just a shell of the man he'd been. So pathetic that he might have reached for the bottle of pills sitting on his nightstand and put an end to it all if that hadn't been even more pathetic. If that wasn't the chickenshit way out.

Mark had never taken the chickenshit way out of anything. He hated weakness, which was one of the reasons he hated having those home health care workers around, taking his pulse and checking his medication.

Within a few minutes, his Ambien kicked in and he slipped into a deep, restful sleep and dreamed the only dream he'd ever had for himself. He heard the roar of the crowd clashing with the slap of graphite sticks on ice and the *shh* of razor-sharp blades. The smells of the arena filled his nose, sweat and leather, crisp ice, and the occasional waft of hot dogs and beer. He could taste adrenaline and exhaustion in his mouth as his heart and legs pounded down the ice, puck in the curve of his stick. He could feel the cold breeze brush his cheeks, steal down the neck of his jersey, and cool the sweat on his chest. Thousands of pairs of eyes, locked on him; he felt their anticipation, could see the excitement in the blur of their faces as he skated past.

In his dreams, he was back. He was whole again. He was a man. His movements were fluid and easy and without pain. Some nights he dreamed that he played golf or threw the Frisbee for his old dog, Babe. Babe had been dead for five years, but it didn't matter. In the dream both of them were filled with life.

But in the harsh light of morning, he always woke to the crushing reality that the life he'd always known was over. Altered. Changed. And he always woke in pain, his muscles stiff and his bones aching.

Morning sun filtered through the crack in the drapery and stretched a pillar of light across the foot of Mark's king-sized bed. He opened his eyes, and the first wave of pain rolled over him. He glanced at the clock on his nightstand. It was eight-twenty-five A.M. He'd slept a good nine hours, but he didn't feel rested. His hip throbbed and the muscles in his leg tightened. He slowly raised himself, refusing to moan or groan as he moved to sit on the edge of the bed. He had to move before his muscles spasmed, but he couldn't move too fast or his muscles would knot. He reached for the bottle of Vicodin on the bedside table and downed a few. Carefully he rose and grabbed an aluminum quad cane by his bed. Most days he felt like a crippled old man, but never more so than in the mornings before he warmed up his muscles.

Steady and slow, he walked across the thick beige carpet and moved into the bathroom. The aluminum cane thumped across the smooth marble floors. For most of his adult life, he'd awakened in some degree of pain. Usually from hard hits he'd received in a game the night before or from related sports injuries.

He was used to working through it. Pain had always been a part of his adult life, but nothing on the scale he suffered now. Now he needed more than Motrin to get him through the day.

The radiant heat beneath the stone warmed his bare feet as he stood in front of the toilet and took a leak. He had an appointment with his hand doctor this morning. Normally he hated all the endless doctor's appointments. Most of his time at the clinic was spent sitting around waiting, and Mark had never been a patient man. But today he hoped to get the good news that he no longer needed to wear the splint on his hand. It might not be much, but it was progress.

He pushed hair from his eyes, then flushed the toilet. He needed to make an appointment to get his hair cut too. He'd had it cut once in the hospital, and it was bugging the hell out of him. The fact that he couldn't just jump into his car and drive to the barber ticked him off and reminded him how dependent he was on other people.

He shoved his boxer briefs down his legs, past the dark pink scar marring his left thigh and knee. Of all the things that he missed about his old life, driving was near the top of the list. He hated not being able to jump into one of his cars and take off. He'd been in one hospital or another for five months. He'd been home now for a little more than one month, and he felt trapped.

Leaving the cane by the toilet, he placed his good hand on the wall and moved to the walk-in shower. He turned on the water and waited for it to get warm before he stepped inside. After months of hospital sponge baths, he loved standing in the shower on his own two feet.

Except for the injury to his right hand and a fracture to his right tibia, most of the crushing damage had been done to the left side of his body. His ability to drive was one thing the doctors assured him he would get back. He looked forward to the day when he didn't have to rely on anyone for anything.

The hot water sprayed across his chest, and he stuck his head beneath the powerful stream. He was fairly sure he'd gotten rid of the health care worker with the two-toned hair and the Pucci.

Water slid into the crease of his smile as he remembered her scandalized gasp. The way she'd said "Pucci," he'd figured it had to be some high-priced designer. She'd said it like his former wife had said, "It's Chanel." He didn't care how much something cost. He knew ugly when he saw it.

He washed his hair and soaped up his body, then reached for the detachable showerhead and turned it to massage. He held it against his hip and left thigh and let the hot water beat the hell out of his muscles. It hurt like a son of a bitch but gave him relief from the sharpest pain. When he was finished, he dried himself and brushed his teeth. A day's growth of beard darkened his cheeks and jaw. Instead of shaving, he moved into the huge walk-in closet and dressed in a pair of blue nylon jogging pants and a plain white T-shirt. He shoved his feet into black Nike flip-flops because tying shoes was a hassle. Yesterday morning before the news conference, it had taken him forever to button his shirt and tie his shoes. Well, maybe not *forever,* but things that he used to do by rote now took thought and effort.

He placed the splint on his right hand and tightened the Velcro before he grabbed his black titanium cane from the couch where he'd been sitting last night.

The original homeowners had a servants' elevator built inside a large closet down the hall. With the aid of his cane, Mark walked out of the bedroom and past the spiral stairs he used to take two at a time. He glanced over the ornate wrought-iron and wood railing as he moved across the landing. Sunlight poured in through the heavily leaded glass in the entry, tossing murky patterns on the marble floor below. He opened the closet door and rode the small elevator down. It opened into the kitchen, and he stepped out. He poured himself a bowl of Wheaties and ate at the kitchen table because he needed something in his stomach or the medication he took would make him nauseous.

For as long as he could remember he'd eaten the Breakfast of Champions. Probably because it's what his father could afford to feed him. Sometimes he couldn't remember what he did last week, but he could recall sitting at his gran's old kitchen table, a white sugar bowl in the center of the yellow tablecloth, eating Wheaties before school. He remembered perfectly the morning in 1980 when his grandmother had set the orange box on the table and he'd stared at the Olympic hockey team on the front. His heart had stopped. His throat closed as he'd looked at Dave Silk, Neil Broten, and the guys. He'd been eight and they'd been his heroes. His grandmother had told him he could grow up and be anything he wanted. He'd believed her. There hadn't been a lot he'd believed in, but he believed his grandmother Bressler. She never lied to him. Still didn't. Not even when it would be easier. When he'd woken from his coma a month after the accident, hers was the first face he'd seen. She'd stood next to his father by the foot of his bed and she'd told him about the accident. She'd listed all his injuries for him, starting with his skull fracture and ending with the break in his big toe. What she hadn't mentioned was that he'd never play hockey again, but she hadn't had to. He'd known by the list of his injuries and the look in his father's eyes.

Of the two adults in his life, his grandmother had always been the strong one. The one to make things better, but that day in the hospital, she'd looked exhausted and worn thin. After she'd listed all his injuries, she'd told him that he could still be anything he wanted. But unlike that morning thirty years ago, he no longer believed her. He'd never play hockey again, and they both knew that was the only thing he wanted.

He rinsed his bowl as the heavy chimes of the front doorbell sounded. He hadn't called for a driver yet, and could think of only one other person who'd show up at such an early hour.

He reached for his cane and walked out of the kitchen and through the hall. Before he reached the front of the house, he could see a kaleidoscope of color through the muted glass. He balanced on his feet and pulled open the door with his good hand. The health care worker stood on his porch wearing her big sunglasses and yellow and red hair. Her piece-of-shit Honda was parked in the driveway behind her. "You're back."

She grinned. "Good morning, Mr. Bressler."

She looked like she was covered in painted feathers. Like a peacock. A peacock with large breasts. How had he missed those? Maybe the pain he'd been in. Most likely the ugly orange jacket.

"You like the shirt?"

He raised his gaze to hers. "You wore it just to irritate me."

Her grin widened. "Now why would I want to irritate you?"

Chapter Three

 Chelsea pushed her sunglasses to the top of her head and looked way up at the man standing in the entryway's natural light. His damp hair was brushed back. It curled around his ears and along the neckline of his bright white shirt. He scowled at her from beneath dark brows; the annoyance shining in his brown eyes made his feelings for her clear. He hadn't shaved, and a dark shadow covered his cheeks and strong prominent jaw. He looked big and bad and dominant. All dark and foreboding, and she might have been a little intimidated if he hadn't had the longest lashes she'd ever seen on a man. Those lashes were so out of place on his chiseled masculine face that she smiled.

"Are you going to invite me inside?" she asked.

"Are you going to go away if I don't?"

"No."

He gave her a hard look for several long seconds before he turned and walked across the stone flooring. As she'd noticed yesterday, he moved slower than men of his age. His cane was a smooth extension of his left hand. What she hadn't noticed was that he used the cane on his left side, the wrong side. She might not have noticed at all if not for the big brouhaha about Gregory House using his cane on the wrong side in the television medical drama *House*. The writers of *House* had made a mistake, but she supposed Mark Bressler used the wrong side because he wore some sort of splint made of aluminum and blue Velcro on his right hand.

"There's nothing for you to do today," he said over his shoulder. "Go home."

"I have your schedule." She closed the front door behind her, and the three-inch heels of her sandals echoed on the marble floor as she followed him into a large office filled with hockey memorabilia. "You have an appointment with your orthopedic doctor this morning at ten-thirty and an interview with *Sports Illustrated* at one o'clock at the Spitfire."

He leaned his black cane against the edge of a massive mahogany desk and turned to face her. "I'm not doing the *Sports Illustrated* interview today."

Chelsea had worked with a lot of difficult employers. It was her job to get them where they needed to be, even when they didn't want to be there. "It's been rescheduled twice."

"It can be rescheduled a third time."

"Why?"

He looked her in the eyes and said, "I need a haircut." Either he was a bad liar or he just didn't care if she knew he was lying.

She pulled her phone out of her handbag. "Do you have a preference?"

"For what? A haircut?" He shrugged and lowered himself into a big leather chair.

Chelsea dialed her sister's number, and when Bo answered she said, "I need the name of a good hair salon or barber."

"Gee, I don't know," her sister answered. "Hold on. I'll ask Jules. He's standing right here." Chelsea walked to the window and pushed aside the heavy drapery to look out. The fight she'd had with her sister the night before still bothered her. If the one person in the world she loved and trusted above all others thought she was a loser . . . was she?

Bo got back on the line with the name and number of a salon in Belltown. Chelsea hung up, then dialed. "Let's keep our fingers crossed," she said as she turned back to the room.

"You're wasting your time," Mark grumbled as he opened a drawer in the desk. "I'm not doing the interview today."

Chelsea held up one finger as the salon picked up. "John Louis Salon. This is Isis."

"Hello, Isis. My name is Chelsea Ross and I work for Mark Bressler. He has an important interview and photo shoot with *Sports Illustrated* this afternoon at one o'clock. Is there any way you can get him in for a cut and blow?"

"Cut and blow? Jesus," the grump behind the desk continued to grumble.

"I'll see what I can do," Isis assured her in a tone usually used by uppity receptionists in snooty salons.

"We'll be grateful if—" The bitch put her on hold.

"Even if I get my hair cut, I'm still not doing the interview."

Chelsea moved the phone away from her mouth. "What's your next objection?"

"I'm not dressed for it," he said, but she knew that was a lie too. She hadn't a clue why he didn't want to do the interview, but she doubted it had anything to do with the way he looked. Which, even she had to admit, was absolutely gorgeous in a casual, scruffy way that only truly good-looking men could get away with. Too bad he was such a jerk.

"Well, since it's just an interview and not a photo shoot, I don't think it matters."

"You said photo shoot."

"Yeah, I may have prevaricated."

"You lied."

Isis came back on the line, and Chelsea returned the phone to her mouth. "Yes."

"We have a two o'clock opening."

"I need to have him cut and blown and on his way out the door by twelve-forty-five."

"Well, I don't think we can help you."

"Let me talk to your manager because I'm fairly sure he or she will want to take credit for making the captain of the Chinooks' hockey team look good in a magazine that is read by millions worldwide." She looked across the room at a big poster of Mark all geared up and shooting a puck. "Or I can just as easily chose another salon if you—" She pulled the phone away from her face and stared at it. "Bitch did it again," she muttered, and moved to the framed poster. Mark didn't look all that different in the poster than he did today. Maybe a little meaner. His brown eyes a little more intense as he stared out from beneath the black helmet on his head. She studied his eyes and then glanced over her shoulder to study him. "What are you doing?" she asked as she watched him pick up the phone on his desk.

"Calling the service to send a car."

"There's no need. It's my job to get you to your appointments. I'll drive you."

"In what?"

"My car."

He pointed the phone at the front of the house. "That piece of shit in my driveway?"

She held up her finger once more as Isis came back on the line.

"We can get Mr. Bressler in at noon."

"Fabulous. What's the address?" She moved to the desk and wrote on a sticky note before flipping her phone closed and dropping it in her bag. "You don't like the Honda, fine. What wheels do you have in your garage?"

He set the phone back in the cradle. "You want to drive my vehicle?"

It wasn't unheard of. She'd driven her former employers around in their cars all the time. The more D list, the more they'd wanted to appear as if they had drivers. "Sure."

"You're fucking nuts if you think I'm going to let you drive my car. I saw the dents in your Honda."

"Minor parking lot dings," she assured him. "Isn't your car insured?"

"Of course." He leaned back in his chair and folded his arms across his wide chest.

"And wouldn't it be more convenient for you to have me chauffeur you than waiting around on a car service all the time?"

He didn't say anything, just scowled.

She looked at her watch. "It's after ten now. You don't have time to wait for a service to pick you up."

"I can be late," he said with the confidence of a man who was used to the world waiting on him.

"I'm offering you an opportunity to make your life easier, and you're being obstinate and unreasonable for no logical reason. Unless you *like* to depend on a car service."

"What's the difference between depending on a service and depending on you? Other than you're more annoying."

She held up three fingers and counted down. "I'm cute, you don't have to tip me, and I'm already here."

He stared at her for several long moments, then slowly stood and reached for his cane. "You're not that cute. If you 'ding' my car, I'll kill you."

She smiled and followed him out of the room. Her gaze landed on his wide shoulders and followed his tapered back to his waist. A wallet bulged the pocket of his dark nylon running pants. There were some men who wore sweats and looked like goofballs. Then there were men like Mark who made them look good, with his long legs and tight behind. He might have had a serious accident six months ago, but his body was still hard from a lifetime of exercise. "Don't you get a little lonely living in this big house by yourself?" she asked to fill the silence.

"No." The way he walked, his cane, and the splint on his hand contrasted with his dominant aura. A clash of strength and vulnerability that was appealing. And which he totally ruined with his rude, abrasive personality. "Until recently, I've rarely been here," he added. "For the last few years, I've been meaning to put it on the market. You interested?"

"Sure. What's your asking price?" She couldn't afford the lawn care.

"At least what I paid for it." They moved through the gigantic kitchen with its intricate stone and tile work and professional-grade appliances. She followed him past the pantry and laundry room, and above a built-in mud bench next to the back door, two sets of keys hung from hooks. One set had a Mercedes emblem, the other unmistakably the keys to a Hummer. "I'm probably going to regret this," he muttered as he grabbed the Mercedes keys with the thumb and forefinger of his bad hand.

Chelsea slid around him and opened the back door, holding it for him as he carefully stepped down. A shiny gold Mercedes S550 sedan sat in the middle of his five-car garage. The lights blinked, the locks deactivated by the key fob. One of her previous employers had driven a S550. Only older. This one was brand-spanking-new. She shut the door behind them. "Ooh. Come to Mama."

"You're going to drive careful. Right?" He turned, and she almost ran into his chest.

"Right." A hand's width separated her Gaultier from plain white cotton, and she ran her gaze up his T-shirt, over his throat and stubbly chin, to his mouth.

"I've driven this car one time," she watched him say before she looked up into his eyes staring down at her. "Three days before my accident, I drove it home from the dealership." He might be a jerk, but he smelled wonderful. Like some sort of manly soap on clean manly skin. He held up the keys, then dropped them into her waiting palm. "I'm not kidding about killing you."

He looked serious. "I haven't had a ticket in about five years," she said as she followed him around to the passenger side. "Well, maybe a parking ticket, but nonmoving violations don't count."

He reached for the front passenger door as she reached for the back. "I'm not sitting back there." The hard splint surrounding his middle finger hit against the door, and he couldn't grasp the handle with his other fingers. Chelsea pushed his hand aside and opened the door for him. "I can open my own freakin' door," he barked.

"I'm the chauffeur. Remember?" Really though, it was just easier and faster if she did it. She watched him slowly lower himself into the car, one corner of his mouth tightening as he pulled his legs inside. "Do you need help with your seat belt?"

"No." He reached for it with his left hand. "I'm not two years old. I can buckle my own seat belt. I can feed myself, tie my own shoes, and I don't need help taking a piss."

Chelsea closed the door and walked around to the side. "Ten thousand dollars. Ten thousand dollars," she whispered.

The new-car smell filled her head as she climbed inside and dumped her purse in the back. Soft beige leather caressed her back and behind. She sighed and pressed the ignition button. The motor purred like a content little kitten. "You have the premium package." She ran her hands over the leather-covered steering wheel. "Heated everything. GPS. A place to plug in your iPod. Nice."

"How do you know about my premium package?"

She ignored the innuendo. "I'm from L.A. We get heated seats and steering wheels even though it hardly ever drops below sixty degrees." She pushed the garage opener clipped to the visor, and one of the doors slid up. When she engaged the GPS system, it lit up and asked in a perky female voice, *"Hello Mark. Where to?"* She glanced at his stony profile as she requested the medical center. Then she buckled her seat belt and looked behind her as she backed the Mercedes out of the shadowy garage and into the sunlight. "Whenever I drive an expensive car out of someone's garage, I always feel like Ferris Bueller. I swear I can hear the music in my head." She lowered her voice and said as deep as possible, "Bow bow— ooohhh yeeeaah."

"Are you high?"

The garage door closed and she slid the car into drive.

"No. I don't take drugs." There'd been a time when she'd toyed with drugs. Experimenting with this and that, but she'd seen firsthand the horrible waste of addiction and she'd chosen not to go down that road. "You'll be happy to know that I passed a drug test to get this job." She eased her foot off the brake, rolled past her Honda, and proceeded down the driveway. "Apparently they're careful about whom they hire."

"Obviously." He leaned his head back and brushed

his thumb along the handle of his cane. "They sent me a nurse who'd rather play chauffeur."

"*Turn right*," the GPS instructed, and Chelsea headed for the 520. "*One mile north. 8.8 miles till destination.*"

"That's annoying," Mark grumbled as he leaned forward, and messed around with the GPS screen until the voice command option was silenced.

The Mercedes rolled along the asphalt as if it owned the road. For a few seconds, she debated whether to tell him that she wasn't a nurse. If he found out later, he might get mad. Then again, maybe if he found out later, he'd like her and it wouldn't matter. She looked at him out of the corners of her eyes, sitting over there like the Grim Reaper. Yeah, right. "Listen, Mark— May I call you Mark?"

"Mr. Bressler is good."

She returned her attention to the road. "Listen, *Mr.* Bressler, I'm not a nurse. Not technically a *health* care worker either." Since he was probably going to get mad anyway, she went for broke. "You've been such a pain in the ass—with all due respect—that no one in the Chinooks' organization bothered to fill me in on what I should do for you. I suspect that no one expects me to last more than ten minutes. I was just handed a schedule and told good luck."

For several tense moments, stunned silence filled the car. "You're not 'technically a health care worker.' Do you have any sort of medical training?"

"I know CPR and I played a nurse on TV."

"You what?"

"I played a nurse on *The Bold and the Beautiful*."

"If you're 'not technically a health care worker,' what are you?"

She glanced across the Mercedes at him. Morning sunlight penetrated the leafy pattern of the tree-lined street and poured in through the windshield. The gray shadows brushed his face and slid across his blinding white T-shirt. "I'm an actress."

His mouth parted in shock. "They sent me an actress?"

"Yeah, evidently."

"Take the 520 West," he advised, even though the navigation system was showing her the same thing.

Behind her sunglasses, she rolled her eyes and took the freeway ramp to Seattle. "I've been the personal assistant to various celebrities for more than seven years. I have a lot of experience putting up with bull crap." Arrogant whiners, the lot of them. "An assistant is better than a nurse. I do all the work, you take all the credit. If something bad happens, I get the blame. There is no down side."

"Except that I have to put up with you. Hovering around, watching me. And you don't even have the qualifications to take my pulse or wipe my ass." He opened the console between the seats and pulled out a pair of silver-rimmed aviator sunglasses.

"You seem to be a healthy guy. Do you need someone to wipe your ass?"

"You offering?"

She shook her head and passed a minivan with a my-kid's-smarter-than-your-kid bumper sticker. "No. I draw the line at any sort of personal contact with my employer." She glanced over her left shoulder and merged into the faster lane.

"You just cut off that van full of kids."

She glanced at him. "Plenty of room."

"You're driving too fast," he said through a dark scowl that might have intimidated other people. Other people who weren't used to dealing with difficult egomaniacs.

"I'm only going five miles over the speed limit. Everyone knows five miles doesn't count." She returned her attention to the road. "If you're going to be a backseat driver, I'm going to make you sit in the backseat like Miss Daisy." It was pretty much an empty threat and they both knew it. Her brain scrambled for a response if he called her on it. The key to assistant survival was to remain physically and mentally nimble and anticipate your bigheaded employer's next move.

"You must not be a very good actress if you're in Seattle babysitting me."

Her nimble brain hadn't anticipated that from him. She told herself there were ten thousand reasons why she shouldn't push him out of the car. "I'm a very good actress," she said instead. "I just haven't had a big break. Most of my roles have been bit parts or have landed on the cutting room floor." She glanced at the GPS and turned on her blinker.

"What have you acted in?"

"A lot of different things." Chelsea was used to that question. She got it a lot. "Did you see *Juno*?"

"You were in *Juno*?"

"Yeah. I was up in Canada assisting one of my B stars, who was working on a movie for Lifetime, when I got the call that the production company needed background people so I showed up." She took the I–5 South exit. "I was in the shopping mall scene. If you look past Ellen Page's big belly, you can see me talking on a cell phone."

"That's it?"

"For my part in *Juno*, yes. But I've done a lot of other films."

"Name something. Other than blink-and-you-miss-it parts."

"*Slasher Camp, Killer Valentine, Prom Night 2, He Knows It's You*, and *Motel on Lake Hell*."

Silence filled the car, and then he started to laugh. A deep rumble that came from his chest. "You're a scream queen. No shit?"

She didn't know that she could be considered a scream *queen*. More like a scream slut. Or the best friend of the scream queen. Her roles had never been big enough to be considered the queen. "I've done other things. Like walk-on parts on *The Young and the Restless* and *The Bold and the Beautiful*. And on *CSI: Miami*, I played one of a series of dead girls that kept washing up on the beach. The makeup was really interesting." She looked over her left shoulder and passed a delivery truck. "Most people assume *CSI: Miami* is filmed in Miami but it's not. It's actually filmed on Manhattan Beach and Long Beach," she continued. "I've done a *ton* of series pilots that never got picked up. Not to mention *tons* of commercials. The last commercial I did was for Hillshire Farms. I wore a cheerleader's outfit and yelled, 'Go meat.' That was about six months ago. When I was in—"

"Jesus!" he interrupted as he reached for the buttons to the radio and filled the inside of the Mercedes with "Slither." The heavy bass vibrated the floor beneath her feet, and Chelsea bit the side of her lip to keep from laughing. He no doubt meant to be rude, but Velvet Revolver was one of her favorite bands. Scott Weiland was a skinny, hot rock god, and she'd rather listen to Scott than tax her brain in a futile effort to entertain a grumpy hockey player.

Too bad Scott was such a junkie, she thought as she tapped her fingers on the steering wheel along with the heavy beat. If she were alone, she'd bust out and sing along, but *Mr.* Bressler was already annoyed with her. And while Chelsea had near perfect recall of song lyrics and movie dialogue—kind of a hidden savant talent—she couldn't carry a tune.

She glanced at the GPS and took exit 165A and merged onto James Street just as the trusty navigation system instructed. Within a few minutes, Chelsea pulled the Mercedes in front of the massive medical center.

Mark turned off the radio and pointed the handle of his cane toward the windshield. "Keep going. The clinic entrance is further down."

"I'll find the parking garage, then I'll come find you."

"I don't need you to find me," he said as the car pulled to a stop beside the curb. "I'll have one of the nurses call you when I'm ready to be picked up."

"Do you have my number?"

"No." He unbuckled his seat belt and opened the door with his good hand. "Write it on something."

Chelsea reached into the backseat and grabbed her purse. She pulled out an old business card and a pen. She wrote her new cell phone number on the back, then looked through the car at Mark. "My new number's on the back," she said as she handed it across to him.

The tips of his fingers bumped into hers as he took the card and glanced over it. He slid his legs out of the car and grabbed his cane. "Don't wreck the car," he said as he grabbed the top of the door frame and stood. He shoved the card into his back pocket and shut the door.

A taxi behind the Mercedes honked, and Chelsea eased her foot off the brake and headed toward the street. In her rearview mirror she caught a glimpse of Mark Bressler just before he entered the building. The bright morning sun shot glistening sparks off his aviators and shone in his dark hair. He paused to watch her—no doubt to make sure she didn't "wreck the car"—before he moved within the deep shadows of the building.

She turned her attention to the road and figured she had a little over an hour to kill. She was in downtown Seattle. There had to be somewhere she could go to scrub her mind free of the past hour. She needed to find her happy place.

She touched the GPS screen and turned on the voice command mode. *"Where to, Mark?"* it asked. Clearly it didn't know that it was supposed to address him as *Mr.* Bressler.

"Neiman Marcus," she said. "I need Neiman Marcus."

Chapter Four

 Mark glanced at the Neiman Marcus bags in the backseat of his car and buckled his seat belt. For her first day on the job, she sure was making herself comfortable.

"Where to, Chelsea?"

He looked at her, then at his navigation system. "What the hell?"

His "assistant" gave the GPS an address in Belltown, then looked across at him and smiled. "I didn't think you'd mind if I programmed my name into the voice recognition. It kept calling me Mark, which was just confusing because I am clearly not you."

"Turn right. 3.6 miles till destination."

He leaned forward, brought up the menu screen, and turned off the sound. "Confusing for who?"

"The GPS."

"The GPS doesn't *get* confused." He leaned back in his seat and closed his eyes. He'd been right about her. She was nuttier than squirrel shit, and she was driving his ninety-thousand-dollar car.

"How was your appointment?" she asked, all cheery.

"Great." Mark opened his eyes and looked out the passenger window at St. James Cathedral. But the appointment hadn't been great. He hadn't received the news he'd been wanting to hear. The doctor had seemed pleased, but the tendons weren't healing as fast as Mark hoped and he had to wear the splint for at least another month. Which meant he couldn't transfer his cane to his right side for better balance. It also meant he had to take the splint off to button his shirt or pants, take a shower, or eat a meal. Although he'd always shot left, trying to sign his name left-handed was like writing with a pen stuck in his toes.

A dull ache radiated from deep in the marrow of his femur and spread to his hip. At the moment, it wasn't bad. Nothing he couldn't handle, but in a few hours it was likely to get worse. He hadn't brought any medication with him because he didn't like to be doped up in public. He didn't want anyone to think he couldn't handle a little pain. He was Mark

Bressler. He'd played hockey with a fractured ankle and a broken thumb. He'd played through concussions and torn and bruised muscles. He could handle the pain. If he was lucky, it wouldn't get real bad until he got back home, where he could park himself in front of his big TV and knock back a bottle of his favorite medication.

The car turned on Madison, and Mark glanced across at his assistant. Despite her big sunglasses, two-tone hair, and hideous shirt, she was cute. Like a kitten was cute, but Mark didn't like cats. Cats were sneaky. One second a cat looked all soft and harmless. All big blue eyes and innocence. One second you were just looking at it thinking, *Huh, that's kind of a cute kitten,* then it sank its teeth into your hand and ran away. A sort of stealth blitz that left a guy stunned and wondering what the hell just happened.

Behind the mirror lenses of his glasses, he lowered his gaze down the side of her neck and shoulder to her breasts. She sure wasn't built like a little kitty cat, more like a porn star. She'd said she was an actress. All porn stars thought they were actresses too. He wondered how much she'd paid for her boobs.

He closed his eyes and groaned. What had his life come to? Looking at a nice pair of tits and wondering how much she paid for them? Who gave a shit!

In another life, *his* other life, he'd be thinking about how he was going to get face-deep in her cleavage. His only thought about kittens would begin and end with how he was going to get her little kitty cat naked and riding his lap.

For most of his life, Mark had been good at two things: hockey and sex. He'd only set out to be good at shooting pucks, but a guy couldn't exactly live his life hip-deep in rink bunnies and not get to know his way around a woman's body. Now he couldn't do one and didn't have any interest in the other. He'd never been a guy whose dick defined his life, but sex sure had been a big part of his life. Except for when he'd been married. Christine had used sex as a reward. When she got what she wanted, he got laid.

Hell, he'd always thought he should be rewarded because he'd been faithful, which, given the amount of time he'd spent on the road with women throwing themselves at him, had been damn tough.

"This appointment shouldn't take more than an hour," his assistant said as she turned onto First Avenue and headed north. "I should have you at the Spitfire and your interview with *Sports Illustrated* right on time."

He couldn't recall ever agreeing to the interview in the first place, but he must have. When he'd talked to his sports agent about it, he must have been high on morphine or he never would have agreed to be interviewed when he wasn't one hundred percent. Normally his agent, Ron Dorcey, wouldn't have pushed it either, but with Mark's name fading from the sports pages, and endorsement deals drying up faster than a puddle of water in the Mojave, Ron had arranged one of the last interviews likely to come Mark's way.

He would have much preferred the interview take place next month or even next week when his head was a little clearer. When he'd had a chance to think about what he wanted to say in what would likely be one of the last articles written about him. He wasn't prepared, and he wasn't quite sure how he'd managed to get himself interviewed *today*. In person.

Wait—he did know. Somehow he'd let a little bit of a woman bully him into doing it. He didn't care that getting the interview over and done was easiest in the long run, not to mention the right thing to do. He'd let her push him around like he didn't outweigh her by a good hundred pounds. Now she was driving his car like her name was on the pink slip.

Earlier, when she'd offered herself as his assistant instead of a health care worker, for one brief moment he'd thought, *Why the hell not?* No more waiting around for a car service might make him feel less dependent. But in reality he felt more dependent and less capable of taking care of himself. Health care workers wanted to manage his pain. Chelsea Ross clearly wanted to manage his life. He didn't need her and he didn't want her around.

Mark brushed his thumb along the cool metal cane. Back to the original plan. No more Mr. Nice Guy. By the time he returned home that afternoon, he'd have her ready to quit. The thought of her peeling out of his driveway brought a genuine smile to his face.

"I got a text from the *Sports Illustrated* reporter a few minutes ago and she's set up in the VIP room," Chelsea said as she and Mark moved toward the entrance of the Spitfire. The sounds of the city surrounded them, and the cool breeze blowing off the bay brushed her face as she glanced up at him out of the corner of her eye. She'd done a good job. She'd had him in and out of the John Louis Salon in time for his *Sports Illustrated* interview. That had to count for something. Had to show him that she was good at her job and that he needed her. "Her name is Donda Clark and she said the interview shouldn't take more than an hour."

He looked good too. The back of his dark hair

barely brushed the collar of his T-shirt and the tops of his ears. He looked clean-cut. Handsome. Manly.

She'd been worried.

The John Louis Salon catered to an alternative clientele. Edgy. Emo. And Chelsea had worried that Mark would come out with guyliner and Pete Wentz or Flock of Seagulls hair.

"After I get you settled with the reporter, I have to run over to the Chinooks' offices." She had to sign some insurance papers, and the offices were only about five blocks away. "Call me if you're done early."

"The last time I saw my cell phone was the night of the accident." From behind his sunglasses, he glanced at her, then returned his gaze to the sidewalk. "I assume it's in the mangled Hummer somewhere."

She knew he had a home phone, but how could anyone live without text messaging for six months? She'd been in Seattle less than two weeks and she'd already changed her number and her plan. "Who's your carrier?"

"Verizon. Why?"

"I'll get you a new phone," she said as she opened the door to the lounge and followed him inside. "And put you on my friends and family plan."

He pushed his glasses to the top of his head and said something about going ahead and killing himself. The scent and sizzle of carnitas and sliders hit her nostrils and made her stomach growl. The dim interior was lit with track lighting, white globes, and chandeliers. Forty-two-inch flat-screen televisions hung among local artwork and flashed with major sports events. The bar's clientele was an eclectic mix of upwardly mobile and laid-back grunge. Knit hats and business suits all mingled inside the sports lounge.

A decent lunch crowd filled the tables and booths as Chelsea followed Mark through the bar. Heads turned as they passed, and she didn't fool herself that all that attention was directed at her. Over the hum of voices, people called out his name. He lifted his bad hand in acknowledgment, the dim light shining on the aluminum of his splint.

Chelsea was used to walking into a restaurant and seeing all eyes turn to her employers. A time or two, she'd purposely created attention for them by posing as a fan or faux paparazzi. This energy was different from anything she'd ever experienced. This wasn't superficial celebrity adoration. This was real and bigger than any of the B, C, or D listers she'd ever worked for.

"Good to see you, Hitman," the bartender called out to him as they passed. "Can I get you anything?"

"No thanks. Not right now."

Chelsea bit the side of her lip. *Hitman?*

The *Sports Illustrated* reporter sat on a red leather sofa in the back of the lounge; her long blond hair curled about her shoulders and shone in the subdued light. The reporter stood as they approached and moved from behind a large cocktail table. She wore a red bird's-eye jacket and pencil skirt that hit her at mid-thigh. She was tall and gorgeous and perfectly proportioned, everything that Chelsea was not. Oh, Chelsea could buy that exact shade of blond and she planned to have her breasts reduced to fit her body, but she would never have those long legs.

"Hello, I'm Chelsea Ross." Chelsea shook the woman's slender hand. "Mr. Bressler's assistant."

"It's nice to meet you," the reporter said, but her eyes were transfixed on the man behind Chelsea. "You're a hard man to pin down," she said as she dropped Chelsea's hand and reached for Mark. "I'm Donda Clark."

He switched his cane to his right hand. "Mark Bressler."

"Yes, I know." She smiled and motioned toward

the seat next to her on the sofa. "I caught the game in Detroit last December."

A tight smile curved Mark's lips. "That was one of the last games I played." He moved to the sofa, placed his good hand on the arm, and slowly sat. The corners of his mouth tightened even more, and Chelsea wondered if he was up to the interview. He seemed so strong, it was easy to forget that he'd been near death just a few months prior.

"I thought Detroit might turn it over after Le-claire drew a double minor in the third frame, but the Chinooks' firepower clearly overwhelmed the Red Wings."

Wow, what an ass kisser. "Can I get anything for the two of you before I go?" Chelsea asked.

"I'd like a Chablis," Donda answered as she sat and dug a tape recorder out of her bag. "Thank you."

"Mr. Bressler?"

He took the glasses from the top of his head and shoved one side down the collar of his T-shirt. "Water."

Chelsea moved to the bar and wondered if Donda noticed the pain etched in the side of Mark's mouth and if she'd write about it.

"What can I get you, sweetheart?" the bartender asked as his gaze landed on her chest. She was so used to guys' reaction to her breasts, it didn't anger her as much as it once had. Annoy, yes. Anger, no.

Chelsea waited a few seconds before his gaze moved up to hers. "House Chablis and a glass of ice water." She looked at the name tag clipped to his blue polo. "Colin."

He smiled. The cocky smile of bartenders world-wide who knew they were good-looking. "You know my name. What's yours?"

She'd been known to date a few cocky bartend-ers. Most of them had been out-of-work actors. "You already know it. It's sweetheart."

He reached for a glass and filled it with ice. "It's nice to meet you, sweetheart. What brings you into the Spitfire?"

"I'm Mr. Bressler's assistant."

Colin lifted his gaze from the glass he slid across the bar and grinned. "I didn't think you were his date. You're not his type."

"How do you know his type?"

"A lot of hockey players hang out here. He used to come in with some of the guys."

He poured the wine, and Chelsea watched him for a few moments. "What's his type?" she asked, only because it was her job to know that sort of thing. Not because she was nosy or anything.

"He goes for models. Like the blond he's talking to."

"Ah." Figured.

"I prefer cute and spunky. Like you."

Cute. She'd always been *cute.* For the most part, she was okay with that. Unless she had to stand next to a gorgeous supermodel and read for the same part. And because she was short, everyone assumed she was "spunky." Or maybe it was her fashion flair. Although everyone always assumed the same about Bo, and Bo had the fashion sense of an undertaker. "What makes you think I'm spunky?"

He chuckled. "It might as well be written across your forehead."

Which told her nothing. She reached for both glasses. "See ya, Colin."

"Don't be a stranger, sweetheart."

She moved back into the VIP lounge and set the glasses on the table in front of the sofa. Mark glanced up at her and slid his sunglasses to one side of his neck. "I'll be back in an hour," she told him. "If you need anything, call."

"I'll take good care of him," the reporter assured her, and Chelsea waited until she turned before she gave in to the urge to roll her eyes. She moved through the bar and out into the warm afternoon air. The Metro rushed past, the sound of the motor and screech of brakes bouncing off the stone buildings. Seattle definitely had a different vibe than L.A.

It had a faster pace. Maybe it was the cooler temperature. Or maybe it was because the Gore-Tex–clad, granola-munching Starbucks drinkers jogged because they actually enjoyed it. Whatever it was, Chelsea liked it well enough. She wouldn't mind living in Seattle until after her surgery. She figured she'd need a few weeks to recuperate before she headed back to L.A. to take another shot at pursuing her dream.

She'd often told friends that casting directors hired her breasts, not her. She'd been forever typecast as a bimbo or a sexually promiscuous character. Once her breasts were no longer a factor, directors would have to take her seriously. They'd have to pay more attention to her talent than to her body.

What if you still don't make it? a tiny pessimistic part of her brain asked. She'd give herself two years. No, five. If she still hadn't landed anything significant by the time she was thirty-five, she'd find something else. She'd be sad, but she wouldn't have any regrets. Not about pursuing her dream. And certainly not about reducing her heavy breasts.

It took her less than ten minutes to walk the five blocks to the Chinooks' offices. She'd been in the human resources offices last week and found it easily. After she filled out her insurance forms, she headed to the public relations department where her sister worked. The second she stepped inside the offices, she could feel that something was up.

Bo sat on the edge of her desk with her hands covering the bottom half of her face. Jules Garcia stood in front of her. "You're worrying about nothing," he said.

"That's easy for you to say. You don't have to fix it."

"You don't have to fix anything."

"Yet."

"Hey all," Chelsea said as she approached.

Bo dropped her hands. "Hey, Chels."

"Hi there," Jules greeted, his gorgeous green eyes appraising her peacock Gaultier. The other night when she'd first met Jules, she'd assumed he was gay. He was just too pretty and too concerned about the way he looked to be straight. His prison-ripped muscles screamed gay, but a few moments in his company had cleared up the confusion. Chelsea had been around a lot of gay men in her life. Straight men too. Jules was that rare breed that didn't easily fit in one camp or the other. Not like Mark Bressler. There was never a question for which team Mark played. His whole body leaked hetero toxins. Jules's sexuality was more covert, disguised behind hair gel and fashion risks. Like the lavender-and-pink-striped shirt he favored today.

"Is something wrong?" Chelsea asked.

Bo handed Chelsea the sports section of the *Seattle Times*. An enlarged photo of several men standing on a yacht, one of them pouring beer from the Stanley Cup onto bikini-clad women, took up most of the front page. The caption read: *Chinooks celebrate near Vashon with Lord Stanley's Cup.*

"They're partying with the Stanley Cup? Can they do that?" Chelsea studied the picture. It was a little fuzzy but clear enough. "I mean, is it allowed?"

"It's actually tradition," Jules assured her. "Each team member gets the cup for one day."

"They can just do what they want with it?" Now she understood some of Bo's concern.

"Within reason," Jules answered. "And a representative of the Hall of Fame has to be with it at all times."

Obviously pouring beer on women in bikinis was considered "within reason."

Bo slid off the side of her desk. "So there's going to be a lot of opportunity for shenanigans."

Jules shook his head. "You worry too much. After they all get their turn, it'll get taken away to have their names engraved on it and everything will settle down."

Chelsea tossed the paper on her sister's desk. "How many players get their turn with the cup?"

"All those who are eligible to have their names engraved on it. Off the top of my head, I think twenty-four," Jules answered. "Including Ty Savage and Mark Bressler. Even though neither played the full season."

"Mr. Bressler gets a day with the cup?" He hadn't mentioned it. Then again, he didn't say much. Except when he wanted to be rude.

"Sure. He was the captain until just before the playoffs. Any player who played in forty-one regular season games or five playoff games is eligible. Bressler played in well over forty-one games and is a huge part of the reason the team made it into the finals. He helped build the team and deserves as much credit for winning as anyone. It's just a shame he didn't get to play in the finals."

"When is his day?" She pulled her BlackBerry out of her bag to make a note.

"I don't know," Bo answered.

"I'm sure he can have it whenever he wants. Has he talked to anyone about what day he wants the cup?"

Chelsea shook her head. "I don't know. I'll ask him."

Jules reached out and brushed the sleeve of her shirt. "Nice."

"Thanks. It's a Gaultier."

"I thought it might be. I have a silk Gaultier in pewter and gold."

Of course he did. "Are you sure you're not gay?" She cocked her head to one side. "Bo has no interest in fashion, and I'd love to find a gay best friend to shop with."

"I have more important things in my life," Bo protested.

"Like what?" Jules and Chelsea asked at the same time.

"Like . . . like my job."

Jules looked from one sister to the other. "If the two of you didn't look alike, I wouldn't know you're twins. You're so different."

Chelsea thought about the fight she'd had with her sister the night before. "Bo is a lot more responsible than I am."

Her sister gave her a tight smile. "I can be kind of uptight."

"That's an understatement." Jules chuckled. "You're bossy as hell."

"Well, someone has to be or nothing would get done around here."

"Right. The whole organization would fall apart without a five-and-a-half-foot woman in PR telling everyone what to do and how to do it."

"I'm five feet, one and a *half,*" Bo said as if they were in junior high and that half an inch was still important. She frowned and pushed her short hair behind her ears. "Why are you here, Jules? Just to fight with me?"

"As pleasant as fighting with you always is, I was going to see if you're free for lunch."

"I have a meeting in ten minutes," Bo grumbled.

He looked at Chelsea. "You free?"

She glanced at the clock on her phone. She didn't get the feeling that Jules asked because he thought she and Bo were interchangeable. He was a nice guy. They both had to eat, but she still had to run it by her sister since he'd asked Bo first. "Do you mind?"

"Not at all."

"Good, because I'm starving." She looked at Jules. "I have to be back at the Spitfire in half an hour."

"I know a sandwich shop not far. You can get something and eat it on the way."

"Okay." Chelsea glanced at her sister, who glared at Jules as if he'd done something wrong. "Are you sure you don't mind?" she asked.

"I'm sure." She turned to her desk and picked up the newspaper. "Some of us have to work."

"And some of us got the day off." Jules moved toward the door. "Sucks to be you."

"Yeah." She sighed heavily. "Sucks to be me."

"I'll see you at home later," Chelsea said as she moved to the door. Bo nodded but didn't turn around.

"Did something happen?" she asked Jules as they moved down the hall. "Bo is acting weird."

"Is she?" He held open the door for her, and as she passed, she caught the scent of his cologne. "I think all this stuff with the cup is making her more uptight than usual. And she's usually wound fairly tight."

"Maybe." She dropped her phone into her purse and pulled out her sunglasses. "What can you tell me about Mark Bressler?"

"I don't know a lot. I knew him a little bit when I worked for the Chinooks five years ago. I only recently started working for the organization again. I was rehired to assist Mrs. Duffy when she inherited the team. That would have been a month or two after his accident."

Chelsea didn't think she'd ever forget the game the other night. Not only because it had been fun to watch but because during the award ceremony, Mrs. Duffy had walked out onto the ice in a pair of pink skates, and the captain of the team, Ty Savage, had dipped her back and tongue kissed her for the world to see. The crowd inside the Key Arena had gone wild. "That was so romantic," she sighed.

"Yeah."

She looked up at him, at the sun shining in his spiky black hair. "You don't think so?"

"Sure." He shrugged his big shoulders. "I just hope Ty doesn't break her heart. She's a nice person, and I'd hate to see her get hurt."

"He retired for her. Not many men would do something like that. He must love her."

They walked a few more feet, and Jules opened the door to a little deli and the two stepped inside. The smell of fresh-baked bread made Chelsea's stomach growl. "Love doesn't always work out," he said.

She knew that well enough. She'd been in love a few times, only to be dumped flat on her behind. But she'd always picked herself back up and moved on. In the past, she'd let lust and love get all mixed up in her head. She'd let a pretty face, hot body, and slick moves convince her that what she felt was love. The kind that lasted forever. The kind her parents had shared. It never had worked out for her, but she was sure she'd find someone someday. "You sound a little cynical."

He shrugged, and they moved toward the counter. "I always go for girls who don't like me or just want to be 'friends.' God, I hate it when a woman just wants to be *friends*."

She wondered if he was talking about his boss. She looked up at the chalkboard menu and asked, "Who just wants to be your friend?"

Jules shook his head. "Never mind." He ordered a turkey and Swiss, tons of veggies, and no mayo. "How's your first day of work?"

Chelsea ordered a ham and cheddar, hold the veggies, yes to mayo. "Are we changing the subject?"

"Yep."

How was her first day? She'd survived and had even managed to find a Betsey Johnson skirt on sale at Neiman Marcus. But . . . "Mr. Bressler is difficult."

"I've heard. In just over a month, he's gone through five health care workers. You're the sixth."

She hadn't known the exact number, but she wasn't surprised. "I'm not a health care worker. My plan is to dazzle him with my assistant skills." So far he didn't seem all that dazzled, but Jules didn't need to know that. "By the time I get him back home today, he will wonder how he ever got along without me."

Chapter Five

Chelsea scarfed her ham sandwich and made it back to the Spitfire at ten after two. She'd used the extra ten minutes to pull the Mercedes in front of the bar so *Mr. Bressler* wouldn't have to walk the extra block. Surely he'd be grateful.

The crowd had thinned out, and she waved to Colin as she walked to the VIP lounge. Deep male laughter filled the back of the room, and it wasn't until Chelsea saw Mark that she realized the laughter came from him. Donda sat on the edge of the red sofa, one of her hands resting on his knee as she spoke, gesturing wildly with her other hand. Several empty appetizer plates and glasses sat on the table in front of them. Chelsea pulled out her BlackBerry and looked at it as if she were consulting a schedule. "We have just enough time to get you to your next appointment," she said. Celebrities loved looking important. Like they were always off to something bigger and better. Most of the time it was a little white lie.

"I just have a few more questions," Donda said.

Chelsea glanced up and looked at Mark. His brows were drawn as if she was speaking a language he didn't recognize. He was probably confused about the little white lie. He'd never had his very own personal assistant and wasn't familiar with how she worked and what she could do for him. Soon he'd be singing her praises. "I'm double-parked in front, but if you need more time, I can come back."

"I think we're done." He reached for his cane.

"Thanks for meeting me, Mark." Donda rubbed her hand a few inches up his leg, and Chelsea wondered if that was professional behavior for a *Sports Illustrated* reporter. She'd bet not. "If I have any follow-ups, I'll be in touch."

He planted his good hand on the arm of the sofa and stood. He sucked in a breath, then clinched his jaw, and Chelsea wondered when he'd last taken his medication. If it had been that morning, she needed to get him home. Though surely he would have brought something with him. But as they moved through the lounge, his steps were a bit slower and more measured than they'd been an hour ago.

"Take care, sweetheart," Colin called out to her. "Come back when you can stay."

She flashed him a smile. "Bye, Colin. Don't work too hard."

As they stepped outside, Mark asked, "Boyfriend?"

"I've only been in Seattle a little more than a week. Not nearly long enough to find a boyfriend." She shoved her sunglasses on her face and moved to the double-parked Mercedes. "Give me a few more days," she said as she opened his door. Then she glanced at the street traffic and ran around to the driver's side before he could complain about her opening his door. "Make it a week," she added as she slid inside the car.

He looked across the car at her and shut his door. "That long?"

She was sure he was being facetious, but she didn't care. "Finding guys to *date* isn't a problem. A boyfriend takes more time," she said as she turned off the hazard lights. "There are lots of hot guys like Colin around. Guys who look good in a pair of jeans and a wife-beater. Those guys are fun, but they aren't real boyfriend material." She belted herself in.

"So poor Colin is off your list?"

"Nah. I'd go out with him." She shrugged. "He thinks I'm spunky."

"That's one word for you." He grabbed his sunglasses from the collar of his T-shirt. "Another word would be 'pit bull.' "

"Yes." She slid the car into drive and pulled away from the Spitfire. "But I'm your pit bull."

"Lucky me." He put on the glasses and buckled his seat belt.

He said it like he didn't mean it, but he would. She glanced at the GPS and continued northeast. "Have you seen the front page of the *Seattle Times* sports section?"

He turned and looked out the passenger window. " 'Fraid not."

Which she found a little surprising since he'd been the captain of the Chinooks until six months ago. "Half the page is filled with a photo of a group of guys standing on a yacht somewhere, and someone is pouring beer from the Stanley Cup on women in bikinis."

He didn't respond. Maybe he was in too much pain. She'd broken her tailbone falling off a table once. At the time, she'd had one too many cherry bombs and had been convinced she was some sort of exotic belly dancer. Which was ridiculous since she'd never had a lesson and danced about as well as she sang. The next morning her tailbone had hurt like a son of a bitch and she could hardly move without swearing. So she could kind of relate to Mark's mood. "At first I was a little appalled, but Jules told me that it's okay and even allowed. Everyone on the team gets a day with the cup to do whatever he wants to do with it. Within reason, of course. There are rules. Although I think they're pretty lax." She glanced at the GPS and took a slight right. "But I guess you already know all that."

"Yeah. I already know that."

"So, what day do you want the Stanley Cup? Just let me know and I'll make it happen."

"I don't want the fucking cup," he said without emotion.

She looked over at the back of his dark head. "You're kidding. Why? Jules says you're a huge part of the reason the team made it into the finals."

"Who the hell is Jules?"

"Julian Garcia. He's Mrs. Duffy's assistant. Kind of like I'm your assistant. Only Jules knows a lot about hockey and I know squat about the game." She shrugged. "Jules said you deserve more credit for building the team than anyone else." Okay, maybe she'd embellished a wee bit. But blowing smoke up celebrity butt was part of her job. In the spirit of smoke blowing, she added, "More credit than Ty Savage."

"I don't want to hear that asshole's name."

Okay. Someone sounded bitter. "Well, you've earned a day with the cup just like the other guys. Probably more because you were the captain and you—"

"I need to stop at a pharmacy on the way home," he interrupted and pointed toward the left. "There's a Bartell Drugs."

She slowed, cut across three lanes, and pulled into the parking lot.

"Jesus Christ! You're going to get us killed."

"You wanted Bartell."

"Yeah, but I thought you'd take a U at the light like a normal person."

"I am a normal person." She parked by the front doors and looked across the car into the mirrored image in his sunglasses. His jaw was clenched like she'd done something wrong. There hadn't been any other cars *that* close, and everyone knew that a miss was as good as a mile. She was pretty sure she'd learned that rule in drivers' ed class. "I thought maybe you need to fill a prescription? Like right now!"

He reached into his back pocket and pulled out

his wallet. "I have my prescriptions delivered." He grabbed two twenties and handed them to her.

She guessed that meant she was going in by herself. Which was okay. It would take them longer if he got out. "What do you need? Toothpaste? Deodorant? Preparation H?"

"Box of condoms."

She closed her eyes and mentally pounded her head on the steering wheel. *Ten thousand dollars. Ten thousand dollars.* "Are you sure you don't want to get those yourself?"

He shook his head and smiled. His straight teeth were unusually white within the shadows of the Mercedes. "As you keep reminding me, you're my assistant. Lucky you."

Buying condoms was so embarrassing. Worse than maxi pads and only slightly better than the monthly Valtrex prescription she'd had to pick up for a certain young actress with a sitcom on the WB. "What size?"

"Magnum. The ribbed kind."

Magnum? But of course he wore magnums. Being a big prick and all. For the hundredth time that day, she forced a smile on her face and turned once again to look at him. "Anything else?"

"Some of that warming KY and a vibrating ring. Make sure it's a big one." He raised his hip and stuck the wallet back in his pocket. "I don't want it too tight and cutting off my circulation."

"No. You wouldn't want that." This was about the longest conversation they'd had and it was about circulation to his penis. She was almost afraid to ask. "Is that it?"

"A bag of Red Vines." He thought for a moment and added, "I guess I better have some Tic Tacs."

Yes, because God forbid his breath wasn't minty.

By the time Mark made it home, his bones throbbed and his muscles ached. It took him only a few minutes to get rid of his little assistant. Most likely because she seemed more than happy to go. With any luck, she wouldn't return. If the look on her face when she'd come back from buying condoms was any indication, she was probably looking up help wanted ads on Craigslist and calling for interviews at that very moment. Sending her into Bartell had been damn funny. A flash of pure brilliance and quick thinking on the fly.

Mark downed six Vicodin straight from the bottle, grabbed his bag of Red Vines, and headed for what the Realtor had called the leisure room at the back of the house. He picked up the remote to the sixty-inch flat screen and sat in a big leather chaise that Chrissy had found somewhere. Most of the other furniture she'd bought was long gone, but he'd kept the chaise because it fit his body and was comfortable.

With his thumb on the remote button, he flipped through the channels without really paying attention. He'd had a doctor's appointment, haircut, and hour-long interview. It wasn't even three yet, but he was exhausted. Before the accident, he used to run five miles and work out with weights, all before hitting the ice for practice. He was thirty-eight years old but he felt like he was seventy-eight.

Dr. Phil flashed across the screen and he paused to watch the good doctor yell at some guy for yelling at his wife. He tore open the bag of licorice and pulled out a few. As far back as he could remember, he'd always loved red licorice. It reminded him of the Sunday matinees at the Heights Theater in Minneapolis. His grandmother had been a huge fan of the movies and had bribed him with Red Vines and root beer. Even though it was something he'd never admit out loud, he'd seen many a chick flick in the late seventies and early eighties. Everything from *Kramer vs. Kramer* to *Sixteen Candles*. He and his gran had always gone to the Sunday matinees because he'd usually had hockey games on Saturday, and also there was less of a chance that one of his friends would see him walking into a sappy movie on Sunday. His dad had usually been working second and third jobs to support him and his grandmother and to make sure Mark had the best hockey skates and equipment. One of the best days of Mark's life was the day he signed his first multi-million-dollar contract and set up his dad so the old man could retire.

Mark took a bite of his licorice and chewed. He'd never known his mother. She'd run off before his third birthday and had died a few years later in some car accident thousands of miles away in Florida. He had a vague memory of her, more faded than the few cards she'd sent. She'd write to tell him that she loved him more than anything, but he hadn't been fooled. She'd loved drugs more than him. Her husband and her son hadn't been enough for her, and she'd chosen crack cocaine over her family and even over her life, which was one of the reasons he'd never been tempted to do drugs.

Until now. Not that he was addicted. Not yet, but he certainly had a clearer understanding of how easily it could happen. Of how drugs took away the pain and made life tolerable. Of how easy it would be to slip over the edge and become a full-blown addict. But he wasn't there yet.

He'd been fighting pain all day, and as the Vicodin kicked in, he felt his muscles ease. He relaxed and thought of the photo in the sports section his little assistant had told him about. It sounded like the guys were having a fine old time, and if he'd won the cup with them, he probably would have been there. But he hadn't and he didn't want to drink from the cup and celebrate as if he had. And giving him a day with the cup anyway felt like pity.

Sure, there had been several guys he knew who hadn't played in the cup finals for one reason or another and had still celebrated. Fine. Good for them. Mark just didn't feel the same way. For him, looking and touching and drinking from the cup was a big, shiny reminder of everything he'd lost. Maybe someday he could get past the bitterness, but not today. Tomorrow didn't look good either.

The reporter from *Sports Illustrated* had asked him his plans for the future. He'd told her that he was just taking life one day at a time. Which was true. What he hadn't mentioned was that he didn't see a future. His life was a big blank *nothing*.

Before the accident, he'd thought of his retirement. Of course he had. He had enough money so that he didn't have to work for the rest of his life, but he hadn't planned on doing *nothing*. He'd planned on getting hired as an offensive coach somewhere. It was what he knew. Seeing plays in his head before they happened was what he'd been good at. Finding lanes through traffic and scoring goals had been a talent that had made him one of the top ten goal scorers for the past six years and was something he'd helped teach the guys on his team. But to coach offense, or defense for that matter, the coach had to skate. There was no way around it, but Mark could hardly walk a hundred feet without pain.

He ate a few pieces of licorice and tossed the bag on the table next to the chaise. As a Burger King commercial came on the air, Mark closed his eyes, and before Dr. Phil returned, he drifted off into a peaceful, drug-induced nap, the remote still in one hand. As with most of his dreams, he was back at the Key Arena, fighting it out in the corners. As always, he heard the roar of the crowd, the slap of graphite sticks on ice, and the *shh* of razor-sharp blades. He could smell sweat and leather and the unique scent of the ice. The cold breeze brushed his cheeks and neck as thousands of pairs of eyes watched from the seats. The anticipation and excitement in their faces were a blur as he skated past. Adrenaline bit the back of his throat as his heart and legs pounded down ice. He glanced at the puck in the curve of his stick, and when he looked back up, he saw her. A clear face in a blurry sea. Her big blue eyes simply looked back at him. The light bounced off her two-toned hair. He turned his skates to the side and stopped.

Everything around him fell away as he continued to stare at her though the Plexiglas.

"Why are you here?" he asked, beyond annoyed that she'd shown up and disrupted the game.

She smiled—the full-lipped tilt of her mouth that he recognized after one day of being around her—but she didn't answer. He skated closer to the wall and his stick dropped from his hands. "What do you want?"

"To give you what you need."

There were so many things he needed. So many. Starting with the need to feel something other than constant nagging pain and the void in his life.

"Lucky you," she whispered.

Mark's eyes flew open and he gasped for breath. He sat up too fast, and the remote fell to the floor. His head spun as he glanced at the clock on the bottom left of his television screen. He'd been asleep for an hour. Jesus, she'd intruded in his life. Now she'd infiltrated his dreams. Of all the faceless people in his dreams, why was her face clear?

He reached down and grabbed his cane resting on the floor. Thank God the dream hadn't been sexual. He didn't even want to think about getting it up for his assistant. Not even in a dream.

The splint on his hand itched, and he tore it off.

Tossing the Velcro and aluminum aside, he slowly stood and made his way from the room. Why *her*? It wasn't that the little assistant wasn't cute. She was plenty cute, and God knew she had a body that could stop traffic, but she was just so damn annoying. The rubber tip of his cane thumped across the stone floor and his flip-flops slapped the heels of his feet. Rested and his pain somewhat dulled, he walked with relative ease.

In the kitchen, the Bartell sack with the condoms, KY, and vibrating ring lay atop the granite island. He didn't know what the hell he was going to do with that stuff. It wasn't like he was going to use it anytime soon. He opened a drawer and shoved it inside.

He didn't know what he was going to do with his assistant either. Too bad he couldn't shove her in a drawer and lock her inside. He thought of her driving *his* new Mercedes like she owned the road. He thought of her face when she'd first slid into the leather driver's seat. She'd looked like she'd been about to orgasm. Under different circumstances, he might have pulled her into his lap. Under different circumstances, he might have thought the way she'd caressed his leather was about the hottest thing he'd ever seen. Under current circumstances, it had been just one more thing to irritate him.

More than likely, the woman would be back tomorrow. His optimism of a while ago faded. For reasons that he couldn't begin to understand, she seemed to actually want to be his assistant. Maybe she was a little off in the head. No, she was definitely off in the head because why else would she buy condoms and KY when she clearly didn't want to?

Chelsea would put up with a lot for ten thousand dollars. "He made me buy him condoms," she told the back of her sister's dark head. "And warming KY."

Bo looked over her shoulder and reached for a half gallon of milk. "Well, he's a hockey player," she said, as if that explained and excused it. "And he always did have a lot of different girlfriends. At least he's using protection."

"And a vibrating ring."

"What's that?"

"A cock ring that vibrates."

Bo glanced about the dairy aisle at Safeway to make sure no one could overhear them before she set the milk in the cart. "They make those?"

"Apparently, and in case you ever need one, there are three different kinds available at Bartell drugstore. The duo, the magnum, and the intense pleasure. The duo has two pleasure buttons, one on each side. The magnum is self-explanatory, and the intense pleasure vibrates faster for—you know, intense pleasure."

"You read each package?"

"It's my job." Although, really, she'd read out of curiosity more than anything else. It wasn't like she was a vibrating ring expert.

"Have you ever . . ." Bo lowered her voice and glanced around one more time. " . . . used one?"

"No." But if she ever got a boyfriend she might. Buying those condoms today reminded her that it had been seven months since her last relationship.

And because Bo was as nosy as her twin, she asked, "Which did you buy Mark?"

"He made me buy the magnum because he was concerned about cutting off his circulation."

Bo's brows rose up her forehead. "Magnum? That's scary."

Chelsea pushed the cart farther down the produce case. "You've seen one?"

"Not in person." Bo shook her head. "Just in the porn movies David used to watch," she said, referring to a past boyfriend. "Do you think he's really a magnum or he just wanted to shock you?"

"I don't know, and I don't want to think about it. It's too disturbing."

"That's true," her sister agreed. "You have to work for him tomorrow, and that's the last thing you want to be thinking about when you walk into his house." They moved a few more feet down the dairy aisle, and Bo glanced at her list. "I know Mark isn't really mobile, but making you buy him condoms and stuff was really uncalled for."

"I thought so, but I've had to do worse."

Bo put her hand on the cart and stopped it next to the butter. Concern etched her brow. "I'm almost afraid to ask, but what?"

"Well, taking back designer dresses to places like Saks with big armpit stains was always embarrassing. Picking up prescriptions for various sexually transmitted diseases was mortifying, and breaking up with someone else's girlfriend or boyfriend was sad."

"Oh." Bo sighed and reached for some cottage cheese.

Her sister looked so relived, Chelsea had to ask, "What did you think I was going to say was worse? That I was working for a madam in the Hollywood Hills?"

"No." They continued beneath the fluorescent lights of the Safeway. "I just hoped that you never had to do anything illegal."

There was illegal. Then there was *illegal*. She'd mostly just committed your ordinary illegal stuff. Run a red light. Drove too fast. Hopped aboard the ganja train at a few parties in the past. "Do we need some butter?" she asked, purposely changing the subject before her sister could ask any specific questions.

Bo shook her head and checked milk and cottage cheese off her list. "Jules never came back after lunch."

"Hmm." Chelsea picked up several containers of fat-free cherry yogurt.

"Did he go to the Spitfire with you?"

"No." She dumped the yogurt into the cart. "Do you want string cheese? We used to love string cheese."

"I don't want any." Bo moved to the eggs. "What do you think of Jules?"

"I think he works hard to look good." She grabbed some key lime yogurt too. "Nothing wrong with that."

"Except he's full of himself."

Chelsea hadn't gotten that impression. "If you work hard on your body, you kind of have the right to brag about it. If I worked out, I'd brag. But I don't, because I hate pain."

"He's rude too." Bo opened the egg carton and checked for breakage. "And obnoxious."

A harried mother with three kids hanging out of her cart wheeled past, and Chelsea looked at her sister. "I didn't think so. Maybe he's a little cynical."

Bo looked over at her as she shut the carton. "Why do you say he's cynical?"

"Because he said something about love not working out. My guess is that he's had his heart broken a few times." She leaned forward and rested her forearms on the handle of the cart. "But haven't we all?"

"He used to weigh a lot, and I think he still sees himself as the fat kid in school."

"You're kidding. He doesn't have an ounce of fat on him now," Chelsea said as Bo put the eggs in the seat of the cart next to their purses. "He's ripped and he has those beautiful green eyes. You should date him."

"Jules?" Bo made a gagging sound.

"You should. He's very cute, and you two have a lot in common."

"What are you planning to do tomorrow?" her sister asked and changed the subject.

"I'm not sure." Chelsea recognized the maneuver and let her. "I've never worked for someone who doesn't have a list as long as my arm and expects the impossible. Mark said something about wanting to move out of Medina. So maybe I'll start looking at real estate options for him. His house is too damn big for one guy anyway."

"Most of the athletes around here live downtown, or on Mercer, or in Newport Hills." She pushed the cart toward the butcher block. "At least I think a lot of the Seahawks and Chinooks still live in Newport. That's how it became known as Jock Rock."

Chelsea made a mental note to check real estate listings in those areas. "What movie are we going to watch tonight?"

"How about something with aliens?" Bo suggested and grabbed a package of hamburger.

Chelsea reached for a produce baggy above the chicken. "Something not cheesy, like *Independence Day*? Maybe a little cheesy, like *Men in Black*? Or heavy on the cheese, like *Critters*?"

"Heavy, like *Mars Attacks!*"

"Good call. A little black comedy and with a dash of political satire, all wrapped up in B-movie parody. Gotta love Tim Burton."

"You aren't going to quote dialog throughout the whole movie are you?" Bo sighed. "I just want to kill you when you do that."

Chelsea grabbed a package of legs and thighs. In L.A., she and her friends had recited lines during movies. It had been part of the fun. At least for them. "You mean like, 'Little people, why can't we all just get along?'"

Chapter Six

Though it wasn't easy, Chelsea controlled herself during *Mars Attacks!* and didn't recite dialog. Afterward, she grabbed her laptop and climbed into bed. She placed the computer in front of her crossed knees and turned it on. A picture of Christian Bale, all duded up in *3:10 to Yuma*, popped up on her desktop. She'd never met Christian Bale but she admired any actor who could play Jesus in one movie and Batman in the next and do both roles justice. Sure, he had a bit of an anger problem. So did Russell Crowe, but that didn't make either of them bad actors. Although she did have to admit that if Christian didn't learn to control himself like Russell had, she'd have to find someone else to love from afar.

She plugged in her Verizon PC card and logged

onto the Internet. She purposely didn't click on her bookmarks. She didn't want to know any of the Hollywood gossip or read what producer was looking to fill what roles in what movie. When she returned to L.A., she'd contact her agency and tell them she was back and to send out her portfolio again.

Everyone in her family thought she had stars in her eyes. Maybe she did, but her feet were firmly rooted in reality. She knew that in Hollywood, landing a role after the age of thirty was about as easy as landing a man. But that didn't mean that her only option was to slide her feet into Crocs, get a cat, and give up.

While she searched properties in the Seattle area and bookmarked the homes and condos she thought Mark might be interested in seeing, she thought about her life in L.A. Parts of it had been exciting and really fun and she missed hanging out with friends. But there was a dark side too. The horror stories of sex and drugs were too numerous to count. Young actors arriving in town, dreaming of making it big, only to be used and discarded like garbage. The desperation at casting calls was truly sickening, and she didn't miss scrambling for bit roles and walk-on parts. She didn't miss standing around movie sets for twelve hours, dressed as a serving wench with her breasts hanging out for a period film. She'd liked working on horror films. She liked being part of a cast. She liked playing a part and becoming another person for a few hours. It was fun and exciting. She looked forward to getting back to L.A. and getting the chance to score roles other than the slutty bimbo.

First, though, she had to stick it out for three months with a crabby hockey player.

She clicked on a few more sites and found several very promising real estate options. She bookmarked them also, then she decided to Google Mark himself. One of her brows lifted in surprise as she looked at over a million results and a dozen fan sites dedicated to "the Hitman."

"Geez." It wasn't like he was Brad Pitt.

On his official Web site, she watched video clips of him scoring goals, skating with his stick held above his head, or dropping his gloves and throwing punches. In interviews, he laughed and joked and talked about how much winning the Stanley Cup would mean to him and the rest of the Chinooks. Each site was filled with various still photos of him, looking all rough and sweaty while he shot the puck. The photos ranged from him having blood on his face to looking clean-cut and smiling in his head shots.

She clicked on a link and she watched a Gatorade commercial of him dressed in nothing but a pair of hockey shorts hanging low on his hips. On her computer screen, he slowly tipped his head back, brought the bright green bottle to his lips, and downed the sports drink. A color-enhanced, neon-green drop leaked from the corner of his mouth and slid down his jaw and the side of his throat. Dark hair covered his big chest, and Bo had been right. The man had an eight-pack. What her sister hadn't mentioned was the dark happy trail that ran down the center of his smooth, flat belly and circled his navel before diving beneath those shorts. Oh baby. Chelsea had worked in Hollywood and she'd seen a lot of hard male bodies. Mark's was one of the most impressive she'd seen outside of a body-building contest on Venice Beach.

She read his goals and point averages, not that she had a real clue what any of that meant, but even Wikipedia said it was impressive, so she supposed it was. She found a fan site with a photo of him tearing down the ice, and she clicked on a link titled "Bressler quotes."

Her gaze skimmed a few quotes about playing hockey before stopping on "I don't celebrate coming in second place." She didn't know him well, but she could imagine him saying something like that. When asked what it was like to be the captain of the Chinooks, he'd answered, "I'm just one of the guys. On the bus or airplane, I just sit in the back, play cards, and try to take the guys' money." The quote that surprised her the most was, "As a kid, I knew I wanted to play professional hockey. My father worked a lot to afford my skates, and Grandmother always told me I could be anything I wanted to be. I believed her and here I am. I owe a lot to them both." Most people thanked their parents, but his *grandmother*? That was different and unexpected. A smile curved one side of her lips. Mentioning his father and grandmother almost made him human. In fact, in all the pictures and video clips he appeared more human than the guy she knew. There was just something different about him now. Something more than the different way he walked and the way he used his right hand. Something dark. Hard.

On another Web site, the owner had put up three different photographs of Mark's mangled Hummer. This time both Chelsea's brows lifted in surprise as she looked at the twisted wreckage. The man truly was lucky to be alive. A fourth photo of him being wheeled from the hospital appeared on a second page. The picture was somewhat blurry, but there was no mistaking those dark eyes glowering from his face.

There.

That was him. That was the guy she worked for. The hard, dark, gloomy man.

She knew that head injuries could change a man or woman's personality. She wondered if it had changed his. If it had, she wondered if he'd ever get those laughing, joking pieces of his life back. Not that it really mattered to her. She was only sticking around for three months until she got that ten grand.

On the official Chinooks' site, the organization had put up a guest book for fans who wanted to express their best wishes for Mark's recovery. More than seven thousand people had signed in to the book to wish him well. Some of the notes were very nice, and she wondered if Mark even knew that so many people had taken the time to write. She wondered if he cared.

Before she closed her laptop and turned off the bedroom light for the night, she Googled plastic surgeons in the Seattle area. She paid attention to where they'd gone to school and how many years they'd been in practice. Mostly though, she looked at before and after pictures of breast reductions. She wasn't a jealous person, but envy stabbed her soul as she studied the photos. For many different reasons, she wanted so badly to be reduced from her double-D cups to a C. She wanted to run and jump without pain. Not that she would, but it would be nice to have the option. She wanted to be taken as seriously as average-sized women. In Hollywood, she'd been hired to fill out the costume, not so much for her acting ability. And in L.A., everyone automatically assumed she had implants, which had always kind of irritated her.

She'd like to have sex without her heavy breasts bouncing around. As she was now, she preferred to have sex with a bra on. It was more comfortable, but not all the men she'd been with liked it.

She'd been a double D since the tenth grade. It had been humiliating and painful, and probably the reason Bo had such a difficult time finding men she trusted. Even now, sometimes men *and* women took one look at her and Bo and assumed they were nymphomaniacs. It still baffled her to this day. She didn't know what having large breasts had to do with sexual promiscuity. The truth was that because of the size of her breasts, she was more uptight about sex than other women she knew.

One of the biggest reasons she wanted a reduction was that she'd like people to talk to her face, not her chest. She'd like, just once, to meet a man who didn't stare at her breasts. A man like Mark Bressler.

A frown dented her forehead. Mark Bressler might not stare at her breasts, but he was a jerk in many other ways. Many just as offensive ways. Like insulting her clothes, her intelligence, *and* her driving skills.

"Hey." Bo stuck her head in the room, and Chelsea shut her computer so Bo wouldn't see the breast reduction befores and afters on the screen. "Jules just called and wanted me to ask you if Mark was going to play in the Chinooks' celebrity golf tournament in a few weeks. He's always played in the past."

"Why doesn't Jules ask him?"

"Because Mark doesn't always answer his phone." Bo smiled. "But now he has you."

"Yeah. Lucky me."

"Last night I visited a Web page that the Chinooks set up after the accident. Your fans can log on and send you a special message. It's really nice."

Mark sat at his desk and looked over the real estate property that his assistant had pulled up on his computer. He was only going along with her plan because he actually did want to move. He'd spent more time in this house in the last month than he had in the last five years. Or at least it seemed like it. The house was a constant reminder of his past and the walls were closing in on him.

He scratched the stubble on his chin with his left hand as he leaned forward for a better look at the square footage of the house on the screen. He'd showered earlier, dressed in his usual T-shirt and jogging pants, but hadn't bothered shaving because he wasn't planning on leaving the house today.

"Did you know about the page?"

He shook his head as he maneuvered the mouse. It was difficult with the bulky splint on his right hand. Maybe someone had told him about the page. He didn't recall. Whether from the drugs or from the hit to his head, his memory of the last six months was sketchy. "Like a memorial page?"

"No. Like a place where they could send you their best wishes for your recovery. Over seven thousand hockey fans have written letters and notes to you."

Only seven thousand? Mark glanced up from the computer monitor on his desk. He looked over his shoulder and raised his gaze past his assistant's big breasts covered in shiny gold ruffles, up her throat, and into her blue eyes. Today she wore a short, crazy-colored skirt, probably "Pucci," and a pair of big wedge sandals that clunked across his floor when she walked. Her clothes were toned down, for her.

"Are you going to answer them?"

It wasn't that he didn't appreciate hockey fans, he

certainly did, but he hated writing a short grocery list let alone seven thousand e-mails. "No."

"You could send out one mass thank-you. I really think it's the decent thing to do."

"Good thing I don't care what you think."

She sighed and rolled her eyes. "I've also been asked if you plan on playing in the Chinooks' celebrity golf tournament this summer?"

She was like a gnat buzzing around his head, annoying the hell out of him. Too bad he couldn't swat her. If he thought for one minute that a good swat on her ass would offend her and she'd go away, he might be tempted. It was just after eleven A.M. and he was tired as hell. His physical therapist, Cyrus, had stopped by earlier and they'd worked out for an hour in the gym upstairs. But that wasn't the only thing causing his fatigue. He hadn't slept well the night before because he hadn't taken his sleeping medication. Partly because he wanted to see if he still needed it and partly because he didn't want any more freaky dreams where the assistant popped up.

She tilted her head to one side, and the ends of her bright reddish-pink hair brushed one side of her soft neck. "Did you hear me, Mr. Bressler?"

"Unfortunately, yes." He turned back to the monitor and looked at the real estate property in Newport

Hills. It was on the water and he wasn't interested. Living close to any water was damn buggy. "I'm not playing this year."

"Why? You've always played in the past."

"I can't play one-handed." Which wasn't necessarily true. If he wanted to play, he'd play holding a club with his teeth.

"I could help."

He almost laughed, and clicked on the next property she thought might interest him. "Yeah? How?" Stand in front of him and hold the club with her right hand while he held it with his left? He thought of her back pressed against his chest, his nose in her hair, and his hand just above hers on his nine iron. His brain skidded to a halt at the double entendre, and an odd weight settled at the top of his stomach.

"I could look into special clubs."

The weight was so unexpected it disturbed him. Probably because he recognized it. He hadn't felt anything like it in a long time, but he knew the heavy pull for what it was. "A club for disabled players? No thanks." The last thing he wanted was to feel any sort of *anything* for the assistant. It wasn't like he was opposed to feeling desire for a woman again, just not this woman.

She leaned forward and pointed to the condo on the screen, and he was forced to look at her small hand and the smooth skin of her fingers and palm. She kept her nails short, and without any sort of color. Usually he liked color. His gaze slid to the delicate blue vein of her wrist. She was so close that if he wanted, he could press his mouth to the inside of her bare elbow. She was so close that he was surrounded by the scent of her perfume. It was kind of flowery and fruity, just like her.

"The view out the windows is spectacular," she said and leaned a bit closer. Her hair fell forward and her soft breast brushed the back of his shoulder. The weight in his stomach slid a few inches lower and if he didn't know better, he'd suspect that he was about to get turned on.

"I don't want to live downtown. It's too noisy."

"You'd be high and wouldn't hear it."

"I don't get the good drugs anymore. I'd hear it," he said, and brought up a house in Queen Anne. Maybe the feeling in his stomach had to do with his medication.

She laughed next to his ear. A soft, breathy little sound that tickled his temple. "I meant high as in elevation."

He almost smiled. Showed where his mind tended to reside these days.

She leaned forward a little more, pressing into him. "This house is almost four thousand square feet. It has a great view of the bay and is all one floor. I thought it might be perfect for you."

He wondered if she was doing it on purpose. Women had been pressing and rubbing up against him since his rookie days. Letting him know they wanted sex in not so subtle ways. But he didn't really think his little assistant was rubbing up against him because she wanted him to push her down on his desk and have sex with her right there.

Or did she?

"The kitchen has been completely renovated and modernized. What do you think?"

What did he think? He thought of her sitting on his desk in front of him, his hands pushing the skirt up her legs, because as much as Mark loved spending time with a nice pair of breasts, he was ultimately a thigh man. A woman's smooth inner thighs were his favorite parts. He loved sliding his palms up soft, warm skin, getting softer and warmer as his hand moved up higher.

"What do you think, Mr. Bressler?"

The weight slowly lowered to just beneath his navel and stopped before reaching his groin. "I don't cook." Six months ago, he would have had a full-blown erection by now.

"You don't have to cook."

The warm heaviness was the most of anything

he'd felt in a long time and the very last thing he wanted to feel for the woman pressing into him. "Tell me again? Why am I looking at real estate?"

"Because you want to move."

He placed his left hand on the desk and stood, balancing most of his weight on his right side. He didn't need her butting into his business and trying to run his life. "I never told you that."

She was forced to take a step back. "You mentioned it."

He turned and leaned his behind on the desk. "If I mention that I haven't been laid for six months, are you going to start lining up hookers?"

Her brows lowered over her blue eyes. "You didn't get laid yesterday?"

God, did she ever react like a normal woman?

"You didn't hook up with Donda?"

The *Sports Illustrated* reporter? "No." He'd never hook up with a reporter, on the off chance she'd write about it.

"Or anyone else?"

Why would she think something like that? "It's none of your damn business."

Her gaze narrowed. "It *is* when you make me buy you condoms and KY and a magnum pleasure ring. God, that was embarrassing and just plain gross. And it was all for nothing!"

He folded his arms across his chest. "I was *thinking* about getting laid." She looked mad. Good. That made two of them. Pushy woman. She needed to back off, and she really needed to stop rubbing against him before he *did* get a hard-on. Or worse, much worse, before she noticed that he couldn't get it up. That he wasn't a functioning man. "But thinking about sex and buying condoms doesn't mean I want to do it with *you*. So you can stop rubbing yourself against me. I'm not that desperate."

Her big blue eyes rounded. "What?"

"You're not my type of woman. I'm not a boob man, and rubbing your breasts against me doesn't turn me on."

"I didn't rub against you."

"You rubbed." He pointed his rigid middle finger at all the ruffles on her blouse. "I don't want to have sex with you. No offense."

Her mouth fell open. " 'No offense'? You've been trying to offend me since the first day we met."

He dropped his hand to the top of the desk beside his right hip. That was true.

"You've been working overtime at it."

No, he hadn't. If he'd been working overtime, he would have said, "Now, don't get all mad and bitter and hurt. I'm sure some men find you attractive. I'm just not one of them. Honestly, I just can't get it up for a woman with a smart mouth, big boobs, and ridiculous hair. It's just totally out of the question."

She blinked. He'd shocked her, and he half expected her to storm out of his house. "That's a relief." A smile curved her full pink lips. "I've quit, or been fired, from a lot of jobs because I refused to have sex with my boss." Her nose crinkled like she smelled something bad. "You wouldn't believe what some men have wanted me to do."

Actually, he probably could. Men were fairly predictable.

"It's disgusting. The last guy I worked for expected a BJ."

And while men and some women were fairly predictable, she was not. She didn't react like he expected because she wasn't a normal woman. She had yellow and reddish-pink hair and dressed like an abstract painting.

She laughed as she shook her head. "It's a huge relief to know I never have to worry about that from you."

For a man who'd never had to work all that hard at getting a woman in bed, her laughter irritated him more than usual. Which said a lot. "Hold on. You're not ugly. I didn't say anything about a BJ being out of the question."

She folded her arms beneath her breasts, and her

arms got lost in gold ruffles. "Well, it is." In fact, he'd never seen such relief on a woman's face. It made her smile huge and brightened her eyes like she'd just won the tri-state lotto. "And since we're being honest, I just have to tell you, Mr. Bressler, that I don't find you in the least attractive either." She lifted a hand out of all those ruffles before tucking it back inside.

"Praise Jesus," he said through a frown as a dull ache settled in the backs of his eyes. This conversation wasn't going where he wanted. She was supposed to be getting mad and he was supposed to be laughing as he watched her walk out the door.

Chapter Seven

Chelsea looked at the tall, arrogant man in front of her. At his powerful arms and big chest. His scowl and his hard gaze. The jerk didn't like a taste of his own medicine. "Really, you have no idea how relieved I am to know that I *never* have to have sex with *you*."

"Yeh, I think I have some idea. You've said it three times now."

"I'm just so glad we have it out in the open." *You're not ugly.* She wasn't the least ugly. In fact, she thought she was pretty darn attractive. He was just a typical jock a-hole who thought he was so special he should date supermodels. "And in the future, if I lean over to show you something and I accidentally touch you, it's not on purpose." And because she really did want to keep her job, she added, "Although I'm sure lots of women would kill to touch you."

His brows lowered over his dark eyes, and combined with the black shadow of his beard, he looked kind of scary. "Just not you."

But Chelsea had faced a lot scarier things than one moody hockey player. For all his weight and bulk and anger, he didn't intimidate her. "No. Not me." Time to change the subject before he got mad and got her fired. Or worse, sent her on another humiliating and senseless errand like buying condoms. "I think your participation in the charity golf tournament is important. First, because it's for charity and the press will give it more attention if you're there. Second, because your fans want to see you."

"Are we back to that?" He closed his eyes and groaned. "God, you're like a tick burrowing into my head. I told you I can't play. I'd come in over par on every damn shot."

A pit bull and now a tick. Flattering. "Your score isn't the point."

"The score is always the point." He reached for his cane and rose to his full height. "I don't play anything that I can't win."

"You don't celebrate second place."

"That's right."

"This event is for charity. The point of playing for any charity isn't whether you win first, second, or third. It's your participation." He opened his mouth to argue but she held up one hand. "Just think about it. I have another week before I have to give them an answer either way."

He moved past her. "Stop interfering in my life."

"I'm just trying to help you." She followed him. "I'm really at a loss here. I don't know what you need."

He stopped suddenly and she almost ran into his wide back and black nylon jogging pants.

"You are the only person I've ever worked for that doesn't have an impossible list for me. You don't have a list at all. Tell me what you need for me to do for you."

His back straightened. "I don't *need* you to do anything for me."

She moved in front of him and looked up into his face. Light from the front of the house slashed across his nose and the top of his chest. His mouth was compressed even more than usual. "The Chinooks are paying me good money to be your assistant."

"Whatever they're paying you, I'll give you double to quit."

Somehow she doubted he'd give her twenty

grand. "It's not just about the money," she lied. "I get satisfaction from my work. You need me and—"

"I don't need you."

"—and," she continued as if he hadn't interrupted, "if you don't tell me what I can do to help you out, I'll just have to keep coming up with stuff on my own."

"Fine. You can write back to all those seven thousand hockey fans you're so concerned about."

It wasn't like she hadn't ever answered someone else's fan mail before. "What do you want the e-mail to say?"

"One e-mail is so impersonal." He continued around the stairs and headed down the darkened hall. "I think you need to answer each individually."

She called after him, her Kate Spade wedges suddenly rooted to the tile. "What?"

"Write to each of the fans individually," he repeated, his voice trailing after him.

Dread weighted her feet, and she forced herself to follow. "I thought a mass 'thank you for your concern,' yada yada, e-mail would be nice."

"Yada yada isn't personal." He moved into a huge room with one of the biggest televisions she'd ever seen, a big leather couch, a large chaise, and three poker tables. She stopped in the doorway.

"Mention how much their letters mean to me,"

he said over his shoulder. "And include something about their own letter so they'll think I read it myself."

"What a tool," she whispered.

He turned and looked at her across the room. "Did you just call me a tool?"

He might have fractured half the bones in his body, but there was nothing wrong with his hearing. She pointed to the poker tables and totally lied. "No. I said, 'That's cool.' Do you play a lot of poker?"

"I used to." He grabbed the television remote from an end table and turned toward the television. "You better get going on those e-mails."

Tool, she mouthed to his back. Then she turned and made her way back to the office in the front of the house. Her wooden wedges thumped across the tile floor like a death knell. "Seven thousand e-mails," she moaned. *Ten thousand dollars.*

She pulled out the chair Mark had been sitting in earlier and called her sister. "I need to know who to contact to get access to Mark's guest book page on the Chinooks' Web site," she explained. "The e-mail addresses of the people who signed it are hidden." After a few minutes of further explanations, she grabbed a pen and a pad of sticky notes from a drawer. She wrote down a name and a number and called the senior manager of the Web site. After some back-and-forth, he determined that she wasn't some wacko trying to get access. He gave her the link to the administration panel, username, and a password she could use. Within minutes she was in. Easy, cheesy, lemon squeezy. Now came the hard part, replying to all those letters.

The first dozen notes expressed the writers' best wishes for Mark's recovery. They were filled with concern, recollections, and hero worship. Chelsea hit reply and wrote basically the same message in all of them:

Thank you for your concern and for taking the time to write. Your caring support means a lot to me. I am doing well and feeling better every day.

Mark Bressler

After forty-five minutes of mind-numbing work, she came across:

Hi Mark,

This is Lydia Ferrari.

Chelsea smiled. Ferrari. Right.

We met at Lava Lounge a few months before your accident. I had on the green mini T-shirt dress and you said I looked like Heidi Klum.

Chelsea rolled her eyes before she continued.

We hooked up in my apartment in Redmond. It was one of the best nights of my life. I gave you my digits but you never called. At first my feelings were hurt but now I'm just sad to hear about your accident. I hope you recover soon.

> *Lydia*

She didn't know which was worse. That Lydia had hooked up with a man she'd met in a bar or that she'd written about it in a public forum. As for Mark's behavior, she wasn't surprised. Disgusted but not surprised. He was a jock.

Dear Lydia, she wrote.

Sorry I hooked up with you and never called. I'm kind of a jerk that way. On behalf of all men everywhere who've said they were going to call and never did, I'd like to apologize. Although really, Lydia,

what do you expect? Get a little self-esteem and quit
hooking up with men you meet in bars.

Chelsea sat back and looked at what she'd written. Instead of hitting reply, she pressed delete
and erased Lydia's inappropriate letter and her response.

The next letter began:

Mark Turdler,

Karma's a bitch. That hit you gave Marleau was il-
legal as hell. I'm glad you're in a coma.

> *Dan from San Jose*

She deleted that one, too. There really wasn't an
excuse for someone to write something so horrible,
and she didn't think she should dignify Dan with a
response.

She answered a few more, then read:

Mark,

My son and I never miss a Chinooks' home game
and a chance to see you play. You are an inspiration
to my eight-year-old son, Derek, who met you at

youth hockey camp last summer. You were his coach and taught him to never give up. He talks about you all the time, and because of your encouragement, he wants to play professional hockey someday.

Mary White

Chelsea lifted her eyes from the screen and looked at the posters and trophies and other memorabilia around the room. A Chinooks' jersey with the number "12" and the name "BRESSLER" written across the shoulders hung behind Plexiglas and beneath a broken hockey stick on the wall. On another wall hung a picture of him wearing a deep blue jersey, his hair matted and sweaty. A huge smile curved his mouth and showed his straight white teeth. In one hand he held a puck with a piece of tape across it. The number "500" was written across the white cloth tape.

All these things had meaning to him and told the story of his life. A life filled with hero worship and hockey, hooking up with random women, and inspiring young boys.

His was a story she didn't know. And truthfully, didn't understand. He had so much. Was so lucky, and yet he was so angry. It was like he'd flipped a switch and closed off the laughing, smiling man she'd watched in interview clips. The Mark Bressler she knew was more like the man she'd seen in other video clips of him, the hockey player throwing punches and fighting it out on the ice.

No, she didn't understand his anger and his somber moods, but she supposed she wasn't getting paid to understand him. She looked at the computer screen and got back to work.

Dear Mary, she wrote.

It was my pleasure to coach Derek last summer. I'm glad to hear he does not plan to give up. I'll come see him play in the NHL someday.

Take care,

Mark Bressler

She scrolled to the next letter and made a mental note to ask Mark about youth hockey camp. He wouldn't like it. He'd probably accuse her of being pushy and trying to run his life. He'd call her a tick, but his life needed someone to run it.

After forty minutes and ten more letters, she rose and stretched her arms over her head. At this rate, it was going to take her forever to get the letters written, and she suspected that's why he'd told her to do it. She dropped her hands to her side and moved through the house toward the leisure room. Light from all the leaded glass windows smeared milky patches across the stone and wood and made her think she was in a villa in Tuscany. She wondered if his former wife had chosen the house, because the little she did know of Mark, it didn't seem to suit his tastes. He seemed like more a modern architecture kind of guy.

The carpet in the huge room silenced the soles of her shoes as she walked inside. On the television, the noon news showed the weather forecast for the next week. The sound was so low she could barely hear it. The curtains were open, and the late morning sun poured in through large French doors, bleaching the carpet a lighter beige and stopping just short of the large chaise where Mark lay, asleep. His right hand rested on his stomach, the blue splint contrasting with the white of his T-shirt. His left hand lay on the leather beside him, palm up, his fingers curled around the remote. The permanent frown between his brows was gone, his forehead smooth. He looked younger, softer, which seemed odd given the strong angles of his face and the dark spiky stubble.

If I mention that I haven't been laid for six months, are

you going to start lining up hookers? he'd asked, and she bit the side of her lips to keep from laughing and waking him up. She'd worked for a comedian once who *had* asked her to get him a hooker. He'd used a certain escort service and had wanted Chelsea to go pick the girl up and drop her off. He'd wanted her to come back two hours later, then take the girl back home. She'd refused, and the comedian had paid for a cab instead.

Unlike the comedian, Mark Bressler obviously had no problems when it came to getting females. He was very good-looking and had a raw sexual aura that surrounded him like a poisonous cloud. Unless he had some sort of fetish, she just couldn't see him dialing up hookers.

She moved to the heavy drapery and shut the curtains. It was a good thing she wasn't easily offended anymore. If he'd made those comments about her large boobs several years ago, she would have burst into tears and run from his house, which she suspected was the reason he'd insulted her.

Again.

She turned, and he rubbed his injured hand across his stomach and chest, the rasp of his splint barely audible over the low voices pouring from the television. He didn't open his eyes, and she wondered if she should wake him for lunch. Instead she tiptoed out of the room. Best not to poke the beast.

She went back to work, answering fan letters. For the next two days she wrote mostly generic responses or deleted inappropriate messages. Wednesday, she took a break from the computer to drive Mark to a doctor's appointment a few miles away, and Thursday she drove him to the Verizon store. Both times he was such a horrible backseat driver, she threatened to drive him around in her Honda if he didn't shut up.

He did. For a few minutes.

"Son of a bitch!" he swore as she drove him home from the Verizon store that Thursday afternoon. "That car almost hit us broadside."

"A miss is as good as a mile," she quoted her mother.

"Obviously not, or your car wouldn't be dented to shit."

Her Honda wasn't "dented to shit." It had a few minor parking lot dings. "That's it. From now on we're taking my car. You call *me* a tick and a nag, but *you* are the worst backseat driver in the entire state of Washington and half of Oregon."

"You don't know every backseat driver in Washington and half of Oregon."

She ignored his comment. "You bitch when I pull

out too fast. You bitch when it's not fast enough. You bitch when I go through a yellow light and bitch when I stop," she said. "For a person who has so much in life, you complain a lot."

"You don't know jackshit about my life."

"I know that you're bored. You need a hobby. Something to do."

"I don't need a hobby."

"I'm thinking you should get involved in youth hockey camp. I know from reading your fan letters that you were a positive influence in the lives of those kids."

He looked out the passenger window and was silent for several moments before he said, "In case you haven't figured it out, I can't skate these days."

"When I went to that Stanley Cup final with my sister and Jules, I noticed that the Chinook coaches just stand behind the bench, act really cranky, and yell a lot. You can do that. You're good at being cranky and yelling."

"I've never yelled at you."

"You just yelled 'son of a bitch' at me."

"I raised my voice in reaction to you almost killing me. I survived one car wreck. I don't want to be taken out now by a little person who can hardly see over the dash."

Maybe that explained why he was so horrible when she drove him around. He was terrified of another car crash. Of course, that didn't explain his asshole behavior at home. "I can see perfectly fine and I'm five-one and a half." She stopped at a red light and looked across the car at him. "In order to be considered a little person and attend the annual LPA national convention, I'd have to be four-ten or under."

He turned and faced her. Both his brows rose above the frames of his sunglasses.

"What?"

He shook his head. "You know the height requirement of little people?"

She shrugged and glanced up at the traffic light. "When you grow up with kids calling you a midget, you look these things up."

He chuckled, but she wasn't amused. The one time he decided to laugh, it was at her. The light changed, and she put her foot on the gas pedal. Once again he'd managed to change the subject. "One of the letters I answered yesterday was from Mary White. You coached her son Derek."

He turned and looked out the passenger window once more. He was quiet for a few seconds, then said, "I don't remember a Derek."

She didn't know if that was the truth or he was

just trying to shut her up. "That's a shame. The impression I got from his mother was that you were a great coach."

"Sometime today, you need to program my phone," he said, subject closed. "I'll give you a list of names and you can look the numbers up."

She'd drop the subject. For now. "Programming a cell is really easy." Because his phone was lost and he hadn't backed up his numbers to the Verizon secure site, he'd lost everything. Yeah, it was easy, but finding all his numbers and programming them into his phone would take time. Time that she would rather spend plowing through the fan letters. "You can do it."

"I don't get paid to do it," he said as they pulled into the garage. "You do."

When they walked into the house, a cleaning service was there vacuuming and washing all those windows. Mark scribbled a list of names, then handed her his cell. "That will get you started," he said, then disappeared into the elevator.

Chelsea plugged in the phone to give it a good charge before she turned to Mark's computer and got back to work. While she answered a fan letter, an e-mail popped in his personal inbox. In case it was a Realtor, she opened his e-mail program. The return address caught her eye, and she opened it.

Coach Mark, it read.

My mom let me read what you wrote I hope you get better really soon I've been practicing my stops like you tot me I'm getting good you should see.

Derek White

Derek White? How had the kid managed to get ahold of Mark's e-mail address? Wasn't he like eight? If he'd been older, she might be scared. As it was, she was slightly alarmed.

Derek, she wrote.

Good to hear from you. I don't know if I'll be at hockey camp this year. If I can't, I'll miss you too. I'm glad to hear that you are practicing and I'd love to see how good you are getting.

Coach Mark

P. S. How did you manage to get my e-mail address?

Chapter Eight

Friday afternoon, Mark looked forward to a day of doing nothing besides watching junk TV. As was true with his life lately, there seemed to be a conspiracy to change his plans. "That double overtime against Colorado in the regular season was grueling. One of the toughest games I've ever played," Sam Leclaire said as he raised a bottle of Corona to his lips. The light in the room caressed the black and purple shiner smudging his right eye.

"It wasn't pretty. Especially with you sitting out a double minor," Mark agreed as he looked at the four hockey players lounging on his couches and chairs inside the leisure room. Through the open glass doors, two more of the guys stood on the veranda outside, hitting golf balls across the yard and into the thick, short hedge. Beyond the hedge was the Medina golf course, and Mark hoped they kept the balls off the green or he'd hear about it from the grounds superintendent, aka Kenneth the Nazi. Kenneth was just one more reason he needed to get the hell out of Medina.

"Hensick took a dive on that one. The pansy ass rolled around like a girl. He embarrassed himself."

Which might have been true, but didn't mean that Sam hadn't tripped Hensick. Then punched him for good measure and gave Colorado the power play.

The guys had shown up at his house half an hour ago, unannounced. He was pretty sure they'd organized this little trip without calling first because they knew he'd tell them not to come. He hated to admit it, but he was glad they'd shown up without warning. He'd known most of these guys for a long time. He'd been their captain, but they were more than just teammates. They were friends. Close as brothers, and he missed shooting the shit with them. He hadn't known how much until now.

Today they all looked rough around the edges. Like warriors who'd just survived a battle. The two defensemen outside looked the worst of the lot. Left guard Vlad Fetisov had a few stitches in his brow, while the team's enforcer, Andre Courtoure, had butterfly tape closing a cut on his chin. Inside the house, second-in-command, alternate captain Walker Brooks, wore a brace on his left knee. Of course there was Sam's shiner, but Sam always had a shiner. He was a good guy. Always laughing and joking, but there was something darker inside. Something he tended to work out on the ice. Which made Sam a liability almost as much as a damn good hockey player.

"The rumor is that Eddie is leaving," forward Daniel Holstrom informed everyone from his position on the side of the chaise. Unfortunately, Daniel had yet to shave off his playoffs beard, and the growth of blond hair on his cheeks and chin looked moth-eaten.

Sniper Frankie Kawczynski raised a bottle of Corona to his lips. "Isn't he already playing in the Swedish leagues these days?"

"Not Eddie the Eagle. Assistant coach Eddie," Daniel clarified.

"What?" Walker looked across the room at Daniel, incredulous. "Eddie Thornton?"

"Thorny?"

"That's what I hear. He's signing on as the assistant coach in Dallas."

"Where did you hear that?" Mark wanted to know.

"Around. I bet it's true. Thorny never did get along with Larry," he added, referring to the Chinooks' head coach, Larry Nystrom.

"Nystrom can be a straight-up hard-ass," Frankie said. He sat in a chair to Mark's left, a big kid from Wisconsin whose height and bulk had deceived many opposing players. Frankie was as nimble as a ballerina, with a slap shot clocked at one hundred and fifteen miles an hour. Just three miles short of the record holder, Bobby Hull. Mark had helped handpick Frankie when Mark and the late owner of the team, Virgil Duffy, had looked over the NHL draft several years ago.

Mark shrugged. "Larry's always been a fair hard-ass."

"True," Frankie agreed. "But remember when he got all apoplectic and turned purple after Tampa Bay handed our balls to us a couple seasons ago? I thought he was going to bust a vessel in his head and blood would shoot from his eyes."

"Apoplectic?" Mark laughed. "Have you been reading again?"

"Unlike most of you guys, I did spend a few years in college before I was drafted."

As much as the guys could get on Mark's nerves, he missed the constant razzing. He pointed to his own chin and asked Daniel, "Why are you keeping the fuzz?" He and the Stromster had played on the same front line for past six seasons. The Swede had been drafted by the Chinooks his rookie year. The same year Mark had been named captain.

"I like it."

"You should have seen Blake's." Sam chuckled and took a drink from his bottle. "He looked like someone had given him a bikini wax on his face. One of those Brazilians like my ex-girlfriend used to get on her patch."

Mark glanced toward the door. The guys didn't know there was a woman in the house. Exactly where his little assistant was, Mark didn't know. When he'd answered the door, she hadn't been in the office at the front of the house.

"It was bad," Walker agreed, "but I thought Johan's beard was—" He stopped, and his attention shifted to the vicinity of Mark's crotch as "American Woman" played from the pocket of his jogging pants. The nylon pocket had slid to his inner thigh, and he looked around at the curious faces. Mark stuck his hand in his pocket and dug around next to his balls. He pulled out his new cell phone as The Guess Who warned American woman to stay away. A picture of Chelsea flashed on the cell's screen. "Yeah?" he answered.

"Hi, it's me."

"I guessed that. Tell me about 'American Woman.'"

"'American Woman' was a song written and performed by the Guess Who and later Lenny Kravitz."

"I know all that. Why is it on my phone?"

"It's my ringtone so that you know it's me. I thought it was appropriate given our relationship."

"Where are you and why are you calling?"

"In the kitchen. I'm taking a break from answering fan letters, and I just wanted to know if you or your guests need anything."

There it was again. Need. "I'm sure the guys could use another beer."

"I figured. How many guys are there?"

"Six counting Vlad, but he's not drinking today." Which Mark knew from his long association with the Russian meant he was hungover. He flipped the phone closed and lifted one hip and shoved it back in his pocket. For the most part, when the guys got together at his house to drink or play poker or both, it was just the guys. He didn't know how they'd react to a female in their mix. "That was my assistant," he told them. "She's bringing more beer."

Sam finished off his Corona and set the empty bottle on an end table. "You have an assistant?"

"More like a pain in the ass." Mark stuck one finger beneath the brace and scratched the back of his hand. "The Chinooks kept sending nurses over here to check my pulse and make sure I took a crap.

I hated having them hover over me, watching me all the time, so I guess the organization thought they'd have better luck if they sent an assistant."

"What's she like?"

"Annoying as hell." Mark leaned back against the soft leather couch. "You'll see."

A few minutes later she walked into the room, all five feet nothing of her, carrying a tin bucket filled with ice and Coronas. "Hello, gentlemen. Don't get up," she said, even though no one had made a move to stand. She wore those big clunky shoes she favored and a short leather skirt with animal print on it—zebra maybe. Her baggy black blouse had a big bow on the front, and her neon pink cell phone was clipped to the sparkly red belt wrapped around her waist. In the short time that she'd worked for him, Mark had noticed that she wore her tops really loose and her bottoms really tight. He wondered if she thought big shirts made her big breasts less noticeable. They didn't. "I'm Chelsea Ross, Mr. Bressler's personal assistant." She bent forward to set the bucket on the coffee table, and Mark watched Frankie's gaze slide to her little behind wrapped up in black-and-white-striped leather. "I've brought beer. Any takers?"

All four gentlemen raised their hands like they were in school.

"You look familiar," Walker said, tilting his head to one side to study her.

Mark had always thought so too.

She grabbed a beer out of the bucket, slid her hands up the bottle, and twisted off the top. "Do you watch *The Young and the Restless*?"

"No."

"Ever seen *Slasher Camp*?"

"No."

She handed Walker the Corona. *"Killer Valentine? Prom Night 2? He Knows It's You?"* She turned back to the bucket. *"Motel on Lake Hell?"*

"Don't forget that 'go meat' commercial," Mark reminded her. "The one where you wore a cheerleader outfit."

She chuckled and pulled another beer from the ice. "Good to know you were paying attention."

Droplets of water slipped across the tips of her fingers, ran down the bottle, and dripped into the bucket. Yeah, he was paying attention. Too much attention, although he didn't know why. "Among Chelsea's many talents, she's a scream queen," he informed the guys.

Daniel looked up at her as she moved toward him. "You're a what?"

"I'm an actress." She handed the Swede the bottle

and flicked the droplets from the tips of her fingers. "I recently moved here from L.A."

"And you've starred in horror movies?" Walker asked.

"I wish." She shook her head and moved back to the coffee table. "I didn't *star* in horror films, but I've acted in a number of them. My biggest role was in *Slasher Camp.* I got the axe, literally, within the first half hour." She dug around in the ice and pulled out a Corona. "The amount of blood was ridiculous. The scene was shot at night in the woods and called for me to be practically nude. They didn't even warm up the fake blood before they splashed it all over my throat. All that gross stuff gushed down my chest and soaked my white underwear. I about froze to death."

Stunned silence filled the leisure room as Mark, and he was sure every other guy within hearing distance, pictured her naked breasts, nipples hard from the cold, covered in fake blood. Jesus, he was getting that heavy feeling again in his stomach.

It was Sam who finally broke the silence. "What was the name of that movie again?"

"*Slasher Camp.* I played Angel, the slutty best friend." She twisted off the cap and dropped it into the bucket. "In a lot of horror movies, the slutty girl is a metaphor for an immoral society and must be killed. You can interchange the slutty girl with the pot-smoking boy, but it's always the same message. Immoral choices must be punished, while the virginal, squeaky-clean lead kills the bad guy and gets to live." She took a deep breath and let it out. "I always drew the line at torture porn like *Turistas* or the *Hostel* films. There's a huge difference between metaphorical stereotypes in society and sexual objectification."

What? What the hell did that mean?

"I don't watch those movies. They scare the hell out of me," Frankie said, then snapped his fingers. "I got it. You look like the short girl in the PR department." He raised both palms as if he was about to hold two melons in front of his chest, quickly thought better of it, and dropped them. "What's her name?"

"Bo." She walked around the table to Frankie. "Bo Ross. She's my twin sister."

"Jesus. Mini Pit." Of course. It was so obvious, Mark wondered why he hadn't connected the two.

She glanced at him. "Who?"

"Mini Pit," Sam explained. "It's short for Mini Pit Bull."

"You call my sister Mini Pit?"

Sam shook his head. "Not to her face. We're too damn afraid."

She chuckled, and Mark was still amazed that he

hadn't made the connection. "Short. Bossy. Annoying as hell. I should have made the connection that first day." The thought of two identically annoying, short, bossy-as-hell women kind of scared the crap out of him. The feeling in his stomach dissipated. Which was a good thing. A very good thing.

She looked over her shoulder at Mark as she handed the beer to Frankie. "It's probably the hair that threw you."

"That's bad, but more than likely . . ." He paused to point to her wild skirt. "It's the brain-numbing clothes you wear."

She moved to the bucket and grabbed another beer. "If your brain is numb it's more than likely the Vicodin."

Sam laughed. He loved shit talk, no matter who was talking it. "He's getting old. His memory isn't great."

"His memory is convenient." She twisted the top and held the beer toward Sam.

"Thanks, Short Boss."

She pulled the bottle back before he could grab it. "Did you just call me Short *Boss* or Short *Bus*?"

"Boss." She shoved the beer toward him and he took it from her. "What are you doing later?"

"Are you hitting on my assistant?" Mark asked before she could respond. He didn't like the idea of any of the guys hitting on Chelsea. Not because he had any interest in her, but because he was doing his best to discourage her from sticking around. If the guys liked her, she'd never leave.

"I've never known a scream queen." Sam grinned and took a drink of his beer. Mark knew for a fact that Chelsea wasn't Sam's type. Sam liked tall, leggy women with big lips. Like Angelina Jolie. His preference was so well-known that everyone razzed him about dating Octomom.

"I'm going to church with my sister," she said, her blue eyes shining with humor. "You're welcome to come along."

"I'll pass."

Vlad and Andre walked through the door from outside, oblivious of Chelsea. "If you go to ze strip clubz," the big Russian was schooling the rookie, "ze Luztee Lady is a good one. Ze best."

"The Lusty Lady is a dive," Andre said. "I prefer the clubs in Canada. Cheetahs in Kelowna has totally nude dancing and the girls are hot. If you go, get a lap dance from Cinnamon. I don't think that's her real name, but she has better—"

"You guys haven't met my assistant," Mark interrupted before the two got into a debate over which nudie bar gave the best lap dances. Although everyone knew that it wasn't Cheetahs. It was Scores in Las Vegas.

"Hey guys." She looked up and smiled. "You must be Vlad."

Vlad wasn't unattractive. Just severe-looking. Women had been known to run in the other direction. Especially if he dropped his pants and showed them the impaler. Although to be fair, he didn't do that much anymore.

Without moving his head, Vlad glanced at Mark before returning his gaze to Chelsea. "Yez."

"Mr. Bressler mentioned that you weren't drinking today." She dug down in the ice and pulled out a bottle of Evian. She moved toward him and gazed up into his face. "So I brought you water."

"Thanz."

"You're welcome." She turned to Andre. "Can I get you a beer?"

Andre wasn't tall like Vlad or the rest of the players, but he was massive and had a low center of gravity, like a cement pylon. Which came in handy when he needed to knock an opposing player off the puck or duke it out. "Ah—yeah. I guess."

Mark didn't know if the rookie enforcer was stunned or embarrassed. Probably both. For the past year or so, there'd never been a female in the house when the boys had gathered. They weren't used to putting their best manners forward while they drank beer at Mark's house.

"I watched you guys play the other night." Chelsea moved to the bucket. "I'd never been to a hockey game before, and I know absolutely nothing about it, but you guys did great."

"Yeah," Mark said dryly. "They won the cup."

She leaned forward a little, and her skirt slid up the backs of her smooth legs. She had the kind of legs he liked on a woman. If she was standing in front of him naked, with her knees touching, there was just enough room to slip his hand between her thighs.

She stood up straight and moved toward Andre, holding a beer. "Why did you hit that guy in the head the other night?"

"When?"

"Second period."

Andre's black brows lowered. "He had the puck," he answered, as if that explained it all. And it did. She gave him the beer, and he said, "Thanks."

Little Miss Sunshine smiled at the rookie. "You're welcome. Does your chin hurt?"

He shook his head and returned her smile. "It was just a little love tap."

She looked at Vlad and pointed to her own brow. "Is that a love tap?"

"Nah. Hurtz like hell."

She laughed, and it occurred to Mark that she not only wasn't running like hell, she wasn't the least bit intimidated by any of the other six big hockey players in the room. She grabbed a bottle of water and moved toward him. "Holler if you need anything," she said, and handed him a bottle of Evian. He reached for it but she didn't let go. His fingers brushed her hand and he almost pulled back. "My number is programmed into your cell. So you don't have to come and find me."

"What's my ringtone?"

She smiled and let go of the water. "Any of you guys need anything else?" she asked instead of answering his question.

"Maybe nachos," Andre answered.

She turned to the enforcer, her back facing Mark. "I don't cook."

"But you're a girl."

Mark reached into his pocket and pulled out his cell.

"That doesn't mean I was born with a burning desire to brown meat and grate cheese."

He hit redial on his phone, and Chelsea's Black-

Berry lit up a split second before the line about "messing with a son of a bitch" played from the vicinity of her waist. She reached for the cell, pushed a few buttons, then turned toward him.

He raised a brow and she explained, "I thought I'd just stick with the Guess Who. Kind of a ringtone theme."

Sam laughed.

"Have fun guys," she said, and practically ran out of the room and down the long hall.

The boys watched her go, and the room fell into silence. Of course Sam was the one to break it.

"She's cute."

Mark watched the white stripes on her skirt disappear from sight. Sure she was an attractive girl, but they didn't know the real Chelsea.

"I like ze short womenz."

"You like any _womenz._"

Vlad shrugged his big Russian shoulders and pointed toward the doorway. "And bringz the beer too."

"Damn. I need myself an assistant." Sam raised his Corona to his lips and took a long drink. "Better than a wife. Less trouble than a girlfriend."

Mark shook his head. "You just saw her good side. She's pushy and annoying. She's a mini pit bull." He pointed his stiff middle finger at them. "Just like her twin sister. Remember that."

At the thought of Bo Ross they all winced, except Andre. "I've always thought Mini Pit was cute. Kind of feisty."

"I like ze feizty womenz."

They room fell quiet for several moments. The guys all looked at one another as if they were waiting for something. Then Walker leaned forward and placed his forearms on his thighs. "Listen, Mark. We all need to know something." He dangled the Corona from one hand and got to the real reason they'd all shown up on his doorstep. "Where were you the other night?" He turned his head and looked at Mark. "We thought you'd be there."

He didn't have to elaborate. Mark knew what night he meant.

"We all talked about it beforehand. If we won, Savage was going to immediately hand the cup to you because you were our captain long before him. He did a hell of a job filling your shoes after the accident. He was great and all the guys like and respect him, but he isn't you. He could never be you, and to his credit, he never tried." Walker looked at the other men in the room. He was the alternate captain. The second in charge when the captain wasn't around.

He was a good man and a leader, and there was a reason he wore the A on his jersey. "Playing without you wasn't easy on anyone. We were worried about you, trying to get used to Savage, and battling for the cup. You were on this team for eight years. You built it and you led us to the playoffs. We didn't win the cup because we had Savage. He's a damn good hockey player and we were lucky to get him. We won because of the hard work we all put into it. The hard work that you put into it, and you should have been there the night we won. Why weren't you?"

They needed an answer, and he supposed he could lie and they'd all go home happy. But they deserved better, and he'd always told them the truth. "I have really mixed feelings about that night," he said, and unscrewed the top to his Evian. "I could lie to you all, but I won't. I'm glad you guys won. Beyond happy for every one of you. You deserve it, and I mean that to my core." He placed his right hand against his chest. "But at the same time, I am pissed that I couldn't win the cup with you. I am pissed that it was Savage and not me. I could have gone that night and pretended it didn't matter. That everything was sunshine and rainbows, but you all would have seen through the bullshit."

He took a drink of water, then screwed the cap back on. "My whole life, that's the only dream I've ever had. The one thing I've ever really wanted, but a freak accident took it from me." He dropped his hand to his side. "Everyone tells me that I should just feel grateful to be alive. Well, I don't. I don't feel much of anything at all. Just anger." A burning ball of anger that he didn't know how to get rid of. "I'm sorry. I'm a selfish dick. I'm sorry if I let you down. You're right. I should have been there with you guys, but I just couldn't."

"Thanks for being honest." Walker sat back. "I can't say that I understand, though. More than anyone in this room, you deserved to be the first man to hold the cup. The fact that you didn't play in the playoffs doesn't change that."

Sam agreed. "That's right."

Mark looked across at Sam. "Just because I wasn't there, doesn't mean I didn't see the game. I watched right here." He pointed to the couch. "And that penalty you drew in the second frame was stupid and could have cost the game. And instead of partying and pouring beer from the cup onto women in bikinis, you'd be bawling your eyes out like a girl."

"Savage was thrown in the box too."

"Savage was hit from behind. You weren't. When are you going to get it into your head that you're not an enforcer? That's Andre's job."

Sam grinned.

Daniel chuckled.

Vlad rocked back on his heels and smiled.

"What?" Mark asked. "What's so damn funny?"

"You sound like your old self," Walker answered.

He would never be his old self. If he ever forgot it, the ache in his hip and thigh was a constant reminder.

"You should talk to someone about the coaching job," Daniel suggested. "At the press conference the other day, Darby said there would always be a place for you in the Chinooks' organization."

"I think he was blowing smoke." The thought of driving to work at the Key Arena turned and twisted the burning anger in his gut.

"I don't believe that," Walker said. "You should think about it."

They'd come here today for an answer. But they'd also come because they wanted him to be okay. He could see it in their eyes. Because they seemed to want to believe it so badly, he opened his mouth and lied. "I'll think about it."

Chapter Nine

"I know what you need?"

He looked into her small face, half covered in shadows. "What?"

She ran her small hands up his bare chest and rose onto the balls of her feet. "This." She kissed the side of his neck. The hot, moist pull of her mouth on his skin slammed into his chest, forcing the air from his lungs. "You need this." Her warm breath brushed across his throat, and he shuddered. His whole body was alive, every cell and pleasure receptor sensitive to her satin touch.

"Yes." He raised his hands and tangled his fingers in her blond and red hair. He brought her head back and gazed into her lust-heavy blue eyes as he lowered his mouth. Down to her sweet, wet lips. She tasted good, like the pleasure he'd been missing in his life. Like sex. Like hot, hungry sex. The kind that ripped a man apart. The kind that left him battered and bloody and willing to die for more.

Her tongue slid into his mouth, slick and wanting. He fed from her long, hungry kisses as her hands slid over his body. Her fingers combed through the short hair on his chest. Touching him and leaving little trails of fire across his flesh.

He raised his head, gasping, and looked into her face, at her lips, pouty and wet, and her eyes, shining with desire. She stepped back and pulled her dress over her head. Except for a pair of white panties, she was naked beneath. He didn't bother to check his response. To go easy. He went to that wild primal place beating in his chest and groin and he pushed her down onto the chaise. Her panties disappeared along with his clothes, and he lay down on her soft, warm body.

"Yes," she whispered as he pulled back and drove into her. Her back arched and she smiled. "This is what you need."

Mark's eyes flew open and he stared up at his dark ceiling. The black blades of his fan disturbed the air and pushed it across his face. His heart pounded in his chest and his groin ached. Desire, both sharp and dull, pulled at his testicles and he slid his hands beneath the sheets just to make sure he wasn't dreaming that part too. He laid his palm across his boxers and on top of an impressive hard-on. He sucked in a breath through his teeth at both the pleasure and the pain. His erection heated the cotton of his underwear and warmed his palm and he curled his fingers around the long, hard length of it. Because of an erotic dream about his little assistant, he was as hard as a steel club. He didn't know whether to be alarmed, or to be horrified, or to fall to his knees on the side of the bed and praise Jesus.

Chelsea cracked open her eyes and winced as the morning light stabbed her corneas. Pain squeezed her forehead, and her mouth felt like she'd eaten socks. She stared into her sister's face on the pillow next to hers, just like when they'd been kids. Had something happened? Where had they been the night before?

"Oh God," she groaned. Karaoke at Ozzie's Road-house flashed before her scratchy eyes, an excruciating memory of her and Bo belting out "Like a Virgin" and "I'm Too Sexy" at the tops of their lungs. There was only one person on the planet with a worse voice than Chelsea. Bo. Bo was worse, and Chelsea was shocked the crowd at Ozzie's hadn't tossed them outside.

She sat up and waited for the pounding in her head to dull before she swung her feet over the side of the bed. With her eyes half closed, she wandered down the hall and into the bathroom. The vinyl floor felt cool beneath her feet, and she stuck her mouth under the faucet and turned on the cold water. She drank like a camel, then rose to look at herself in the mirror. Black smudges circled her eyes and her hair stuck out on one side. She looked as good as she felt and reached for the Tylenol. She downed three Caplets and wandered back toward the bedroom.

"Good morning, sunshine."

Chelsea stopped and peered down the hall at the half-naked man standing in the kitchen. "What are you doing?"

"Eating breakfast," Jules answered as he poured milk over a bowl of cereal.

"Why are you eating breakfast here?"

"I'm not surprised you don't remember. Bo called me last night and I met the two of you. I was the only one in any condition to drive."

Chelsea retraced her steps, grabbed a terry-cloth robe from the back of the bathroom door, and continued toward the kitchen. Tiny bits and pieces were starting to come back to her. "Why are you still here?" she asked as she tied the fluffy belt around her waist.

"Since I live in Kent, and it was after two in the morning, you and your sister told me to crash in Bo's room." He reached into a drawer and grabbed a spoon.

It was too bad she was hungover and her eyes hurt because she really couldn't fully appreciate Jules's developed chest or each muscle of his six-pack. She pointed to his tight leather pants. "Are you trying to be Tom Jones or Slash?"

"We talked about this last night when you accused me of having a metrosexual meltdown." He took a bite. "But again, I'm not surprised you don't remember. You were totally wrecked."

"I remember." Unfortunately, more than just bits and pieces of the night was starting to come back. The singing. The drinking. The flirting with college boys and tourists.

Jules pointed his spoon at her. "You look like shit."

"Perfect. I feel like shit."

"Want some granola?"

"Maybe." She moved past him and grabbed a Coke out of the refrigerator. There was nothing like a sugary Coke to help with a hangover. Unless it was a Quarter Pounder with cheese and extra greasy fries. Pure hangover heaven.

"How's Bo this morning?"

Chelsea raised the Coke to her lips and chugged

half the can. "Still asleep," she said when she lowered the soda. She had a vague memory of her sister and Jules making out while Chelsea was busy flirting with a tourist from Ireland. She'd ask Bo about it later. She poured herself a bowl of cereal and joined Jules at the kitchen table.

"How are things working out with Bressler?" he asked.

"The same. He resents that I'm there and gives me crappy stuff to do." She took a bite, and the crunching in her head was so loud she could hardly think past the pain. "A bunch of hockey players came to his house and drank beer yesterday."

"You mentioned it last night, but you never said who showed up."

Chelsea thought of all those huge men in one room. She had to admit that she'd been a little intimidated. Not so much by their size. Most people were taller than she and Bo, but she'd seen them play hockey. She'd seen them slam into the boards so hard, the wood and Plexiglas shook. She'd seen them slam into other players equally hard. Walking into that room yesterday had been like walking into a wall of testosterone, but Chelsea was an actress. She'd auditioned in front of casting directors and producers, and she'd learned a long time ago to master her nerves. To appear calm and cool on the outside, no matter what she walked into. "There was the big Russian guy, Vlad," she answered.

"Did he drop his pants?"

"No."

"Good. I'd heard he doesn't do that as much as he used to. Who else?" Jules took a bite and waited for her to answer.

"Let's see. A guy with a black eye." Within a few seconds of meeting the players, she'd discovered they really weren't intimidating in person. They'd seemed like nice guys. Well, except for Mark. Although, surrounded by his teammates, Mark had been more relaxed. And yes, nicer. For him.

"There are quite a few guys with black eyes."

"I think his name was Sam."

"Sam Leclaire. He scored sixty-six goals this season. Ten of those—"

"Stop." Chelsea held up one hand. "Spare me the stats." She'd had to listen to him and Bo argue goals, points, and penalty minutes all the way home from Ozzie's, and frankly, she'd wanted to shoot them both.

Jules laughed. "You remind me of Faith."

"Who?"

"The owner of the Chinooks. When anyone starts talking stats, she goes all cross-eyed and zones out."

Chelsea remembered now. The beautiful blond

who'd been given a long, slow tongue kiss by the new captain, right in the middle of the Key, while an arena full of fans screamed and cheered them on. "Shouldn't the owner of the team know about stats and stuff like that?" Chelsea tried another bite; this time she chewed slowly.

"She just inherited the team last April. Before that, she was like you and knew nothing about hockey. But she's picked up the important stuff real fast." He shrugged. "Now she has Ty to help her."

"The captain?"

"Yeah. They're in the Bahamas."

"Doing what?"

Jules raised his green eyes from his cereal bowl and just looked at her.

"Oh." She put the spoon down, unsure if her stomach could take more. "If she has Ty to help her out, are you worried about your job?"

He shook his head and shrugged again. "Not really. I think Ty's going to take a job as a scout or have some role in player development, so she'll still need an assistant. I'm going to talk to her about my role when she gets back."

"When's that?" Personally, she'd hate to think her job was up in the air. Well, any further in the air than it already was with Mark Bressler.

"Hopefully before the big celebration party."

"There's a celebration party?"

Jules sat back. "The cup celebration at the Four Seasons next month. The twenty-fourth maybe? It's been put together in the past week, but I'm sure Bressler got an invitation. Or will shortly."

Of course he hadn't mentioned it.

"If you don't get an invite, everyone is allowed one guest. You can go with Bo."

Speaking of her sister, Bo moaned long and loud as she moved down the hall toward them.

"Damn you, Chelsea," she croaked. "I haven't been this hungover since the last time I visited you in L.A." She shuffled to the table and sat down. "Did you make coffee?"

Chelsea shook her head and handed her sister the Coke.

"I did." Jules got up and poured Bo a cup.

"We're getting too old for this," Bo said as she laid her head on the table.

Chelsea secretly agreed. They were both thirty, and at some point in anyone's life, partying to excess lost its appeal. It just got pathetic, and before a girl knew it, she was one of those women who lived life on a bar stool. She tried another bite of her cereal and chewed carefully. Chelsea didn't want to become one of those women with gravelly voices and overly processed hair. She didn't want bad teeth and leathery skin. She didn't want a boyfriend named Cooter who was doing ten to twenty for armed robbery.

Jules set the coffee in front of Bo, then returned to his place across the table. "You girls smell like the old Rainier brewery before they shut it down."

Bo raised the coffee to her lips. "You're not allowed to talk about beer for two days."

"Okay." Jules laughed. "Mini Pit."

Last night, when Chelsea had told Bo that the hockey players called her Mini Pit, Jules had laughed until he'd choked. Neither twin had found it quite that funny, but to make Bo feel better, Chelsea had confessed that they called her Short Boss.

"Not today, Jules." Bo set the coffee down. "Where's your shirt?"

Jules grinned, raised his arms, and flexed like he was in a body-builder competition. "I thought you girls might enjoy the gun show."

"Please," Chelsea moaned. "We're already sick."

"I just vomited in my mouth," her sister added.

Jules laughed and lowered his arm. "I'll put the guns away until later."

"God, I hate it when you're all cheerful. Why aren't you hungover?" Bo wanted to know.

"Because I was your designated driver. You don't remember?"

"Barely."

Chelsea wondered if her sister remembered making out with Jules. She wondered now if maybe she shouldn't bring it up. Ever. There were times when not remembering was best. Like the time several years ago when she'd streaked at a party in the Hollywood Hills. Chelsea had never been one to run like a gazelle, and it hadn't been pretty. Too bad she hadn't remembered that until the next morning. Sheesh, now that she thought of it, maybe she was impulsive. Especially when she drank.

"Do you remember singing 'Kiss'?"

"The Prince song?" Chelsea asked. She didn't recall singing Prince. Madonna and Celine Dion had been bad enough.

"Yeah. And you girls really got into 'I Will Survive.'"

Apparently they'd had quite the song list. Why hadn't anyone stopped them? They'd undoubtedly been horrid. Chelsea turned and looked at her sister. "Do you remember 'I Will Survive'?"

"No. I hate that song. Why would I sing it?"

"You really got into it." Jules added to their misery. "You two belted out that song like it was your own personal anthem or something."

Bo whispered, "It's probably a good thing that parts of last night are a total blank."

"Yeah," Chelsea agreed.

"Don't tell me that you two have forgotten everything." Jules picked up his spoon and continued eating. "You *have* to remember the threesome. Making it with hot twins has always been a personal fantasy of mine." He looked up and grinned. "One that, I think it's safe to say, I share with most men on the planet. I gave you girls some of my best moves, and I'll be crushed if neither of you remember it."

Bo rested her forehead in her hand. "Don't make me kill you, Jules," she said through a tortured sigh. "Not today. I'm just not in the mood to clean up the mess."

After Jules left, the girls moved to the couch and settled in for a little R&R. Recuperation and reality television. A small cooler filled with Coke sat on the coffee table, and they kicked up their feet and tuned in to the brain rot that was *New York Goes to Work*.

Chelsea pointed at the reality star who'd made her first appearance on *Flavor of Love*. "She used to have such a cute body, but she ruined it with those big stripper implants."

Bo nodded. "Sister Patterson should have smacked her upside the head. Why would any woman do that to themselves?"

It was a rhetorical question. "I can completely understand reduction though." Chelsea decided to test the waters and see if her sister's opinion had changed. "Boobs get in the way of everything."

"Yeah, but have you seen the way they do the reduction?" Bo asked as New York shoveled pig manure. "It's a form of mutilation."

Chelsea guessed that answered the question. "It doesn't look that bad. Not like it used to. The scar isn't even very big."

"Don't tell me you're thinking about that again? They carve out huge chunks of your flesh. Like a pumpkin."

Bo sounded just like their mother. There was no talking to her about it, so she let it go.

"Remember when we sent in an audition tape for *The Real World*?"

Chelsea laughed. They'd been nineteen and learned the MTV reality show was going to be shot in Hawaii. They'd wanted to go in the worst way. "Yeah. We thought for sure they'd pick us because we're twins."

"We were so sure we'd get chosen, we started picking out swimsuits."

"I was going to be the bad twin that flirted with the male cast members and you were going to be the one to lecture me about saving myself for marriage." Believing they'd needed a hook to make themselves memorable to the casting directors, they'd played up the whole good-twin, bad-twin scenario on their submission tape. Bo had pulled her hair back and put on a pair of fake glasses to look the part, while Chelsea had dyed her hair purple and borrowed a friend's leather biker jacket. On the outside it might appear as if they were still playing those roles, but Chelsea wasn't playing at anything. She was just being herself. Chelsea Ross. Twin sister and loving daughter. Actress and assistant to a hockey super-star with a terminal case of bad mood-itis. As she watched New York artificially inseminate a pig, she wondered what her life would look like in a year. Hangovers always tended to make her kind of moody and introspective about her life.

In a year, she'd be living in L.A., going to auditions again. She'd be chasing her dream, but she wanted to do things a little differently this time so she didn't get burned out. She didn't want to work as an assistant to the stars anymore.

Maybe she'd start an event-planning business. Hire her *own* assistant to boss around. Not that she'd be mean or unreasonable. She knew what that was like. She'd worked with a lot of event planners in the past, and she liked to arrange and organize fun things. She was good at it, and she generally liked to be around people. That sort of enterprise wouldn't take a lot of startup money, and hopefully she'd have more free time to go to auditions.

And by this time next year, she'd like to have a man in her life. A nice man with a hard body. An image of Mark Bressler popped into her head. No, a *nice* man.

Bo's brain must have been on the same wavelength. Something that didn't surprise Chelsea. "Do you ever wonder if we'll find someone?" her twin asked.

"We will."

"How can you be sure?"

Chelsea thought about it and said, "Because, if women on *My Big Fat Redneck Wedding* can find men, then we can too."

A look of horror entered Bo's blue eyes. "Those men pig wrestle, eat roadkill, and wear camouflage 24/7."

Chelsea waved away her sister's concern. "I think it's fairly safe to say that neither of us will get married under a beer can arbor to a camo-wearing redneck yelling, 'Git 'er done.' We do have some standards."

Bo bit the side of her lip. "You flirted with some guy in a git-'er-done trucker's hat last night."

"That wasn't flirting, and he wasn't a redneck." She knew because she'd checked out his teeth. None of them had been stained or missing. He'd just been some guy trying to be tragically hip. "And I didn't make out with him like you did with Jules."

"I'd never make out with Jules," Bo said, and turned her attention to the television. "Look. New York is roping a goat."

"Oh no. Don't try and distract me. I saw you."

"Probably some other short girl with dark hair."

"You're right. It must have been some other woman who looks exactly like my twin sister."

"Fine." Bo sighed and turned her pale face toward Chelsea. "I've been known to get drunk and call Jules."

"How often?"

"Two or three times."

"If you like him, why do you have to drunk-dial him?"

"I didn't say I liked him." Bo scowled as if they were ten again and boys were yucky. "Jules has a huge ego and dates a lot of different women. We're just friends. Sort of."

She remembered what he'd said once about liking girls who didn't like him. "Maybe he wants to be more than friends."

"Then why hasn't he ever called and asked me out? No. He just wants a booty call."

Chelsea's mouth dropped. "You've given him the booty?"

"Not yet, but I'm afraid I will." She pushed her short hair behind her ear. "Did you see his body? I don't know how much longer I can hold out before I go all *Basic Instinct* on his ultra-fine behind."

"Like stab him with a pick?"

"No. Like throw him down and jump on him."

She liked Jules. "Maybe you should let him know how you feel."

"I don't know how I feel." Bo reached into the cooler and pulled out a Coke. "Sometimes I don't even like him. Sometimes I like him a lot. But it doesn't really matter. I could never date Jules."

"Why?"

Bo popped the top. "Because we work together. You can't date someone you work with."

Chelsea rolled her eyes, forgot she was hungover, and winced. "That's ridiculous."

"No. It's not. It'd be like you dating Mark Bressler."

"There is a difference between work with and work for." She could never make out with her surly employer, let alone *date* him. He was a rude hard-ass, and those were his good qualities. The thought of a booty call with Mark was . . . was . . .

Was not as disturbing as it should be. The thought of her sliding her hands all over his muscles should freak her out. For some reason it didn't. Instead, the thought of touching him triggered thoughts of deep-kissing his mouth. Of looking into his dark brown eyes as she combed her fingers through his hair. Of putting her lips to his warm neck and pressing her hot, sticky skin to his.

The fact that these thoughts *didn't* disturb her, disturbed her more. Sure, he was a handsome man, but she'd never had a thing for big guys. Macho guys who used their bodies and punched each other in the head. Yeah, hockey players wore helmets, but she'd seen the tapes of Mark hitting other players and getting hit himself.

And she'd certainly never had a thing for superstars and athletes. Certainly not superstar athletes. Athletes were the worst kind of superstar. A lot of them partied hard in the offseason and deserved their bad reputations. She'd never read anything bad about Mark, but she figured if she looked hard enough she would. She doubted he'd been an angel.

It didn't matter that Mark no longer played professional hockey. When he was in public, he was still treated like a star athlete. He was given the sort of deference that she'd always found so disgusting.

So why didn't the thought of sliding her hands

on his rock-hard body disturb her? She didn't know. Maybe because it had been a while since she'd slid her hands over anyone but herself. Maybe Bo was having the same dilemma. Or maybe it was Bo's sexual frustration being transferred to Chelsea. It really was true that she could sometimes feel her sister's physical pain. When they'd been younger, if one of them fell off her bike, the other felt it. It didn't happen as much these days, but last year when Bo had broken her clavicle skiing, Chelsea had felt the pain in her shoulder and they hadn't even been in the same state at the time. So she supposed it was possible that she was attuned to Bo's hot, pent-up lust. Especially since they were lounging together on the very same couch.

She turned and looked at her sister, sitting there all innocent, watching junk TV and drinking a Coke. "You have to go get laid by a random stranger."

Bo pointed to the television. "Can I wait for a commercial or do I have to git-'er-done right now?"

"You can wait."

Chapter Ten

Luckily, Chelsea didn't have to depend on her sister to cure herself of her not-so-disturbing thoughts. Mark took care of it by being his usual disagreeable self.

Thank God.

Monday morning when she arrived for work, he stood across the kitchen, looking at her as if he was trying to figure something out. Something he was extremely unhappy about it. She left him alone and worked on his fan letters, which seemed to grow by the day.

Tuesday he seemed even less happy, and by Wednesday, he acted like she'd committed some unforgivable sin. Like she'd kicked him in the leg or wrecked his Mercedes.

Thursday morning she spoke with a real estate agent and put together a few listings that Mark had expressed an interest in seeing. Then she looked for him in the big rambling house. After five minutes of searching, she climbed the long, curving staircase. She'd never been on the second floor, and stood on the landing and looked about. She glanced through the open door of the master bedroom. Rumpled white sheets and a thick blue comforter lay in a tangle on the unmade bed. A pair of jogging pants and flip-flops rested on the floor next to an over-stuffed couch, and beyond the bed, a second door led to a bathroom with stone floors.

A series of clangs drew Chelsea's attention and she moved down the hall. She passed several empty rooms and stopped in the doorway of the last room on the right. It was filled with a big home gym, a workout bench, and rows of free weights. She knew that he worked with a physical therapist up there, but today he was alone.

Mark sat at the leg press, pushing the bar with his feet, while he watched his progress in the wall of mirrors. Soundgarden poured from hidden speakers and filled the room with "Black Hole Sun." Sweat dampened the hair on his head and bare chest. He wore a pair of gray cotton shorts and white running shoes. An ugly pink scar gouged the skin of his left thigh to his knee. For several moments, Chelsea watched him through the mirror, his powerful legs pressing out a steady rhythm. She lifted her gaze to the moist, hard planes of his muscular chest and shoulders, to the determined grimace flattening his lips.

She reached for the control switch next to the door and turned down the volume of "Black Hole Sun." The weights dropped with a loud clang as Mark jerked his head around and looked at her. His dark gaze landed on her face. He stared at her for several heartbeats before he asked, "What do you want?"

She held up the papers in her hand. "I just wanted to give you some information I printed out about the houses you were interested in seeing."

He lowered his feet to the floor, grabbed a bar in front of him with his good hand, and stood. He pointed to the workout bench a few feet away from him. "Leave them there."

Instead of doing as he asked, she rolled up the papers and tapped them against her leg. "Have I done something today to make you angry?"

He reached for a white towel and wiped his throat. His brows lowered as he watched her from across the room. "Today?" The corners of his mouth turned down and he shook his head. "No, but the day isn't over."

She moved to the weight bench and set the papers on top. She had to talk to him about a few things. He would call it prying. She called it doing her job. "Did you get an invitation to the big Stanley Cup party?"

He scrubbed his face. His muffled "Yes" came from within the towel.

"Are you going?"

He shrugged one big, bare shoulder. "Probably."

"Do you have a suit?"

He chuckled and hung the towel around his neck. "Yeah. I gotta suit."

She sat on the bench next to the papers and crossed one leg over the other. Today she'd worn an orange lacy tunic, a brown leather belt, and a pair of beige capris. Sedate for her. She wondered if he'd notice. "Do you need a car service to pick you up?"

"You're not going to insist on driving me?"

"I don't work weekends." She shook her head. "But even if it wasn't on a Saturday night, I'm going with my sister."

"The mini sisters." One brow rose up his forehead. "That should be interesting."

She wondered if he meant "interesting" in a good way. She decided not to ask. "Have you given any more thought to the charity golf tournament?"

He tilted his head to one side but didn't answer.

"Coaching youth hockey?"

He held up his bad hand, and she noticed he wasn't wearing his splint. "Stop."

"I just hate to see you sitting around when there is so much more you could be doing."

Mark reached above his head and grasped the chin-up bar. His right middle finger pointed toward the ceiling, and damp curly hair darkened his armpits. "Let's talk about you for a change."

Chelsea placed a hand on the front of her blouse. "Me?"

"Yeah. You want to get all up into my life. Let's get into yours."

She grasped the bench with her hands and locked her elbows. "I'm just your average, ordinary girl." *Staring at fine pecs covered in short, dark hair.* Normally Chelsea wasn't a huge fan of chest hair, but looking at Mark, she could become a convert. The fine hair growing on his chest surrounded his flat male nipples, then tapered to a fine line running down his bare sternum to his navel. Just like in the sports drink ad.

"Uh-huh."

"There's not a lot to get into." He'd lost the defined edges of his eight-pack, but his belly was still tight as a drum. Defined ab muscles bracketed his stomach. A thin slice of white elastic was visible just above the waistband of the shorts hanging low on his narrow hips.

"Let's get into it anyway."

The kind of elastic that meant he wore briefs. More likely a pair of boxer briefs because she just couldn't picture him in tightie whities. Not that she should be picturing him in his underwear. That wasn't right. She worked for him. Well, maybe not technically, but . . .

"You think that I should do something with my life. What are you doing with yours?"

"At the moment, I'm your assistant."

"Isn't there 'so much more that you could be doing' other than driving me around and butting into my life?"

She raised her gaze before her interest wandered lower and she started to speculate about his magnum package—again. "I have plans."

"Like?"

She looked up into his brown eyes. "I'm working and saving money."

With his good hand he motioned for her to continue. "Saving for?"

"I'd rather not say."

A slow smile curved his lips. "Something personal?"

"Yes."

"There are only a handful of things that a woman won't talk about." He lifted a finger off the bar. "The actual number of past lovers for instance. You all want to know the exact number of women that a man has had sex with, how often, and every juicy detail. But you don't want to share the same information."

"That's because there is still a double standard when it comes to casual sex."

He shrugged one shoulder and leaned forward, still holding on to the bar above him. "I get that, but women shouldn't ask me about my sex life if you all don't want to talk about yours." He straightened and dropped his hands to his sides. "Some things are private." He moved to the weights and lowered the pin. "Maybe I don't want everyone to know my personal business."

Too late. That letter from Lydia Ferrari had been posted in the guest book for several months before Chelsea had deleted it. She figured she should probably tell him about it because someone else might. "Do you know a Lydia Ferrari?"

His brows lowered, and he moved to the seat he'd been in when she'd come into the room. "Like a car?" He grabbed the bar above his head and lowered himself.

"No. At least I don't think so. She wrote a letter on your guest book page."

He spread his hands wide and pulled the bar to his chest. "I don't know her."

"She claims that you met her at Lava Lounge, had sex with her at her apartment in Redmond, then didn't call."

The weight stopped mid-air, and he looked at her through the mirror. "What else did she write?"

"That it was the best sex of her life and her feelings were hurt when you didn't call her back."

He raised the bar and lowered it, the muscles in his arms and back hardened and flexed. "She was a freak."

"You *do* know her."

"I *remember* her. Hell, it's hard to forget a woman with that many sharp body piercings." His jaw tightened as he pulled the weight.

"Where was she pierced?"

"All over. I was half terrified I'd end up with some missing skin and lasting scars."

"Obviously the terrified half wasn't below your waist."

A deep chuckle escaped the smile cracking his lips. "Is the letter still posted?"

"I deleted it."

"Thank you."

"You're welcome." She watched him for several moments, then said, "You don't seem all that upset that 'everyone' knows your 'personal business' with Lydia Ferrari."

"First of all, I doubt that's even her real name." He sucked in a breath and let it out. "Second, women say stuff like that all the time. Even if I've never met them."

Chelsea was just about to point out that he *had* met Lydia when he added, "I'm used to it."

"And it doesn't bother you?"

He shrugged. "People are going to say and write whatever they want and they don't care if it's the truth. Everyone has an agenda. When I said I didn't want to talk about my personal business . . . I meant I don't want to get into it while I'm naked and about to get busy. It can ruin the mood." He took a deep breath and blew it out. Chelsea thought the subject of Lydia Ferrari was over but then he added, "Considering what that woman was into, I just thank Jesus for what she *didn't* write."

She chewed her bottom lip, fighting the battle not to pry. She lost. "What?"

"None of your business, Ms. Nosy Toes." He moved his hands closer in on the bar. "We're talking about my business again and you still haven't told me yours."

"Why, when I ask questions, am I prying and a 'Ms. Nosy Toes'?"

He sucked in a breath and let it out as he worked the weights. "The second thing women don't generally want to talk about," he said instead of answering her question, "is plastic surgery. A lot of women have it, but none of them admit it." He looked at her over his shoulder. "Are you saving to get your nose done?"

"What?" Chelsea gasped. "There's nothing wrong with my nose." She raised a hand to her face. "What's wrong with my nose?"

"Nothing. My ex got her nose done but she wanted to keep it a big secret." He returned his gaze to the mirror. "Like everyone who knew her wouldn't take one look at her face and figure out the obvious."

She dropped her hand to her side. "No. Not my nose."

"Your butt? Karlsson's wife had fat sucked out of her thighs and shot into her butt."

"It's called a Brazilian butt lift. And no, I don't want that." She stood and moved to a rack of free weights. What the hell? What did she care if he knew? It wasn't like she cared about his opinion or that he could take any sort of moral high road. Not after he'd admitted to having sex with a woman even after he feared she'd turn him into a human pin cushion. She ran her hand across the top weight. "I want to save enough to have breast surgery."

The weights crashed down, and his gaze lowered to her chest. "Don't you think you're big enough?"

She frowned and shook her head. "I want breast *reduction* surgery."

"Oh." He looked back up into her face. "Why?"

Typical. She knew he wouldn't understand. Heck, her own family didn't understand. "I don't like having large breasts. They're heavy and get in the way. It's hard to find clothes that fit me, and I get back and shoulder pain."

He stood and reached for the towel still around his neck. "How small would you go?"

She folded her arms across her chest. "I'm thinking a full C."

He nodded and wiped the side of his face. "C's a good size."

Geez. Was she really talking about her breast surgery with Mark Bressler? A man, and he wasn't howling about the travesty of going smaller? "You don't think it's a bad idea?"

"What do you care what I think? If your back hurts, and you can do something about it, you should."

He made it sound so reasonable.

"How big are you now?"

She stared at the floor between his shoes. "I'm a double D."

"On someone taller that might not be a problem, but you're a small girl."

She looked up. At him standing a few feet away. Big and bad and half naked. His damp hair sticking to his head and chest. If she didn't know Mark, didn't know what a surly jerk he could be, she might be in danger of falling in love with him. Of throwing herself against his hot, sticky chest and kissing him full on the mouth. Not for how he looked, which was pretty damn good, but for understanding how she might feel.

"What?"

She shook her head and glanced away. "My family doesn't want me to do it. They all think I'm impulsive and will regret it."

"You don't strike me as all that impulsive."

She looked back at him, and her lips parted. All her life she'd been told she was impulsive and needed direction. The urge to kiss him full on the mouth just got a little stronger. "Compared to everyone else in my family, my life is chaotic. Out of control."

He tilted his head to one side and studied her.

"Things around you might be chaotic, but you're in control." One corner of his mouth lifted a little. "My life used to be like that. Now it's not."

"You look in control to me."

"That's because you didn't know me before."

"Were you a control freak?"

"I just liked things done my way."

Of course he had.

"I lost control of my life the day I woke up in the hospital hooked up to machines and strapped down to a bed."

"Why were you strapped down?"

"I guess I was trying to pull the tube out of my throat."

Even seeing the scars, it was hard to look at him now and see how sick he'd been and how close he'd come to dying. He was strong and in control more than he thought.

"Have the surgery if that's what you want." He shrugged one bare shoulder. "It's your life."

"Bo thinks it's mutilation."

"You're not Bo."

"I know but . . ." How could she explain it to someone who wasn't a twin? "When you live your whole life looking like someone else, changing that is scary. Weird."

"You're talking about boobs. Not your face." He

reached for his cane leaning against the weights. "But maybe I'm the wrong person to give my opinion. I'm a thigh man." The cane fell from his hand and landed on the carpet with a soft thud. "Shit." He grabbed on to the weights for balance and slowly lowered himself.

Without thinking about it, Chelsea moved forward and knelt on one knee. She grabbed the cane and looked up. His face was just above hers, and something dark and intense entered his brown eyes.

"I wish you wouldn't do that," he said, his voice a rough whisper against her cheek.

"Do what?"

He rose and towered over her. "Rush around treating me like I'm helpless."

She stood also, so close that nothing but an inch of air separated the front of her lacy blouse from his hard chest and fine dark hair.

He stared into her face as he reached for the cane. His hand wrapped around hers, and his warm, strong grasp sent a tingle up her wrist to her elbow. "I'm not a child."

She was so close she could see a darker line around the edges of his irises and all the little variations within the deep brown of those eyes surrounded by those thick, enviable lashes. "I know."

His hand squeezed around hers. His gaze lowered to her lips. "I'm a man."

Yes. Yes he was. A half-naked man with big sweaty muscles and smoldering eyes. Suddenly she felt kind of hot and light-headed. Probably from all the testosterone she was inhaling. "I know."

He opened his mouth as if he was about to say something. Instead he dropped his arm to his side and walked around her. She had a feeling that if he could have run, he would have sprinted from the room.

"Don't you want to see the real estate listings I've put together for you?" She grabbed the papers off the workbench and took a few steps toward him.

"I don't need to. You know what I'm looking for." He stopped in the doorway, practically filling it with his broad shoulders. "Set something up and call me."

"You want me to call you about real estate showings?"

"Yes." He placed a hand on the white door frame and turned his face to one side. Light and shadow cut across his profile. "You have my cell number. There's no need for you to wander around looking for me again."

Her gaze lowered from the back of his dark hair to the indent of his spine. "I don't mind."

"I do."

"But . . ." She shook her head. "What if you're just in the next room? Should I still call?"

"Yeah. We don't need to talk in person."

What? Had she missed something? How had the conversation gone from her wanting to kiss his face to her wanting to smack him in the head?

And why wasn't she the least bit surprised?

Chelsea called him five times that day. Mostly just to annoy him.

"Do you have an aversion to maroon carpet?" she asked. "I found a house you might be interested in, but it has maroon carpet."

"Just set up a showing." *Click.*

She waited a half hour, then called again. "Do you need your suit taken to the dry cleaner's?"

"No." *Click.*

At noon she dialed and asked, "How about a sandwich?"

"I can make my own damn sandwich!"

"I know." She smiled. "I just thought if you were making one for yourself, you could make me one too. I like ham and cheese. Lettuce on the side with a dab—"

Click.

He never appeared with her sandwich, which

annoyed her even further when she heard him in the kitchen loudly banging around. She answered more letters on the computer and waited until two to phone him again. "There's a squirrel in your driveway."

"Are you fucking kidding me?"

"No. I'm looking at it."

"You're calling me about a fucking squirrel?"

"Yeah. Sure. Do you want me to get an exterminator to put out some rodent traps? Squirrels have been known to carry rabies, you know."

He muttered something about her being nuttier than squirrel shit, then—*click.*

Shortly after that, a shiny red truck pulled into the driveway, and Mark sped away in it. Probably with one of his hockey buddies at the wheel. She called his cell but it went directly to voice mail. Jerk had turned off his phone.

The next morning when she arrived at work, she called to see if he'd turned it back on. This time she did have something important to tell him.

"I've set up three house showings for Monday after your dentist's appointment."

"I hate the dentist."

"Everyone hates the dentist." She flipped through the notes she'd taken when she'd spoken with the Realtor. "There's a four-bedroom in the Queen Anne district. A five-bedroom on Mercer Island, which I'm told isn't all that far from where you live now. And a stunning six-thousand-square-foot home in Kirkland."

"Fine. Is that it?"

"No. I think you should look at a condo on Second Avenue. I know you said you didn't like the noise downtown, but you really need to see it."

"No." *Click.*

She waited a half hour and called. "I brought some grapes. Do you want some? They're really fresh and delish."

Click.

She waited an hour and then: "What does it mean to fall head over heels? If you fall, shouldn't it be heels over head?"

He swore so loudly it sounded like he was in the room. "I'm going to kill you," he said from the doorway.

Chelsea jumped and spun around in her chair. "Crap!" She clutched a handful of Pucci dress above her heart.

"I swear to God, I will strangle you with my bare hands if you call me with bullshit just one more time." He looked like he meant it too. His eyes were squinty yet shooting fire at the same time. He wore jeans for a change with his white T-shirt. A pack of smokes rolled up in one sleeve would have completed the look.

She slid her fingers to the side of her throat and felt her racing pulse. "You scared me to death."

"I'm not that lucky." He gave her a hard stare for several moments, one that she was sure he'd used on his hockey adversaries. One that she was sure worked. "I'm expecting a call on the house phone in about fifteen minutes. It's my agent. Don't pick it up." He walked away, and his voice trailed behind him. "And for the love of God, don't call my cell."

She wisely bit her tongue. She reminded herself that she wanted this job. *Needed* it. For the rest of the day, she kept herself busy. She scheduled an appointment for an appraiser to come look at Mark's house next week, right after the cleaning crew left.

At three, the real estate agent called Chelsea's phone. A house in Bellevue had just been put on the market within the past hour. It wasn't even listed yet, but she was sure once it was, it would go fast. Probably before Monday. After Chelsea hung up with the agent, she stared at the cell in her hand. She didn't want to die. She didn't want be strangled . . . but if she didn't tell him about the house, she wasn't doing her job. And the new listing wasn't a "bullshit" call. She took a deep breath and dialed fast. It rang somewhere in the house but he didn't pick up. She dialed again and followed "American Woman" around the stairs and toward the back of the house.

She found Mark asleep in the leisure room. Once again, the sound on the television was turned way down and he lay on the wide chaise asleep. She stood near the doorway and called his name. "Mr. Bressler."

He didn't stir and she moved toward him. His right hand was resting on his chest, and he wasn't wearing his splint. "Mr. Bressler." He scratched his chest through his T-shirt but still didn't wake up. She leaned over and touched his arm. "Mr. Bressler. I need to talk to you."

Slowly his lids lifted and he looked up at her. Confusion knitted his brow and he asked in a voice all rough and smoky from sleep, "Why are you dressed again?"

Chelsea froze with her hand on his shoulder. "Huh?"

"That's okay." A beautiful, *sweet* smile curved his lips. He looked at her as if he was actually pleased to see her—as opposed to how he'd looked at her earlier—ready to kill. Seeing his smile reach his eyes, she could almost forgive him anything.

"I need to talk to you, Mr. Bressler."

"And I need to talk to you." He reached for her. One second she was looking down at him, and in the next, she was on the chaise next to him, looking up into his face.

The wind left her lungs with a soft *oomf.* "Mr. Bressler!"

He gazed down at her from beneath heavy lids. "Don't you think it's time you call me Mark? Especially after all the things you let me do to you?"

"What things?"

He chuckled and lowered his face. "This," he said just above her mouth. "Here." His lips slipped across her cheek and he whispered into her ear. "Everywhere."

They hadn't done this. She'd remember if he kissed her. Especially "everywhere." She raised her hand to his shoulder to push him away. Beneath her palm, his hard muscles bunched and turned rock-hard.

"Yes," he whispered against the side of her neck. "Touch me again."

Again? His soft breath caressed her skin and spread warmth across her chest. He kissed her just below her ear, and it felt good. Nice. Like slow, lazy sex on a hot summer day. Definitely something she shouldn't be feeling for her employer. "I thought you didn't like me very much."

"I like you too much." He opened his wet mouth

against the side of her neck and softly sucked her skin.

Her throat got tight. "I don't think we should do this," she managed.

"No. Probably not." He kissed the hollow of her throat, worked his way to her chin, and said just above her lips, "But what the fuck." Before she could protest, his mouth covered hers and robbed her of breath. His warm palm cupped her face, his thumb brushed her cheek. Sexual awareness shimmered like a heat wave across her chest and down her belly. The sudden and unexpected desire heating up her body stunned her.

This wasn't wise. It wasn't a good idea. In the past, she'd easily managed to rebuff employer sexual advances. She should stop him. Instead of doing the wise thing, she slid her hand from his shoulder to the side of his neck, and a groan vibrated deep in his chest. "Kiss me, Chelsea. Open your beautiful mouth for me."

And she did, responding to the rough texture of his voice and the pleasure of his touch. Her lips parted, and he kissed her. Soft, slow, with his wet mouth and tongue, teasing a response out of her. Turning her into the aggressor as any last thought of resistance melted away beneath his hot desire. Her tongue slipped inside his mouth, slick and welcome. He tasted good to her, like need and lust and sex. She slid her fingers into his hair and held the sides of his head in her hands. Her body arched toward him, wanting more of his solid warmth as he fed her wet kisses. A deep, sensuous moan escaped her mouth and touched his lips.

He pulled back and looked into her face, his breathing heavy. Within the shadows of the room, he blinked and his brows lowered. "Chelsea."

She liked how he said her name. All smoky with lust. She moved her hands to the back of his head and slowly brought his mouth down to hers once more. She gave him slow, hungry kisses that tightened her chest and knotted her stomach.

His palm slid down her side and she held her breath, waiting for him to grab her breast. When he didn't, she relaxed and slipped her hand from the back of his head, down the side of his neck and shoulder. She touched the hard planes of his chest, and her fingers grasped the front of his shirt. The knot in her stomach moved lower as Mark slid his hand over her hip and down her leg. He found bare skin, and he slipped his hand beneath the edge of her dress and palmed her thigh.

Somewhere in the distance a bell rang. Chelsea didn't know if it was real or imagined. She didn't care. All she cared about was Mark's mouth on hers and his hand caressing upward. She turned toward him, and he grasped her behind in one of his big, warm hands. His thumb brushed across her lace panties and slipped beneath the elastic edge.

The bell rang once more, and Mark lifted his head and looked down into her face. His gaze moved across her face, down her arm and side, to his hand cupping her butt cheek.

"Shit." He removed his hand and rolled onto his back.

Desire still pounding through her veins, Chelsea wondered if he'd meant "shit" because he'd had to stop. Or "shit" because he shouldn't have started.

He raised one arm and covered his eyes. "Please let this be another nightmare."

She guessed that answered her question. She swung her legs over the side of the chaise and stood. The fact that he considered kissing her a nightmare hurt more than it should have, given the nature of their relationship. It wasn't like they were boyfriend and girlfriend. She worked for him. It *was* a nightmare. Still, he didn't have to be so rude. Especially not after the kiss had been so good.

"How in the hell did that just happen?" He lowered his arm and looked at her. "You're not even supposed to be in here."

It sounded suspiciously like he was trying to blame her, and she was the innocent party. Well, maybe not *innocent*. "I had something important to talk to you about and you wouldn't answer your cell phone."

He sat up and reached for his cane resting on the floor. "Another rabid squirrel sighting?" He stood and turned to face her from the other side of the chaise. The front of his shirt was still rumpled from her grasp. "Grapes that you just couldn't wait to tell me about?"

"You make it sound as if I planned what happened." She placed a hand on her chest. "I'm the innocent party here."

"If you're so innocent, how did I end up with my hand on your ass and your tongue in my mouth?"

She gasped. "This wasn't my fault! You grabbed me and pulled me down next to you." She pointed at him. "And then *you* kissed *me*."

A frown pulled at the corners of his mouth. "You didn't seem to mind."

Chapter Eleven

Mark looked across the chaise at his assistant. Her hair was messy and her lips a bit swollen. His fingers tightened around the handle of his cane to keep from grabbing her again. To keep from pushing her down and sliding his hand up her smooth thigh to her tight little butt.

"Well, at first I was in shock. Then I was just waiting for you to relax so I could get away." She shrugged her shoulder like the little actress she was. "I was just about to knee you in the nut sac and run."

He laughed. No wonder she was out of work. She just wasn't that convincing. Not when he could still hear her long, needy moan in his head.

The doorbell rang once more. "I'm not expecting

anyone," he said. "Did you set anything up without telling me?"

"Of course not. Maybe it's the Realtor. She's really excited about a house in Bellevue."

He held his hands wide and didn't need to look down to know there was an obvious bulge in the front of his jeans. "You're going to have to get that."

Her gaze slid down his chest to the zipper closing the front of his Lucky's. For several long seconds she stared at his erection as red crept up her cheeks. "Oh." She spun on the heels of her sandals and practically ran from the room.

Mark watched her go, then leaned over to grab the remote from the end table. He turned off the television and tossed the remote on the chaise. He'd been dreaming of her. Again. He'd been dreaming of her and then she'd become a living, breathing part of that dream. When he'd first awakened and looked up at her, he'd been confused. In his dream she'd been naked, and they'd been having mad, crazy sex. Then he'd opened his eyes and she was wearing that horrible Pucci dress.

He moved to the French doors and looked out into his backyard and the golf course beyond. Pulling her down beside him and kissing her neck was all a dreamy haze, reality mixed with fantasy. But the sound of her hungry moan had cleared the confusion, and he'd lifted his head to look at her. He'd had a fleeting thought that he should stop, but then she'd pulled his head down to hers and kissed him with her wet mouth and smooth tongue. Any thought of stopping instantly vanished, replaced by darker, hotter thoughts. Thoughts of doing all the naughty little things he'd been doing to her naughty little body for the past week in his dreams. He didn't know if that made him lonely or obsessed or sick. Maybe it made him all three.

"There's someone here to see you."

Mark turned back to the room, ready to tell her to get rid of whoever had shown up on his porch. He opened his mouth, but the words never passed his lips. His gaze landed on a skinny kid with short red hair stuck to his head, bright copper freckles on his face, and gold-rimmed glasses. Mark's memory after the accident might be spotty, but he remembered the boy in the doorway. It was hard to forget a kid who completely lacked basic hockey fundamentals. The kid skated like a windmill, chopped at the puck, and whacked the other kids in the shins. "Hello, Derek. How's it going?"

"Good, Coach Bressler."

What was the kid doing here, and how had he found Mark? "What can I do for you?"

"I got your e-mail. So I'm here."

Mark raised his gaze to Chelsea, who stood by the boy's side. Her face was carefully blank. He knew that look. She was guilty as hell. "I'm kind of forgetful because of the accident," he told the boy. "So you'll have to remind me what I wrote in the e-mail."

Derek held up a pair of inline skates, tied together. "That I should come show you my hockey stops."

Chelsea's jaw dropped and she shook her head. "You did *not* write that."

He tilted his head to one side and folded his arms across his T-shirt. "What else didn't I write?"

Chelsea's eyes narrowed as she stared down at the kid by her side. "You didn't write that he should come here and practice, that's for sure."

Derek looked up at Chelsea, and behind the lenses of his glasses, his eyes narrowed too. "How do you know?"

"Well, I . . . I . . . I spell-check all Mr. Bressler's e-mails before he sends them out. Because of his memory problem, and all that."

It was a bad lie, but the kid bought it. He nodded and turned his attention to Mark. "I could help, maybe. My mom helps me with flash cards."

The last thing Mark needed was for the kid to show up tomorrow with flash cards. "Thanks for the offer, but I'm much better now. How did you get my address?"

Derek pushed up his glasses with his free hand. "The Internet."

The kid's answer was alarming. If an eight-year-old boy could find him, who else could?

"I'm sure you've broken some sort of law. First by somehow hacking Mr. Bressler's e-mail and now by finding his house."

"I didn't break any law! His e-mail is on the paper we got last year. And I just put his name in Whosit and got the address."

What was Whosit?

Chelsea shook one finger at Derek. "Even if you didn't break any laws, which I'm not so sure about, it's rude to just show up at people's houses. Does your mother know where you are?"

Derek shrugged one skinny shoulder. "My older sister is at the mall and my mom's at work. She won't get off until six."

"Where do you live?" Mark asked.

"Redmond."

"How did you get here?"

"Bike."

No wonder the kid's hair was stuck to his head. "Do you want some water or a soda?" He couldn't have the kid die of dehydration before he sent him back home.

Derek nodded. "Do you have Gatorade? Like we drank in hockey camp?"

"Probably." He tightened his grip on the cane and headed toward the door. "And you need to call your mom and tell her that you're here."

"Do I have to, Coach? Can't I just leave before she gets home?"

"No." Mark moved to the threshold and motioned for Derek to precede him. The boy moved out of the way, and Mark gazed down into Chelsea's face. "You and I will talk later."

She stuck her chin up in the air. "I never told him to come over and practice."

He looked into the variegated blue in her eyes. "Not about that."

"About what?"

He lowered his attention to her mouth. "About what happened before Derek rang the doorbell."

"Oh, that."

"Yeah, that." Although he really didn't know what there was to say about *that*. Other than he was sorry and it wouldn't happen again.

He tore his gaze from his assistant's mouth and followed the kid down the hall. Derek's socks slid down his skinny shins as he walked. "Are you in hockey camp this year?"

Derek shook his head. "My mom said we don't got the money this year."

Mark knew that a lot of kids got their hockey camp fee paid for through one of the Chinooks' various organizations. He was fairly sure Derek had been one of those kids last year. "Didn't you get a scholarship?"

"Not this year."

"Why?"

"Don't know."

Mark walked beside Derek into the kitchen. The light bounced off the kid's red hair, glasses, and the white, white skin between all those freckles.

"What name did we pick out for you last year?" he asked as he moved to the refrigerator and opened it.

Derek set his skates on the floor beside his feet. "The Hackster."

"That's right." At camp, each kid got a hockey name. Derek was the Hackster for the way he hacked at the puck. Mark pulled out a bottle of green Gatorade and opened it with the palm of his right hand.

"Does it hurt?"

Mark looked up. "What?"

"Your hand."

He tossed the cap on the granite island and flexed his fingers. The middle one stayed perfectly stiff. "It kind of aches sometimes. Not as much as it used to." He handed Derek the bottle.

"Does your middle finger bend?"

Mark held up his hand and showed the kid. "Nope. It stays like this no matter what."

"That's cool."

He laughed. "You think so?"

"Yep. You can flip people off and not get in trouble." Derek took a long drink until he ran out of breath and lowered the bottle. "The school can't call your mom," he said between gasps, " 'cause it's not your fault."

True. In his case, the school would have called his grandmother, who would have told his father, who would have skinned his behind.

"Are you going to play hockey again?"

Mark shook his head and looked down at the cap on the granite island. His agent had called him earlier that afternoon about possibly commentating for ESPN. "Afraid not." While he wasn't ruling it out, he'd wait for a solid offer. He wasn't all that excited about sitting in a studio and talking about the game rather than being on the ice where the action took place. But as his agent had pointed out, job offers for Mark Bressler were drying up as fast as endorsement deals.

"My mom took me to a playoffs game against Detroit. We won three to one." Derek took another drink, then pushed his glasses up. "Ty Savage put a hit on McCarty in retaliation for the hit McCarty put on Savage in game four. It was a good game, but it would have been better if you'd been there." Derek looked up. His eyes glazed with hero worship. "You're the best player ever. Better than Savage."

Mark wouldn't go so far as to say he was *better* than Ty Savage. Well, maybe a little.

"Even better than Gretzky."

Mark wasn't so sure he was better than Gretzky, but one thing he was absolutely sure of: He'd never been comfortable in the hero role. He'd played hockey. He'd never saved a life or put his own life on the line. He'd never been a damn hero, but it seemed important to Derek. "Thanks, Hackster."

Derek set his bottle on the island. "Do you want to see my stops?"

Not really, but when the kid looked at him like that, he couldn't say no. "Sure." He pointed to Derek's skates. "You can show me on the front drive." It was long enough that the kid wouldn't run into anything, except Chelsea's car. But really, what was one more dent?

Derek grabbed his skates, and the two of them headed toward the front of the house. As they moved past the office, Chelsea stuck her head out of the door.

"Can I talk to you, Mr. Bressler?"

He put his hand on Derek's shoulder. "Go ahead and put your skates on outside. I'll be out in a minute."

"Okay, Coach."

He watched Derek close the big door behind him before he approached his assistant. He was sure she'd want to talk about the kiss. "I'm sorry about grabbing you earlier," he said, getting it over with. "It won't happen again."

She pushed up the corners of her lips. "Let's just forget it ever happened."

"Can you do that?" In his experience, women didn't tend to forget something like that. They liked to pick at it and dissect it for days.

"Oh yeah." She chuckled and waved a hand over her head as if the memory had been swept away. Her movement raised the hem of her hideous dress up her thigh. The laugh was a little too fake to convince anyone, least of all him. "Not a big deal. I'd already forgotten it."

Liar. He took a step closer and stopped a few inches from her, forcing her to tilt her head back and look up at him as if she was waiting for his kiss. "I'm glad you're not going to make a big deal out of it. I was half asleep." Now it was his turn to lie. "And all doped up." He hadn't taken any Vicodin since that morning.

Her smile fell. "I think we've already established that we are not even remotely attracted to each other. You think my face is okay, but not my body. And while I find you . . ." She held up one hand and tilted it from one side to the other. " . . . okay, you're rude and your personality sucks. And I like a man with a good personality."

He doubted that like hell. "Right."

"I do," she tried to argue.

"You're talking like a homely girl." And she was far from homely. "Only homely girls like guys for their personality."

She pointed at him. "That's exactly what I'm talking about. That was really rude."

He shrugged. "Maybe, but it's true."

She frowned and folded her arms beneath her breasts. "What happened earlier isn't what I needed to talk over with you. An agent from Windemere called regarding a house in Bellevue. It's about to go on the market, and the agent wanted to show it to you first."

"Set it up for next week."

"She wanted to show it today."

He shook his head and moved to the front door. The less time he spent with his assistant at the moment, the better. "I've got a date with the Hackster."

"The kid is trouble."

Derek wasn't the only one. Mark looked over his shoulder at his cute little assistant with the sassy hair and smart mouth. The woman was nothing but trouble.

He opened the front door and closed it behind him. Derek sat on the porch fastening his skates. "That girl's mean."

"Chelsea?" He put the tip of his cane on the stair below and stepped down. Chelsea was many things. Annoying being the most prominent, but she wasn't mean.

"She gave me the stink eye."

Mark laughed. "She didn't give you the stink eye." Although she had given Mark the stink eye on one or more occasions. The day she'd found out that sending her to buy those condoms had been a fool's errand came to mind. "She just told you what you didn't want to hear. You shouldn't just show up at someone's house. It's rude." He pulled his cell out of his pocket and handed it to the boy. "Call your mom."

Derek finished buckling his skates. "Oh, man."

"Did you think I'd forgotten?"

"Yes." The kid punched the seven numbers and waited for the axe to fall. The grim line of his mouth turned to a smile and he whispered, "It's going to her voice mail."

Lucky break.

"Hi Mom. I went on a bike ride and ran into Coach Mark. I'll be home by six. Love you. Bye."

Mark let Derek's little lie go for now.

The kid shut the phone and handed it to Mark. "I can skate backward now. I've been practicing in my basement."

Mark dumped his phone in his back pocket. "Show me."

Derek stood, and his ankles fell inward. He held his arms out to the sides and slowly moved his skates back and forth until he rolled to the center of the drive. He used a one-foot drag to stop. Much better than the snowplow he'd been using last summer, but his balance still sucked.

"That's pretty good."

Derek smiled as the late afternoon sun caught fire in his hair and bounced off his white forehead.

"Watch this." He bent his knees, hunched over, and put pressure on the insides of the skates. He rolled back a couple of inches and beamed like he'd just scored a hat trick. What Derek lacked in skill, he made up for in heart. Heart was the one indefinable element that made a good player into a great player. No amount of drills could teach heart.

"You're getting there." Too bad heart wasn't enough. "But you're bent over looking at your feet. What's the number one rule in hockey?"

"No whining."

"Number two."

"Keep your head up."

"That's right." He pointed his cane at the boy. "Have you been practicing your step-overs and jumps?"

Derek sighed. "No."

He lowered his cane and looked at his watch. "Keep your head up and get going to the end of the driveway and back."

Chelsea pushed back the heavy drapes and watched Derek lift one knee and then the other. He marched toward the end of the driveway, his arms out from his shoulders. As he attempted to turn around, he fell on his skinny behind.

"Keep your head up," Mark yelled.

Derek dusted himself off and marched all the way back. He reminded Chelsea of Rupert Grint in the first Harry Potter movie. Only geekier.

Mark met him in the center of the drive and handed him a half-full bottle of Gatorade. Chelsea couldn't hear what Mark said to the boy, just the deep timbre of his voice. Derek nodded and drank.

Mark took the bottle and returned it to the shade of the porch. "Two small. One big," he called out to the kid, and Derek began jumping in place. He immediately fell.

Chelsea let go of the curtain and moved from the office. She walked outside and stood next to Mark. "I thought he was going to show you a few stops and go home. Why are you making him march and jump up and down?"

"The kid needs to learn balance." He pointed his cane at the boy and hollered, "Now change it up. Small jump. Big jump. Small jump. Big jump. Bend your knees, Derek."

"Who are you? Mr. Miyagi?" She held her hands up in front of her, palms out. "Wax on. Wax off. Bend your knees, Derekson."

He chuckled. "Something like that." He walked to the center of the driveway, a slight hitch in his otherwise fluid steps and his cane a smooth extension of his arm. Chelsea folded her arms beneath her breasts and sat on the porch. Mark pointed down the driveway, said something about pushing and gliding. Falling down and getting back up again.

"Use your hips. Head up," Mark called after him. After about fifteen minutes of pushing and gliding, the kid was clearly winded. His cheek had turned a bright red, one of his knees was skinned, and Chelsea almost felt sorry for him. Almost, but the little liar had made her look bad.

He collapsed on the porch next to Chelsea and reached for his Gatorade. "I'm getting good," he said before he upended the bottle and drained it. Chelsea was no expert, but even she could see the kid had a long way to go before he approached "getting good."

The boy looked up at Mark, his eyes filled with exhaustion and hero worship. "Maybe I could come back and practice some more."

Right, like Mark would want the kid hanging around. He didn't like anyone hanging around.

A frown line creased Mark's brow as if he had a sudden headache. "Check with Chelsea to see which days I'm free next week."

Chelsea was shocked. "You're free Wednesday and Friday."

Derek set down the bottle and unbuckled his skates. "I have summer band practice on Wednesday."

Of course he did. He probably played the tuba.

Most of the skinny band-os she'd ever known had played the tuba. Kind of like most of the short guys she'd ever known had driven trucks.

"How about Tuesday and Thursday?" Mark countered.

"You're house hunting those two mornings."

"I can come in the afternoon," Derek said as he tied his shoes. He stood and shoved his skates into a backpack he'd hidden next to the porch. He zipped the backpack closed and threaded his stick arms through the straps.

"Have your mom call me." Mark placed his right hand on the kid's sweaty head. "When you get home, drink lots of water and get lots of rest."

"Okay, Coach."

Chelsea bit the side of her lip. Inside his crusty, cantankerous, jerk-wad, wrapped-up-in-rhino-skin exterior, he was a softie.

She stood as Derek moved to the front of the garage where he'd left his bike. "Shouldn't we give him a ride?"

"Hell no." Mark scoffed. "He needs to build up the strength in his legs. He's as weak as a girl. Riding a bike will be good for him." He turned to look at Chelsea, at her two-tone hair and wild dress. He had an assistant who was more trouble than she was worth, and now a skinny, star-struck, wimpy kid stopping by twice a week. How in the hell had that happened? "It's getting close to five."

"I was just about to leave. Need anything before I go?"

There she went again. Asking him what he needed. "Not a thing." He moved back out into the driveway as Derek rode away.

"See you Monday, then," Chelsea called after him.

He raised a hand and moved to the garage door. He punched the code into the key pad, and the door slowly rose. If he was going to help the kid out, he needed his coach's whistle. He ducked beneath the door and moved past his Mercedes. This week he hadn't taken as much medication. His grasp was coming back in his right hand, and he was sure he could drive again soon. He flipped on a light and continued toward the shelves in the back.

The last time he'd seen his whistle and stopwatch, he'd shoved them in a gym bag. He leaned his cane against the wall and looked up at the floor-to-ceiling shelves. His gaze leveled on a blue equipment bag, and the air left his lungs as if he'd been punched in the chest. The bag was old and worn and had logged thousands of air miles. He didn't need to look inside to know that it held his skates and pads. His helmet and jersey. His hockey shorts and socks were in there. Probably his protective cup too.

When management had come to him in the hospital to tell him the guys wanted to keep his stuff in his locker, he'd told them to pack it up and take it to his house. The guys had had enough to think about besides him. They hadn't needed the daily reminder, and he hadn't wanted to someday walk into the locker room and pack it all up.

Next to the equipment bag lay his long stick bag. And he didn't need to see the Sher-Wood sticks inside to know that each blade had been manufactured especially for him, with a half-inch curve depth and a 6.0 lie. White grip tape wrapped around the handles, candy-caned down the black shafts, and wrapped heel to toe. His old life was in those two bags. Everything that he was and ever wanted to be. All that was left after nineteen years in the NHL was in those bags. That and the hero worship of one eight-year-old boy with skinny legs and weak ankles.

He'd told the boy he'd coach him twice a week, and he wasn't quite sure how that had happened. One second he'd been thinking about getting inside out of the heat, and in the next he'd told the kid to check with Chelsea to see which days worked out best. He hadn't even been thinking about coaching Derek, but the kid had looked up at him like Mark had once looked at guys like Phil Esposito and Bobby Hull. That look had dropped him quicker than a cheap shot to the cup.

He was a sucker. That explained it.

Of course, another explanation was that he didn't have a lot going on in his life. He reached up and grabbed a smaller gym bag from one of the upper shelves. He had no job and no family. He was thirty-eight, divorced, and had no kids. His grandmother and father lived several states away. They had their own lives, and he saw them only about once a year.

What he did have was a house that was too big, a Mercedes he couldn't yet drive, and an assistant who was driving him insane. The crazy part was that he was beginning to like Chelsea for no explainable reason. She had a smart mouth, and physically she wasn't his type of woman. He was at least a foot taller than she and had to outweigh her by a hundred pounds. And as a general rule, he was attracted to women who liked him, not who looked at him as if he was a dickhead. Although he supposed he couldn't blame her for that. He *was* a dickhead, which, surprisingly bothered him more than it used to.

He unzipped the bag, and inside was a whistle,

a stopwatch, and a ball cap the kids from last year's hockey camp had given him, with "#1 Coach" embroidered across it.

He took a few youth-sized sticks and orange cones off the shelf. Derek White didn't have the innate skill to ever play professional hockey. He just wasn't an athlete, but there were a lot of guys who loved the game and played in the beer leagues. Guys who were passionate and still had a lot of fun. Mark couldn't remember the last time he'd laced up his skates with the sole purpose of having a good time.

He put the hat on his head and adjusted it a few times until he found the perfect spot. It felt good. Right. Like nothing had felt in a real long time. He'd loved hockey. Loved everything about it, but somewhere along the line, it had stopped being fun. Playing had been about winning. Every game. Every time.

From outside, he heard Chelsea's car pull out of the driveway, and he moved toward the back door. He'd known his assistant for less than two weeks. Twelve days. It felt longer. She took charge of his days and invaded his sleep.

The other day she'd told him that he looked in control of his life. Hardly. Before the accident, he'd been in control on and off the ice. He'd controlled his personal life as well as his chaotic career. He'd controlled the sometimes out-of-control antics of his fellow teammates, and he'd controlled who walked into his home.

A nagging ache settled in his hip and thigh as he moved through the door and into the kitchen. He reached inside a drawer and pulled out a bottle of Vicodin. Now he controlled neither. He opened the bottle and looked down at the white pills spilling into his palm. It would be so easy. So easy to take a handful. To pop them into his mouth like PEZ and forget all his problems. To let the strong opiate do more than take away his pain. To let it numb his brain and pull him into a nice, cozy place where nothing mattered.

He thought of Chelsea and their conversation about control. He dumped all the pills back in the bottle. He still needed them for pain, but a lot of the time, he hadn't been taking them for the pain in his body. If he wasn't very careful, he'd end up liking them too much.

He thought of Chelsea playing hockey in her little skirt. If he wasn't very, *very* careful, he might end up liking her too much too.

Chapter Twelve

Friday night when Bo got home from work, she handed Chelsea a business card. On the front was the name and information of a media company that the Chinook organization used to produce all their commercials. Handwritten on the back was the name and number of the talent agency they used.

"I thought you might be interested," Bo said. "Most of the time we use the players in our advertising, but sometimes we use local actors."

She looked the card over and checked out the agency on the Internet. She'd be in Seattle for several more months. Depending on where she decided to have her breast surgery, maybe longer. She had to figure out something to do with her time, other than watch TV, go to nightclubs, answer Mark Bressler's fan e-mail, and set up appointments with real estate agents. So why not? If she didn't like the talent agency, she'd know within moments of walking in the doors. No harm, no foul. She'd take her résumé and leave.

On her way to work Monday, she called the agency and set up a meeting for Tuesday when Mark would be coaching Derek. An hour later, she switched cars and drove Mark to see the house in Bellevue. The seven-thousand-square-foot mansion on the waterfront in Newport Shores was filled with hand-crafted parquet flooring and massive oak timbers. The huge windows at the rear of the house looked out over a large backyard with a cabana and spa next to the swimming pool. It had a bar and a temperature-controlled wine room. As for opulence, it was on par with the house he currently lived in and had the added bonus of being priced a million dollars less.

Mark stood in the pantry about the size of Bo's entire apartment and said, "I don't need a house this big."

Chelsea was pretty sure she'd told him the total square footage before they left his house.

"And I don't want to live behind gates," he added.

He'd never mentioned his aversion to gates, but if he'd looked at the information about the house that she'd printed out for him, he would have known. After they left the estate, she looked at him across the Mercedes and asked, "Do you sit around and think up ways to be difficult or is it a natural reflex? Like breathing."

He put his mirrored glasses on the bridge of his nose. "I thought I was being nice today."

"Seriously?"

"Yeah." He shrugged.

She shook her head. "I didn't notice." She paid more attention as she drove him to the dentist. And she supposed if sitting in uncomfortable silence equaled being nice for him, then yeah, he was nice. But an hour later on the way home from the dentist, he totally blew it with his horrid backseat driving again. Oddly enough, she found it more relaxing than his efforts to be nice.

"The light's about to turn red."

"It's still yellow," she pointed out as she sped through the intersection. "I thought you were going to be nice."

"I can't when I'm worried about getting killed. Are you sure you have a valid driver's license?"

"Yes. Issued by the state of California."

"Well, that explains it."

Behind her sunglasses she rolled her eyes and changed the conversation. "Did you have cavities?"

"It wasn't that kind of appointment. He just wanted to check my implants to make sure they are still okay."

Chelsea knew about dental implants. She had a friend who'd knocked out her front teeth in a surfing accident. The dentist had drilled screws into her upper jaw, then stuck porcelain crowns on the spikes. If a person hadn't known she'd had her teeth knocked out, you wouldn't be able to tell. "How many do you have?"

"Three implants and four crowns." He pointed to the top left side of his mouth. "I'm lucky."

She wondered what he considered *un*lucky.

Tuesday afternoon she took her portfolio to the talent agency in downtown Seattle. She met with the owner, Alanna Bell, who reminded Chelsea a little of Janeane Garafalo. But the Janeane of ten years ago, before the actress had turned all bitter about life.

"What's your real hair color?" Alanna asked as she riffled through a file folder.

"The last I checked, it was brown."

"I could find more work for you if your hair isn't two colors. Would you be willing to dye it if I asked you?"

She looked at all the posters and signed photographs on the wall of Alanna's office. The vibe in the agency felt good. Right, and she should know. She'd met her fair share of sleazy agents. "I'd consider it, yes."

"I see you've studied at the Theater of Arts."

"Yes. As well as a few years at UCLA."

Alanna handed her a monolog from *White Olean-der*. Chelsea wasn't a huge fan of cold readings, but it was part of the business. She took a deep breath, cleared her head of everything but the words in front of her, and read: "The Santa Anas blew in hot . . ." When she was through, she set the paper on the desk and waited as she had countless times before. But this time there was something different. Strangely enough, sitting in the agent's office a thousand miles from Hollywood, cold reading, she felt the teasing nibble of the acting bug. Only it was calmer than it had been in years. She didn't have to prove anything to anyone here in Seattle. Least of all herself. There was no pressure to meet the right people or compete for the right part that would launch her career. Here she could just act. She could relax and have fun with it. Something she hadn't done in a while.

"I might have some background work for you this weekend." She glanced down at Chelsea's résumé. "HBO is sending up a crew to shoot around the Seattle Music Experience."

Chelsea groaned inside. She wasn't a fan of standing around in the background for hours, but it was a start and wouldn't interfere with her real job. "Sounds great."

"I assume you have a union card?"

Chelsea dug it out of her wallet and slid it across the desk. After several more moments, she shook Alanna's hand and drove to Medina. Keeping her head in acting and exercising her craft before she returned to L.A. was a good idea. She'd heard of well-known actors and actresses who, after a few big movies, had left the spotlight to act in off-Broadway shows, only to return rejuvenated and with a clearer head. She'd never understood it before, but now she did. Her own head felt clearer. Chasing the dream for ten years had robbed her of the joy of acting. The fun of getting to play someone else for a while.

She drove down Mark's street and pulled up next to the curb. It was a little after two, and Mark stood in the middle of his long driveway, one hand on his cane, the other on his hip. Instead of his regular uniform of white T-shirt and jogging pants, he wore a dark green polo and jeans. A beige ball cap shaded his eyes and cast a shadow across the lower half of his face. Derek stood several feet away, hockey stick in his hands, pushing a puck from side to side. Chelsea parked on the street to give them plenty of room. A slight breeze ruffled her hair and the bottom of her Burberry kilt skirt as she walked toward him. A pair of dark glasses shaded her eyes from the sun.

"How long do I have to do this?" the boy asked.

"Until you can do it and keep your head up," Mark answered, looking so big and imposing next to such a skinny kid.

Chelsea stopped in front of him and pushed her sunglasses to the top of her head. "Do you guys need anything?"

He looked at her, and the shadow from his hat slid down his nose to the bow of his top lip. "Like what?"

"Water? Gatorade?"

Slowly, one corner of his mouth lifted. "No. That isn't what I need."

"Then what do you need?"

From within the shadow of his brim, his gaze lowered from her eyes to her mouth, down her chin and throat to the front of her white blouse. His attention felt almost like a physical caress. Her stomach got all light and her breath got stuck in her lungs as his gaze paused mid-chest before sliding to her skirt and bare thighs. Within the shadow of his hat she felt the heat of his brown eyes, and she half expected him to say that what he needed was her.

"How was your meeting?" he asked.

"What meeting?"

"With the talent agent." He turned to watch Derek and she could breathe again. "Isn't that where you went?"

Oh, *that* meeting. "It was good. She wants me to

do background work at that Seattle Music Experience by the Space Needle."

"What's background work?" he asked without taking his attention from Derek.

"It's just like it sounds. It means I stand in the background looking like I'm doing something important." She pushed her hair from her face. "She asked me to dye my hair one color."

"Head up and roll your wrists," he called out to Derek. "Did you tell her no?"

She glanced up at him and her mouth parted in surprise. "You hate my hair."

"I don't hate it."

"You said I looked like a Russian just off the boat."

"I was talking more about your clothes." He looked down at her, and once again the shadow of his hat slid to the bow of his top lip. "Your hair's not so bad. I've gotten used to it."

"Is this you trying to be nice again?"

"No. If I was trying to be nice, I'd tell you that you look good."

Chelsea glanced down at her white blouse and Burberry kilt. "Because it's more conservative than what I usually wear?"

He chuckled. "Because your skirt's short." He pointed his cane at Derek. "You can stop now. I think you're ready for some passes." He walked into the garage, and when he returned, he had a hockey stick in his right hand. He thrust it toward Chelsea. "Derek, you're going to feed passes to Chelsea."

"Me?"

"Her? She's a girl."

"That's right," Mark agreed, and she half expected him to say something sexist. "She's little and quick, so you better watch yourself."

She took the stick and pointed to her feet. "I'm in three-inch heels."

"You don't have to move. All you have to do is stop the puck."

"I'm wearing a skirt!"

"Then I guess you're going to have to be really careful not to bend over." Beneath the shadow hitting his top lip, he grinned. "I wouldn't mind, but we have to keep it clean 'cause Derek's a minor and I promised his mom."

"The things I do for this job." She kicked off her shoes and lowered her sunglasses to the bridge of her nose.

Mark walked several feet away and pointed to Derek. "Move down ice. Bring the puck up and just feed it to her."

Derek moved down the driveway, barely able to stay up on his skates. Not only couldn't he skate, but he got tangled up with his stick. A few times he nearly fell, and when he finally did shoot, it went wide and Chelsea had to run after it.

"You're watching the puck," Mark told him. "Keep your head up and your eyes where you want the puck to go." He tried again, and once again he barely stayed on his skates and Chelsea had to run after the puck. After the fourth straight time, she was getting a little irritated.

"I'm tired of running after your pucks," she complained as she brought the puck to the middle of the driveway.

"Derek, what is the first rule of hockey?"

"No whining, Coach."

Chelsea frowned and looked from Derek's flushed face to Mark. "Is that in the official rule book?"

"Yes. Along with the importance of trash talk." Keeping his right leg straight, Mark bent down and picked up the puck. "So let's hear some chatter," he said as he handed it to the kid.

"Okay, Coach." This time as Derek skated toward her, he said, "Your hair is stupid and you have a stink eye." He shot, and the puck hit Chelsea's stick and bounced off.

"I have a what?"

"Stink eye."

She raised a hand to the lenses of her glasses. "I do?"

Derek laughed and Mark shook his head. "No. Trash talk doesn't have to be true. It just has to be distracting." He picked up the puck and tossed it to Derek. "That was a good one. You do better when you're not trying so hard."

This time when he skated toward Chelsea, she was ready for him with something she figured was age- and Derek-appropriate. "You're so skinny, you can hula hoop with a Cheerio," she said, thinking she was pretty clever.

Derek shot. It went a little wide but she was able to stop it without have to run too far. He shook his head. "That was stupid."

This from the kid who said she had a stink eye? She looked at Mark and he shrugged. "Maybe you should work on your trash talk."

She wasn't the only one. Other than stink eye, Derek didn't have any other insults in his repertoire, and after he'd called her that three more times, she was ready to whack him with her stick. So when he got tangled up in his skates and fell, she wasn't exactly feeling bad for him.

"Ouch." He rolled onto his back and looked up at the sky.

"Are you okay?" Mark asked as he walked toward the kid.

"The stick hit my nuts."

"Ohh." Mark sucked in a breath through his teeth. "That sucks. Ringing the berries is the worst thing about hockey."

The boy didn't look too hurt. He wasn't writhing in pain or anything, and Chelsea could think of a few things worse than berry-ringing pain. Like the puck hitting your face and getting your teeth knocked out.

"It really hurts."

"I thought there was no whining in hockey," she reminded them.

Mark scowled as if she'd said something really insensitive. "You can whine about a smashed nut."

"Is that an actual clause in the rule book?"

"If it isn't, it should be. Everyone knows that." He got down on one knee beside the kid. "Are you going to be okay?"

Derek nodded. "I think so." He sat up, and Chelsea was pretty sure if she hadn't been standing there, the kid would have cupped himself.

"Then let's call it a day," Mark suggested, and helped Derek stand up.

Chelsea was certainly ready to quit. She walked back to where she'd left her shoes and dusted off the bottoms of her feet. She leaned on the stick as she slipped her feet inside her pumps.

Derek changed out of his skates and shoved them into his backpack. He handed Mark his stick and carefully climbed onto his bike. "Are you going to be okay to ride home? Do you need a ride?" Mark asked, and Derek shook his head.

"I'm all right, Coach."

She guessed it was okay to make him ride his bike if he was exhausted. Just not with a "smashed nut."

As Derek rode away, Mark moved toward the garage doors. "What do you have planned for the rest of the day?" he asked her.

"Answering your fan e-mails." She followed him, letting her gaze travel from the back of his hat, down his neck and wide shoulders, to his tapered waist and hard butt. The man made everything look good. "Why?"

"Some of the guys are coming over to play poker tomorrow night. I thought if I wrote you out a list, you could go to the store and pick up some beer and snacks."

"Now?"

"Yeah." He took her stick and placed it on a shelf in front of a big gym bag. "I'll give you some cash." He pulled his wallet from the back pocket of his jeans and opened it. "Well, that sucks. I only have a five," he said, and returned his wallet. "I guess that means we both go."

She lifted a brow. "You shop? For your own groceries? Aren't you too big a star?"

"You have me confused with one of your celebrities." He moved to the back door and reached inside the house. He came back with a set of keys and tossed them to her. "There's a Whole Foods down the street."

"Are you going to backseat drive?"

"No."

She stood her ground and refused to get into the car. "Promise?"

He raised his right hand and looked like he was flipping her off more than swearing an oath. "Not even if you sideswipe a tree and kill me."

"Don't tempt me." She opened the door and slid inside. The seat was so far back, she couldn't reach the steering wheel, let alone the pedals. "Have you been driving?"

"No." He looked away and shut his door. "I was looking for something the other day."

"What?"

"Something."

He didn't want to tell her, fine. As long as he didn't turn into the backseat driver from hell, he could keep his secret. And surprisingly, he was true to his word. He didn't complain at all about her driving. Not even when she tested him by coming to a rolling stop at a stop sign.

Whole Foods was one of those stores that took

great pride in selling natural and organic foods to people who could afford it. The kind of place that had a killer deli and a kick-butt bakery. The kind that Chelsea generally avoided if she was shopping on her own dime.

She grabbed a cart and they hit the beer aisle first. Mark loaded up on local brew. Everything from Red Hook and Pyramid to beers she'd never heard of. He grabbed bags of blue chips and organic salsa. He bought crackers and three kinds of cheese. Prosciutto and thinly sliced salami.

"Do you know how to make nachos?" he asked as they headed toward the milk case.

"No." There were certain boundaries she didn't cross with employers. Slaving away in their kitchens was one of them.

"It can't be that hard."

"Then you do it."

"I tried it once." He shoved a quart of sour cream and a gallon of milk into the cart. "And I burned my hand and couldn't wear my glove for a week."

"Poor baby."

"You can say that again. That burn was pretty much the reason I didn't win the Art Ross Trophy in 2007."

"The what trophy?"

"Art Ross. It's the trophy given to a player who

has the most points at the end of the regular season. Sidney Crosby won it that year. Beat me by five points, all on account of nachos."

She chuckled. "Is that even true?"

He smiled and held up his bad hand like he was a Boy Scout again. He reached for bags of shredded cheese. "It'll be easy. You won't even have to grate the cheese."

"Sorry. Making nachos is above my pay grade."

He dropped the bags of cheddar into the cart. "What is your pay grade?"

"Why?"

"Just curious about what keeps you coming back every day."

"My deep and abiding commitment to people in need," she lied.

He shook his head. "Try again."

She laughed. "I get paid fifteen bucks an hour."

"Fifteen bucks an hour to answer e-mails and drive my car? That's easy money."

Spoken like a typical pain in the backside. "I have to put up with you *and* now Derek."

"Derek's an eggbeater. You should make human resources give you hazard pay."

He must not have been told about the bonus. She wondered whether she should tell him. The Chinooks' organization hadn't ever told her not to mention it to anyone. She didn't think it was a secret, but something held her back. "Maybe I will if he ever connects with my shin."

"First he has to stay on his feet." He smiled, and it spread to the tiny creases in the corners of his eyes.

"Hello, Mark."

He looked over his shoulder at the tall woman behind them. His smile fell. "Chrissy."

"How are you doing?" The woman had platinum-blond hair and turquoise eyes. She was stunning, like a supermodel, but like a lot of models, she wasn't perfect. Her nose was a little too long. Like Sarah Jessica Parker in *The Family Stone*. Not the Sarah Jessica of the *Sex and the City* movie. That Sarah Jessica was way too skinny.

He spread his arms. "Good."

While Chrissy checked out Mark, Chelsea checked out Chrissy's vintage Fendi satchel with the classic Fendi clasp in black. The purse was so difficult to find, it was practically an urban legend.

"You look good."

"Still with the old man you married?"

Ouch. That sounded bitter, and Chelsea figured that Chrissy must be a former girlfriend. She was the sort of woman Chelsea would expect to see with him.

"Howard's not that old, Mark. And, yes, we're still together."

"Not that old? He's got to be seventy-five."

"Sixty-five," Chrissy corrected.

Sixty-five wasn't old unless you were thirty-five. Which was how old the woman looked. But who was Chelsea to judge? She might have married an old guy to get her hands on that vintage Fendi too.

The woman's attention turned to Chelsea. "Who's your girlfriend?"

That someone would mistake her for Mark's girlfriend was humorous. "Oh, I'm—"

"Chelsea," he interrupted her. "This is Christine, my ex-wife."

Wife? She remembered Mark had said something about his ex-wife getting a nose job. She wondered how big it had been before. "It's nice to meet you." She stuck out her hand.

Chrissy's fingers barely touched Chelsea's before she dropped her arm to her side and turned her attention back to Mark. "I heard you were in a rehabilitation hospital until last month."

"I got your flowers. Very touching. Does Howard know?"

She adjusted the strap of her Fendi bag. "Yeah, sure. Are you still living in our house?"

"My house?" He slid his palm to the small of Chelsea's back. She jumped a little at the weight of his hand. The warmth of his touch heated her skin through the cotton of her blouse and spread tingles up her spine and across her butt. This was Mark Bressler. The guy she was paid to work for. She shouldn't be feeling anything. "I'm moving as soon as I find a new place," he added. "Chelsea's helping me out with that."

"Are you in real estate?" she asked Chelsea.

"I'm an actress."

Chrissy laughed. "Really?"

"Yeh," Mark answered for her. "Chelsea's acted in a lot of different stuff."

"Such as?"

"*The Bold and the Beautiful, Juno, CSI: Miami,* and some 'go meat' commercial."

She was shocked he'd remembered. "Hillshire Farms," she clarified. She glanced up at him, then returned her gaze to his former wife. "I've mostly acted in the horror genre."

Chrissy raised one disdainful brow. "Slasher movies?"

Mark's voice was a deep velvet rumble when he said, "Chelsea's a real screamer. You know I've always been partial to screamers." He smiled, a slow, sexy curve of his lips.

"That was one of your problems."

"That was never a problem."

Maybe it was his smile. Maybe it was the warm touch of his hand, but Chelsea couldn't help it. Her mind went there and she wondered exactly what the man did to make women scream. She'd never screamed. She'd come close once, but never actually screamed out loud.

Chrissy's eyes narrowed. "I see the accident hasn't changed you. You're still the same old crude Mark."

"See you around, Chrissy." He removed his hand from Chelsea's back and pushed the cart in the opposite direction from his ex.

Chelsea walked beside the cart and looked up at him out of the corner of her eye. "That was interesting."

"For who?" he asked, and moved down the cereal aisle.

"Me. She's exactly the type of woman I'd expect you to marry or date."

"What type is that?"

"Tall. Pretty. Expensive."

"I don't have a type." He dumped two boxes of Wheaties into the cart. "At least not anymore."

Chapter Thirteen

Mark carried the last bags of groceries into the kitchen and set them on the island. He leaned his cane against the granite top and grabbed a gallon of milk and a couple of packs of cheese. Earlier, his thigh had started to bother him and he'd popped several Vicodin before Derek had arrived on his bike. Now with the pain dulled, he moved with relative ease.

"You don't have to put my groceries away," he told Chelsea as she opened several cupboards until she found where he kept his salt.

"What else am I going to do for an hour?" The hem of her skirt rode up the backs of her legs as he watched her put away a box of sea salt.

Mark opened his mouth but forgot what he was

going to say. His eyes were glued to her butt and his feet were stuck to the floor like he was a kid again, waiting desperately for a glimpse of female bottom. Instead of a grown man who'd had more ass than he could recall. She lowered her arm, and he moved to the refrigerator and opened the door. "You should probably wear pants the next time Derek is scheduled to come over." He shoved the milk and cheese inside, but left the door open and returned to the island.

She turned and looked at him. Her brows creased as if she wasn't going to like the answer to her "Why?"

"I think I'll have you play in the net."

Her mouth parted and she shook her head. "No way. That kid said I have a stink eye."

"I told you that's just trash talk. Every hockey player has to learn to trash talk. I learned before I joined the traveling team."

"How old were you?"

He reached for the sour cream and meat and returned to the refrigerator. "Ten."

"Were you any good?"

He smiled. "I was good at a lot of things on the ice. Starting shit was just one of my many talents."

She grabbed the counter behind her with both

her hands and crossed one foot over the other. "Like making women scream."

"What?" He shoved everything in those little drawers and shut the door. "Are you talking about my conversation with Chrissy?"

"Yes. That was kind of inappropriate in the middle of Whole Foods."

He'd just been trying to get a reaction out of his former wife and he had. He'd recognized the irritation in her eyes. Not because it hadn't been appropriate conversation in the middle of a grocery store, but because he'd reminded her of all the times he'd made her scream. Interesting thing was, he'd stopped caring what Chrissy did or thought a long time ago.

"Are you still in love with her?"

"God no." So why had he purposely riled his former wife? He wasn't altogether sure, but it had had something to do with the way his ex had looked at his assistant. Mark recognized that look. Like she was better because she was porking an old guy for better seats at country club events.

Chelsea pushed herself away from the counter and walked toward him, the heels of her pumps a light, sexy *tap tap* across the tile. "How long have you been divorced?"

"A little over a year."

She picked up his boxes of Wheaties and moved to the cupboard next to the stove. She opened the door and stood on her tiptoes. Her heel slipped out of one shoe and the hem of her skirt slid up her thighs. The cereal belonged in the pantry, but who was he to stop the show. "What went wrong?" she asked as she reached way above her head with a box in each hand.

"Chrissy loves money. Lots of money." He moved up behind her and took the cereal from her. "She left me for someone with more money and a better seat at the country club."

"An older, wealthier man?"

"Yeah." He easily slid the boxes in place.

She dropped back down and looked at him over her shoulder. "I can't imagine being with a man just for his money."

"Then you're not like most women." At least not like the women he knew.

He'd been fighting a hard-on since she'd walked up the driveway toward him, the wind blowing in her hair and lifting the bottom of her skirt. Hell, he'd been fighting it since that very first dream a few weeks ago. He put his hands on her shoulders and pulled her back against him. He closed his eyes and rubbed his hands up and down her arms. He didn't want to fight it anymore.

"Mr. Bressler?"

"Mark." She was warm and soft and her little butt pressed into the zipper on his Lucky's.

"Mark, I work for you."

"You work for the Chinooks."

She turned and looked up at him through clear blue eyes. He wondered how long it would take him to make them get all drowsy with lust again. "You can get me fired."

"And why would I do that?"

Instead of answering his question she said, "I'm your assistant. There's a boundary that can't be crossed."

"We crossed it the other day."

"That was wrong of me. I shouldn't have done that."

Until the night of his accident, he'd always been extremely self-disciplined. He relied on that discipline now and took a step back. "Why did you?"

She slid past him and moved to the center of the kitchen. "Well, I . . ." She looked at her feet and shook her head. "I'm not quite sure. You're a nice-looking guy." An orange lay on the granite island, and she picked it up. "It makes no sense. I've worked for nice-looking guys before, and I've never done anything at all out of line." She rolled the orange between her small hands and his lower belly tightened. "Never wanted to."

He walked across the kitchen toward her. "Not once?"

"No." She turned toward him, and confusion wrinkled her brow. "All I can think of is that maybe it's because I haven't had a boyfriend for over seven months. Maybe longer."

"How long since you had sex?"

"I don't remember."

"If you can't remember, it must have been bad sex. Which, in most cases, is worse than no sex at all."

She nodded. "I think maybe it's just all pent up inside."

Oh God. He reached for her free hand and brushed his thumb across her fingers. "That's not healthy." He should know. He had so much built-up lust he was about to explode. Yes, he was a man who was used to extreme self-discipline. Absolutely, but he was also a man who was used to getting what he wanted. "You have soft hands." And he wanted her hands on him. All over his body. Her mouth parted but she didn't say anything. He pressed her palm against his chest and slid it up to his shoulder. "And a really soft mouth. I think about it a lot."

She swallowed, and the pulse in her wrist pounded beneath his thumb. "Oh."

He raised his free hand and brushed his knuckles along her smooth jaw. "I would never get you fired, Chelsea. Not for the things we might do, or might not do. I'm really not that big a tool." He lowered his mouth to hers and smiled against her lips. "Most of the time."

"We should stop before things go too far."

He slid his palm to the side of her neck and tipped her head back. "We will," he said, but there was no such thing as too far. There was only her naked and him finding release between her soft thighs. "But the thing is, I like you and you must like me. At least a little. You're still here after I called you retarded, lied about you being unattractive, and made you buy that pleasure ring."

"I guess I like you a little." Her breathing got a bit shallow and she said, "And you need me."

He did need her. For the next fifteen minutes, he needed her real bad. He fit his free hand in the curve of her waist and she sucked in a breath. Her lips parted in an invitation that he had absolutely no intention of resisting. He kissed her. Slow. Easy. Her mouth tasted sweet, like candy. Sweet, decadent candy, and he fought the urge to push her down and kiss her inner thighs. To work his way up to her slick candy center and to see if she tasted sweet and decadent there too. Instead, the kiss continued, a slow, easy exploration of her mouth, giving her a chance to stop if she wanted. Giving her the chance to turn away and leave him with an aching hard-on and a broken heart.

The orange fell from her hand and hit the floor. She rose onto her toes and wrapped her arms around his neck. Her breasts pressed into him, the soft weight settling against his chest. He slid his hand from her waist to her behind. Slowly he brought her closer until the front of her skirt brushed his fly. He felt like he was fifteen again. When the slightest brush against his groin turned him hard as steel and got him off. But unlike being fifteen, he had more control. Barely.

Without raising his lips from hers, he lifted her and sat her on the island. Her mouth clung to his, giving and receiving wet, feeding kisses while her fingers combed through his hair. He slid his hand up her side and cupped her breast.

She jerked her mouth from his and stilled. Lust lowered her lids and clouded her blue eyes. "My breasts are big," she stated the obvious.

"I know. We've talked about your breasts several times."

"They're not very sensitive." She licked her swollen lips. "Some men are disappointed by that."

He unbuttoned the top of her shirt. "Some men aren't me." He looked into her eyes and unbuttoned until the blouse lay open to her waist. "I've only ever been good at two things. Hockey and sex." He looked down at her. At her large breasts in a silky white bra, and at her flat belly. "My hockey career is over. So that only leaves me with one thing I'm good at." The waist of her little plaid skirt rested just below her navel. "Take your shirt off." When she did as he asked, he lowered his face to the side of her neck and spread kisses across her throat and shoulder. He might feel like he was fifteen again, but he wasn't a bumbling kid who didn't know his way around a bra. He easily unhooked it, pulled the straps down her arms, and tossed the bra aside. Narrow pink lines dented her shoulders, and he kissed the imperfections marring her perfect skin. He continued down her chest to her deep, deep cleavage, where she smelled like power and tasted like sin. Dark pink nipples lay in the centers of each heavy breast. In perfect proportion to her size. Slightly puckered, waiting for his attentions. She arched her back, and he cupped one breast in his hand. He brushed his thumb back and forth across her nipple several times before it tightened in response. He touched the tip of his tongue to the tip of her breast and pressed inward. When he got the response he was after, he rolled her nipple beneath his tongue, taking his time and working it over until it turned into a hard little pebble. His scrotum got so tight, his stomach ached with the pleasure of it. Then he sucked her into his mouth and he didn't know which moan was louder, his or hers.

Her head fell back and she gave a sexy little "Ohhh. That feels good. Do that." She squirmed against the front of his jeans and he about exploded in his pants. He kissed her other breast until her breathing got choppy and he knew there was no turning back. She would give him what he wanted. Let him do all the things he'd been thinking about doing to her.

He slid his mouth down her soft stomach to her belly button. He wanted to kiss her thighs and satisfy the hungry, clawing need that demanded release. A box of condoms lay in the drawer beneath Chelsea, just waiting for him to open them up and slide one on.

He pushed up her skirt as the first twinge of pain gripped his thigh. He stilled, hoping it would go away. "Goddamn!" It knotted his muscles, and he grasped the granite edge to keep from falling on his ass. "Shit!"

"What?"

The pain radiated up his hip and he couldn't move.

"Are you okay?"

He hung his head and tightened his grasp on the stone. "No." As carefully as possible, he lowered himself to the floor before he fell. He sat with his back against the island, one hand gripping his thigh. He pulled air in through his nose and breathed it out through his mouth. He didn't know which was worse. The pain in his body, or the humiliation of his body giving out on him before he could satisfy himself and the half-naked woman on the counter. Probably the latter. The pain in his body would ease. The humiliation would be with him for a while.

"Mark." Chelsea knelt beside him, her bra on and her shirt buttoned over her breasts. "What can I do?"

"Nothing." He took another deep breath and gritted his teeth. "Just give me a few minutes."

"Did I . . . did I do something to hurt you?"

Until that moment, he'd thought his humiliation was complete. "No."

"What happened?"

His muscles began to relax, and he looked into her pretty face, her lips still swollen from his kiss. "Sometimes I forget my limitations. When I move too fast or just the wrong way, I get a cramp in my thigh."

"Can I massage it for you?"

"No."

"But if you're in pain, I could rub your leg."

He laughed as the pain receded from his hip. "My leg isn't the only place I'm in pain. If you want to rub me, go ahead and massage my hard-on."

She bit the side of her lip. "That's not in my job description."

"Honey, everything we were just doing wasn't in your job description."

She sat back on her heels. "I shouldn't have let you talk me into taking off my shirt."

"There wasn't a lot of talking."

"I know." Her cheeks flushed pink like the bottom of her hair. "Sometimes I have issues with impulse control, but I can't have sex with you. It's wrong."

"No, it's not."

"Yes, it is." She shook her head and pushed her hair behind her ears. "I work for you, and there are boundaries that I just can't cross. Please don't ask me to. I don't want to lose this job."

They were back to that. He took a deep breath and

let it out. The last of the pain eased from his body, but he knew that one wrong move and it would return. He leaned his head back and closed his eyes. "I told you that you won't get fired."

"I'd still have to leave. It would just be too weird after that. It would be like I got paid to come here and have sex with you. I know that after what just happened you might not believe this, but morally and ethically, I just can't do that."

Morally and ethically, he did not have a problem with having sex with his assistant. None at all, but he'd never been the type of guy to pressure a woman who didn't want sex. Not even when he wanted it so bad his teeth hurt and his balls ached.

"I don't know what else to say."

He glanced over at her. Suddenly he felt tired. And old. Like he'd just gone two rounds with Darren McCarty in overtime. "You don't have to say anything. I took a bunch of Vicodin just before you got here and lost my mind."

She stood, and he looked up her bare legs. "Does it usually make you lose your mind?"

No, she made him lose his mind. "It makes me forgetful, and I forgot that I can't have sex with you." But he wouldn't forget again. He had blue balls and she was about to walk out the door. Just like last time. She was cute and sexy and he liked her, but there were a lot of cute, sexy women that he liked. Cute, sexy women who wouldn't let things like morals and ethics stand in the way of a hot, raunchy roll in the sheets.

If not for a leg cramp, Chelsea would have had sex with Mark. Right there on top of the granite island. There wasn't a doubt in her mind about that. He hadn't been the only one to lose his mind that afternoon in his kitchen. And just like there wasn't a doubt in her mind that she would have done him, there wasn't a doubt in her mind that it would have been good.

Real good.

Scream at the top of her lungs, rock the gates of heaven, and beg him not to stop, good.

She didn't know what it was about him, other than his good looks and hot body. Other than the heat of his brown eyes and the touch of his skilled hands and mouth, that made her forget everything. Forget her ethics and plans and who she was and what she wanted to do with her life.

She'd worked for fantastic-looking men before. Men who'd made it known in subtle and not-so-subtle ways that they wanted to have sex with her. She'd never been tempted. To them she'd just been a woman they found attractive. A body. It hadn't been personal.

Mark was different. There was just something in the way he looked at her sometimes. Not as if he *wanted* her, but as if he *needed* her. It surrounded him like some sort of hot magnetic force that drew her in and drained her brain. It made her all raw nerve endings and warm urges. It made her throw caution and good judgment to the wind, along with her clothes, and want to press her naked body against his. To touch him all over and feel him touch her.

I've only ever been good at two things. Hockey and sex, he'd said. *My hockey career is over. So that only leaves me with one thing I'm good at.*

She'd never seen him play hockey, but she imagined his approach to both was the same. She imagined he used the same thoughtful precision to score goals as he did to score with women. He stayed with it and took his time. Didn't rush and did whatever it took to get the job done.

In the cooler section of Whole Foods, she'd wondered what the man did to make women scream; now she knew. And now that she knew, she worried that getting through the next few days, heck, the next three months, was going to be torture.

But she needn't have worried. The next day at

work, Mark returned to his previous pattern of behavior and ignored her. He ignored her the day after that too. In fact, over the course of the next few weeks, the only real time he spoke to her was when she took him to appointments or chauffeured him around to look at real estate. He looked at so many properties, she didn't think he'd ever find anything. The property was either too big or too small. If he liked the floor plan, he didn't like the area or vice versa. Either it was too secluded or the houses were too close. He was like the Goldilocks of house hunters and couldn't find something that was just right.

Often his friends picked him up, or he spent time in the weight room upstairs or on the golf course just outside the backyard. On the rare occasions he did speak to her, he was so extremely polite, she wanted to hit him on the arm and tell him to knock it off. To send her on a stupid errand or insult her clothes and hair.

Instead, he asked about safe stuff, like her acting. She told him about the background work she'd done for HBO. She'd been hired for a commercial shoot in a local coffee shop, and she'd tried out for the part of Elaine Harper in a local production of *Arsenic and Old Lace*. She didn't get it, which was a little disappointing but okay. The play wasn't set to open until

September. She wasn't sure how much longer she would be in Seattle after September.

Perversely, the less attention he paid her, the more attention she paid to him. The more he ignored her, the more things she noticed about him. Like the way he tended to draw out the O's when he talked. Or how when he was irritated, his "yeah" got chopped to a "yeh." She noticed how his voice sounded through the glass as she stood in the office and watched him coach Derek on the driveway. His coaching style was equal parts encouragement and exasperation, and he was in turn amused and annoyed by Derek's utter lack of coordination.

She noticed the way he smelled. Like some lethally good combination of soap and deodorant and skin. And she noticed the way he walked. He no longer wore his splint, and he'd switched his cane to his right hand. His strides seemed easier. Less thought out. Smoother. She noticed he seemed more comfortable and that pain rarely bracketed his mouth. And she noticed that he fell asleep less during the day but that he often looked tired by the time she left at five.

All that she noticed about him, but he didn't seem to notice much about her. Sometimes she wore clothes so bright, she thought for sure she'd get a reaction.

Nothing. It was like that afternoon in his kitchen had never happened. As if he'd never touched her and kissed her and made her want more.

Yet . . . yet there were a few times when she thought she caught a glimpse of something in his eyes. That hot need burning just beneath the surface. That barely controlled desire, but then he'd turn away and leave her wondering if she was crazy.

Over the next month, she came to view him as something decadent. Something she craved like brownie fudge ice cream. Something bad for her, but the more she told herself she couldn't have it, the more she seemed to crave just one bite. And just like brownie fudge ice cream, she knew that should she ever indulge, one bite would not be enough. One bite would lead to two. Two to three. Three to four, until she'd feasted on the whole thing and there was nothing left but regret and a bad stomachache.

She also knew just where she'd start feasting on Mark. Right where the collar of his T-shirts hit the base of his neck. She'd kiss the hollow of his throat just below the slight bump of his Adam's apple.

Working for him was as hard as it was easy. She didn't have to make sure he got invited to the right parties or arrange events as she had for her past employers. She didn't have to call up designers and make sure he had the right clothes. He was very low-maintenance, but his very laid-back attitude was what often made him difficult.

Three days before the Stanley Cup party, he suddenly remembered that he had to buy a shirt. Chelsea drove him to Hugo Boss and sat in a chair next to the trifold mirror as he tried on several dress shirts. Since the accident, he discovered that he'd lost an inch around the neck, chest, and waist. Which meant he had to buy a new suit and have it altered by the party. He picked out a two-button wool jacket and pants of classic charcoal. To go with it, he tried two different shirts. First a charcoal and black, then a stark white.

The salesman brought him a selection of ties, and he picked out a simple blue-and-green stripe with the stark white. Chelsea watched him through the mirror as he flipped up the collar and wrapped the tie around his neck. Even though he'd regained a lot of the dexterity in his fingers, his stiff middle finger kept getting in the way.

"Shit," he swore after the third attempt.

Chelsea stood and moved in front of him. "Let me," she said, and pushed his hands aside. The backs of her knuckles brushed against the thick broadcloth of his shirt as she adjusted the length.

"You've done this before?"

She nodded and concentrated on the silk fabric

in her hands instead of on his mouth just inches from her forehead. "A million times." She crossed the wide end over the narrow and wrapped it twice. "Half Windsor or full?"

He shook his head. "Whatever."

"I like the half. It's less bulky." He smelled wonderful, and she wondered what he would do if she tilted her face up just a bit. Her fingers brushed his chest and her thumb touched his throat and she thought about rising onto her toes and kissing his warm skin. If she undid all those buttons and slid her hands all over his bare chest . . . Of course she would never do it.

"Stop looking at me like that," he said just above a whisper. "Or I swear I'll push you against the wall and have sex with you right here."

She raised her gaze up his throat and mouth to the stormy anger in his eyes. "What?"

He knocked her hands away. "Forget it." He grabbed one end of the tie and pulled it from his neck.

He was clearly mad about something she'd done. Wisely, she moved away and waited for him at the counter, where he dropped more than three thousand dollars on a suit, two dress shirts, and a tie.

On the ride to Mark's house, an awkward silence filled the car. At least it was awkward for Chelsea, and she left work early. When Bo got home that night, the sisters looked in Chelsea's closet for dresses to wear to the Stanley Cup party. Chelsea didn't have three thousand dollars to blow on clothes, but she did own a small but impressive selection of designers.

After thirty minutes of indecision, Bo reached for the black Donna Karan stretch taffeta. It had a bow sash and a deep V in the back, and Chelsea had worn it to an Oscar party in Holmby Hills three years ago. Of course it fit Bo perfectly, and she looked wonderful in it.

Chelsea didn't have to think about which dress she'd wear. Last year she'd found a Herve Leger beige sheath at a consignment store. It was made of rayon and spandex, with gold jeweled straps. She'd never had the chance to wear it, until now.

The day of the cup party, the twins pampered themselves. Chelsea had the hot reddish-pink lowlights taken out and her hair dyed a nice summer blond. She had her hair straightened while Bo got hers curled. Together they got their fingers and toes done at a local day spa. Chelsea had learned a long time ago that one of the best and most inexpensive places to get her makeup professionally applied was at a makeup counter. The twins drove to the mall in Bellevue, and Chelsea got her face done at MAC while Bo chose Bobbi Brown.

The last time Chelsea had had so much fun with Bo had been the night of their senior prom. The dance had ended in disaster with their dates deciding that they wanted to switch twins, but she and Bo had had a great time until that point.

"Your boobs look huge in that dress," Bo said as she slid her feet into a pair of red pumps and sat on the bed.

"My boobs are huge. So are yours." Chelsea turned sideways and looked at herself in the full-length mirror. The dress wasn't her usual style. It hugged her like a second skin, and the color was very sedate.

"Can you sit down in that thing?"

"Of course." She slipped her feet into a pair of jeweled sandals with five-inch heels and sat next to Bo to buckle the straps around her ankles. That morning she'd called a plastic surgeon and made an appointment to talk to him. She'd been waiting for the right moment to tell Bo. They'd been having such a good time, she figured now was as good a time as any. "I'm going to use the money I get from the Chinook organization to have breast reduction surgery," she blurted.

"Shut up."

She looked up, then returned her attention to her shoes. "I'm serious."

"Why would you do something so horrible to your body?"

"It's not like I'm cutting them off. Haven't you ever wanted smaller breasts?"

Bo shook her head. "Not enough to mutilate myself."

"It's not mutilation."

Bo stood. "Why do you always have to be different?"

"I'm not doing it to be different. I want to do it so that I'm not fifty and slumped over like Mom." She finished with her shoes and rose to her feet. "I'm having a consultation with a local plastic surgeon week after next. I want you to go with me."

"I won't support you this time." Bo shook her head. "I don't even want to talk about it."

Chelsea grabbed her beaded clutch off the dresser. The one person in the world who should understand and support her decision, didn't. The only other person in the world who'd seemed to understand, currently wasn't talking to her at all.

Chapter Fourteen

 The Sycamore Room inside the Four Seasons glowed with golden candlelight. Gold tablecloths and fine white china adorned round tables with centerpieces made of exotic flowers. Beyond the floor-to-ceiling windows, the city sparkled, and scattered lights shone like diamonds on Elliot Bay.

On a raised dais at the front of the room sat the holy grail of hockey: the Stanley Cup. Light bounced off the polished silver like it was a disco ball, and Chelsea had to admit, even from her seat at the back of the room, it was an impressive sight. Almost as impressive as Jules's indigo-and-white-striped suit and fuchsia shirt.

As dessert was served, Coach Nystrom stood at a podium next to the trophy and talked about the hockey season. The highs and the lows. He talked about the death of the team owner, Virgil Duffy, and the accident that almost took Mark's life.

"We were devastated. Not only on a professional level, but more importantly on a personal level. Mark Bressler played for this organization for eight years, led it for the past six. He's one of hockey's all-time great players, a leader, and a fine man. He's family, and when we learned of the accident, everything just stopped. None of us knew if a member of our family would live or die. But as worried as we were about Mark, we couldn't stop. We had the rest of the team to think about too. We had to think up something fast if we were going to have a shot at saving the season. We had to find someone who could step in and fill Mark's considerable shoes. A man who would respect our players and our program. We found that man in Ty Savage."

As the coach talked about Ty, Chelsea leaned to her left and whispered in Jules's ear, "Where's Mr. Bressler?" She and Bo had arrived as the first course was being served and there were more than a hundred people in the room, most of them a lot taller than the sisters.

"Owner's table in the front."

She knew from the few conversations she'd had with Jules, not only was he the owner's assistant, he was her good friend. "Why aren't you at the owner's table?"

"I was invited but I wanted to sit with you and Bo."

She leaned forward a little and looked at her sister seated on Jules's left. Bo's mouth was drawn tight. Maybe tonight hadn't been a good time to tell her about the doctor's consultation.

Applause broke out and drew Chelsea's attention once more toward the front. Two men stood and approached the podium. Both had dark hair that brushed the collars of their dark suits. Both had wide shoulders. One was Mark Bressler. Chelsea didn't need to see his face to know it was him.

Pride lifted her chest and tumbled in her stomach. He was strong and had survived a lot. She watched him move easily toward the dais. If she hadn't known about the accident, she wouldn't have been able to tell tonight. His steps were smooth, his gait sure—until he came to the steps leading up to the podium. He paused for several seconds before he grasped the railing and took the few stairs up. He looked healthy and handsome in his white shirt, striped tie, and wool suit. She was proud of him, yes. But there was something else too, something hot and achy and totally off limits, tumbling and swelling in her heart.

"Good evening," Mark said, his voice deep and confident. "My grandmother always told me that if you take care of family, your family will take care of you. This past eight months, my Chinooks' family has certainly taken good care of me. For that, I am truly grateful."

The light above his head shone in his hair and bounced off his white, white shirt, and the feeling in Chelsea's chest grew a bit more. "It has been both an honor and a privilege to play for the Chinooks these past eight years. Everyone in this room knows it takes more than one person to win games. It takes more than great players. It takes good coaching and dedicated management willing to listen and invest in the team. So I want to say thanks to the late Mr. Duffy, the coaches, the trainers, and the rest of the staff. Most of all, thanks to the girls in the travel office who always made sure I had a room away from the elevator."

"We love you, Mark," a woman yelled.

"Thanks, Jenny." He chuckled. "I need to thank everyone who contacted me after the accident to wish me well. I want to say thanks to every guy I've ever played with. Most of you are in this room. I especially want to thank the guy I never played with, Ty Savage. For the past six years, Savage and I met regularly in the face-off circle to exchange pleasantries. Most of the time, he questioned my paternity while I questioned his sexual orientation. But one thing I never questioned was his skill. On the ice and as a leader. I know that everyone else in the Chinooks' organization has thanked him for the superb job he did leading the team to victory under difficult circumstances." Mark turned and looked at the man standing slightly behind him. "I would like to add my thanks."

Ty stepped forward and the two shook hands. Chelsea remembered the day Mark had called Ty an asshole, and she wondered if he'd changed his mind. The two men said a few words to each other, then Ty leaned toward the mic. "Stepping into the Chinook captaincy was both easy and one of the most difficult things I've ever done. Easy because Mark was a great captain who led by example. Difficult because he was a hard act to follow. As everyone knows, no one on this team deserves their name on that cup more than Mark."

The room exploded in applause, and after several more speeches were given, people moved forward toward the Stanley Cup to get a better look at hockey's top prize. Chelsea stayed in the back with Bo and Jules, but her gaze remained on the man who stood next to the shiny trophy. Even from the length of the room, he appeared relaxed. At ease and in his element. Chelsea had never known Mark Bressler, the hockey player. The elite athlete. Other than what she'd read on the Internet and gleaned from fan letters, she didn't know that side of him or that part of his life. She wondered if she would have liked him. Because despite his rude and obnoxious personality, she liked him more than she should.

"Can't you relax for one night?" Jules asked Bo, pulling Chelsea's attention from the front of the room. "Have some wine. Chill. It's a goddamn party."

Bo stood and grabbed her clutch off the table. "I'll be right back. Some of us have to work. I have to talk to the photographers from the *Times*," she said, and walked out the open door behind them.

Jules picked up his wineglass and drained it. "Come on. There's someone I want you to meet."

Chelsea stood and grabbed her small purse. "Did something happen between you and Bo?"

He adjusted his paisley tie and took her elbow. "Your sister is moody as hell."

Bo? Bo was a lot of things. Uptight and driven topping the list, but she wasn't moody. "Did something happen?" Chelsea felt a bit like a salmon swimming upstream as the two of them made their way to one of the tables in the front.

"I told her she looked pretty, and instead of just

saying thank you like any normal woman would do, she got all mad. She said I was only saying that because she was wearing a designer dress."

She smiled. "Ah." The crowd inside the Sycamore Room began to filter out toward the ballroom where the serious party was about to begin. "It makes perfect sense, now. In the fifth grade, Bo had a little crush on Eddy Richfield. So she punched him on the arm. He ran away crying, and the romance never blossomed."

Jules looked down into her face. "Is there a point to that story?"

Chelsea nodded and pushed her smooth hair behind one ear. "Bo doesn't react like other women."

"Tell me about it."

"And she always takes a swipe at guys she really likes."

"Why?" he asked as they approached the owner of the Chinooks, Faith Duffy. The woman was even more beautiful up close.

"To see if you'll run away crying."

"That doesn't make sense."

"That's Bo." Faith turned toward Chelsea Ross, and Jules introduced the two.

Faith smiled and held out her hand. "It's so nice to meet you, Chelsea. Jules has told me good things about you."

She shook the team owner's hand, and a few feet away, Mark's deep laughter reached across the distance and spread little tingles down her spine. Her back was to him, but she didn't need to see him to know he stood within a group of people admiring the cup a few feet away.

"I was in the Key the night the Chinooks won," she told Faith. "Bo and I both thought that kiss at the end was one of the most romantic things we've ever seen."

"Romantic and shocking." Faith smiled and looked around. "Where is Bo?"

"You know her." Jules let out an irritated breath. "Always working an angle." A frown pulled at his brows and he reached for Faith's left hand. "Is that an engagement ring?"

"Ty asked me to marry him."

"And you didn't tell him hell no?"

Ty moved behind Faith and slid his hand around her waist. "Why would she do that?"

She leaned back against Ty and smiled. "I was going to ask you to be my bridesmaid, Jules."

Ty laughed, and Jules's frown turned stormy. "Funny."

"I'm not joking. I want you to be in the wedding."

While the three of them talked wedding plans, Chelsea excused herself. Most of the room had cleared out, and she walked the few feet toward the dais. She stopped next to Mark and felt the hot swell in her chest again. She would love to tell herself that it was only pride that made her ache, but while she was a good actress, she was a very bad liar. Especially to herself.

He didn't say anything as he stared at the symbol of his accomplishment. His life goal. His dream. He looked at it like he was mesmerized. Hypnotized by its shininess. Or maybe he was just ignoring her again.

"It's bigger than I thought," she said. "Probably pretty heavy, too." She could only imagine the emotion he must be feeling. She knew that if she ever won an Oscar or even an Emmy, she'd be freaked out. Probably become catatonic. "I don't know a lot about hockey, but seeing all those names inscribed on the cup kind of inspires awe. Like the first time I stood at the Lincoln Memorial. It's so grand and filled with history." He still didn't speak. "Don't you think?"

Without looking at her, he said, "Your dress is too tight. That's what I think."

"What?" She turned to look at him. "That's crazy. It covers me almost to my knees."

"It's the same color as your skin."

"I thought you'd like it because it's all one sedate color."

Mark glanced down into her upturned face. Into her big blue eyes and pink lips. He did like it. A lot. He'd like it a lot more if they were alone. "You look naked." *And beautiful.*

"I don't look naked."

"Hey, Short Boss."

Mark groaned inwardly.

"Hi Sam," she said.

"You look hot."

Mark had an irrational urge to kill Sam. Or at the very least, punch him in the head. It had been a long time since Mark had punched anyone in the head. It might feel good.

Chelsea smiled up at the defenseman. "Thanks. So do you."

"What do you say to you and me hitting the other room? I'll buy you a drink."

Mark folded his arms across his chest. "It's an open bar, numb nuts."

Sam laughed and put his hand on Chelsea's elbow. "Free booze. Even better."

"Didn't you bring a date?" he asked the man he used to consider a friend.

"No. I stagged it. Some of the other guys too."

Great. A bunch of horny hockey players and Chelsea in a naked dress. He watched them walk away as bitter acid ate at his stomach. The feeling was rare, almost foreign to him, but he recognized it for what it was. He was jealous as hell and he didn't like it.

"Mini Pit dyed her hair."

He looked across his shoulder at goalie Marty Darche. "That's not Mini Pit. That's her twin sister, Chelsea."

"She looks naked in that dress."

"Yeh." His gaze slid down her spine to her tight little butt. He didn't need Marty to elaborate to know in which direction the man's thoughts were running.

The goalie elaborated anyway. "Do you think her tits are real?" he asked out of the side of his mouth.

They were, and Mark felt another urge to punch yet another teammate in the head. "Big breasts like that cause shoulder and back pain," he heard himself say. He sounded like such a girl, his neck caught fire.

The goalie laughed like Mark was joking. "I wonder if I got her drunk if she'd play knocker hockey?"

"Don't be a dick, Marty."

"What?" Marty looked at Mark as if he'd suddenly grown a horn out of the middle of his forehead. Like he didn't recognize his former captain.

In the past, comments like that wouldn't have

bothered him. Hell, he might have made one a time or two. Or three. But there were rules. You didn't talk that way about a teammate's wife or girlfriend. "Nothing. Forget it." Mark shook his head and walked away. Chelsea was not his wife or girlfriend. She was his assistant, and he'd been trying like hell to treat her like she worked for the Chinooks' organization and wasn't some living, breathing sexual fantasy they'd implanted in his house just to drive him batshit insane. He'd been trying to get the picture of her half naked sitting on his kitchen island out of his head. Mostly he'd been failing, and her touching his chest the other day, and looking up at him like she wanted to have sex right there at Hugo Boss, hadn't helped. Not one bit.

He moved from the Sycamore Room into the crowded foyer. Music flowed through the doors of the ballroom as the band hit their first set.

"Hey, Bressler."

Mark turned to his right and came face to face with one of the greatest enforcers to ever play in the NHL. "Rob Sutter. How in the hell are you?" He stuck out his hand.

"It's been a long time." Rob had been the Chinooks' enforcer until a groupie shot him and ended his career in 2004. "Mark, this is my wife, Kate."

"It's nice to meet you, Kate." Mark shook the

hand of a pretty redhead with big brown eyes. He dropped his arm to his side. "What are you up to these days?"

"We have a sporting goods store and a grocery market in a little town in Idaho," Rob answered. "My oldest daughter lives with us now, and we have two little boys."

"Rob is teaching them all to fly-fish," Kate said. "It's very comical."

Rob smiled. "It's like the Three Stooges." His smile leveled out and his brows lowered. "Listen. I was sorry to hear about your car accident."

Mark looked down at the toes of his black leather shoes. "It changed everything."

"I know what you mean." And if there was one other person on the planet who did know what it was like to have your life shattered, it was Rob "The Hammer" Sutter. "One day you have everything and the next you don't."

Mark looked up.

"I thought my life would never be good again. Now it's better than I ever imagined. Sometimes God has His own plan. Sometimes shit happens for a reason."

Lord, he missed the Hammer. No one else could get his face slammed into the boards and get all philosophical about it afterward like Rob. "You sound like a Hallmark card."

Rob grinned. "When you care enough—"

"Stop or you're gonna make me cry."

"Pansy-ass girl." Rob chuckled and shook his head. "You always were an emotional wreck around your period."

"Rob?"

Both men looked at Kate. Her brows were lowered as if she didn't recognize her husband.

Rob blinked several times and his cheeks turned red. "Sorry, Kate."

Mark laughed. "Have you seen Luc?"

Rob looked around. "Martineau? Not yet. Ran into Fishy though."

Mark hadn't seen Bruce Fish since he'd retired a few years ago. Together, he and the Sutters moved across the foyer to the ballroom where a decent band was playing. Inside, round tables set with tea lights dotted the perimeter of the dance floor while two bars served the thirsty crowd. His gaze skimmed the dimly lit room and landed on a familiar little beige dress. She stood in a small group of people, laughing at Sam as if he was the king of comedy.

He turned to Kate. "It was great to meet you." Then he shook Rob's hand. "Good to see you again."

"Take care of yourself."

As Mark made his way across the room toward her, he ran into Hugh Miner and his wife, Mae. Hugh was a legend in Seattle hockey. A wild man who'd played between the pipes for the Chinooks until he got traded to Dallas a year after Mark signed with Seattle.

When he glanced in Chelsea's direction, she was gone. His gaze skimmed the room, and he spotted her on the dance floor grinding with Walker Brooks. He leaned closer to Hugh's wife to hear what she was saying, but he kept his eyes on Chelsea. So, maybe she wasn't grinding. Exactly. But she was dancing with her arms in the air and undulating her hips like she was a damn belly dancer or something. She wasn't all that coordinated, but she looked so good in that dress that it didn't matter that she really couldn't dance.

After Mark talked to Hugh and Mae, he got stopped by general manager Darby Hogue, who told him that the assistant coach position was still available. He wanted Mark to come and talk to him about it Monday. Mark said he would, but at the moment his mind was somewhere else. Somewhere approximately twenty feet away. While he listened to Darby, he watched Chelsea dance with Frankie, then Sam.

"Forget it," he muttered, and headed to the closest bar. He wasn't going to chase her down. Especially since he didn't have anything to say and didn't want to dance.

For the most part, hockey players were fairly decent on the dance floor. They had natural timing and rhythm in their bodies. Even though it wasn't his favorite way to pass time, Mark wasn't bad himself, but that didn't mean he was about to drag his ass out onto the dance floor. He felt good tonight. Good enough to leave his cane at home. He hadn't taken any medication, and on a scale from one to ten, his pain was only a three. Almost nonexistent, but even if he did feel an overwhelming urge to grab her up and drag her out onto the floor, there was no guarantee that he wouldn't fall on his behind. Like the day in his kitchen when he'd had her close to naked and his hand inches from her crotch. He'd been about five minutes from having sex with her, but instead he'd ended up on the floor gasping in pain and choking on humiliation.

He took a long drink from a bottle of Beck's and watched Jules lead her out on the dance floor. Jules was young and healthy and wouldn't fall on his ass. Jules pulled her close, and the acid in Mark's stomach rose up his chest and ate at a spot just below his sternum.

He lowered the bottle and watched her smile.

Somehow, in a matter of two short months, he'd gone from trying to get rid of her, to looking for her in a crowd. From avoiding her because he didn't like her, to avoiding her because he liked her too much. She was the one person on the planet who made him feel whole again. Like a man.

Jules spun her, then brought her back against his chest. Suddenly Mark felt tired and old. He set the beer on an empty tray and moved toward the door. It was ironic as hell that the one person on the planet who filled him up, reminded him that he was empty.

Chapter Fifteen

Chelsea glanced over Jules's shoulder as the band sang a decent version of "Harder to Breathe." She felt the weight of his hand on her waist and the warmth of his palm against hers. She liked Jules. He was a good-looking guy with an impressive body, but it was another good-looking guy with an impressive body she looked for in the dark ballroom. A few moments ago, she'd spotted Mark at the bar. He wasn't there now.

"John Kowalsky was inducted into the Hall of Fame a few years back," Jules told her. "He was one of those guys, like Bressler and Savage, who dominated with size but whose slap shot was clocked at over a hundred miles an hour."

"Where's he?"

"I just told you. We're you listening?"

No. "Sorry. The music's loud."

"He's the big guy dancing with the tall brunette to your left. This room is filled with hockey legends."

Jules sounded really excited, like he was about ready to bust an important vessel. Like he just might start spouting statistics. "So, are you ever going to ask my sister out on a real date?" she asked before he made her endure that particular snorefest.

Jules paused in mid-step. "We argue too much."

"That's because you guys are sexually frustrated." Chelsea stopped and looked up into his green eyes. "You're like cats yowling and scratching at each other. For God's sake, go find my sister and just do it already." Jules opened his mouth to say something and closed it. The music stopped, and Chelsea moved to one of the round tables and grabbed her purse. She headed out into the foyer and glanced around for the restroom sign. She spotted Mark standing in a group of men and several women a few feet away. His head was bent to one side while he listened intently to Faith Duffy. He'd brushed back one side of his charcoal suit jacket and shoved a hand into the front pocket of his wool pants. As if sensing her presence across the foyer, he lifted his gaze and looked at Chelsea over the woman's shoulder. His brown eyes stared into hers, then lowered to her mouth. He smiled and said something to the owner of the team, but his gaze slid down Chelsea's throat to her chest. A hot shiver ran down her spine, and her footsteps slowed. She forced herself to keep walking. One foot in front of the other, moving farther and farther away. Down the long foyer until she was inside the cool bathroom stall. Of all the available men on the planet, why did she have to feel something for the one man off limits to her?

She used the bathroom, then set her purse on the counter next to the sink while she washed her hands. Of all the men on the planet, why did her body have to respond to him? She didn't fool herself that what she felt was love. She didn't love him any more than he loved her. What they had between them was nothing more than lust. The intense kind that burned hot and furious but ultimately burned out quickly.

She dried her hands and opened her purse. A tube of pink lipstick lay in the silky bottom and she bushed it across her mouth. She didn't need that kind of complication in her life. She knew what she wanted. She had a plan, and he was the one person who could ruin it all. Best to take a page from his book and avoid him. Which of course wasn't going to be possible. Especially when he stood in the hall across from the bathroom, leaning his back against the fire escape door. The door to the bathroom swung shut behind her, and his intense gaze reached across the distance and pinned her feet to the floor.

"Are you looking for the men's restroom?"

He shook his head. "I'm looking for you."

"Oh. Do you need something?"

His gaze lowered to her throat. "Yeh."

A tight little ball of nerves tickled her stomach, and she forced herself to walk toward him. "What?"

He blinked and looked back up into her face. Instead of answering, he asked, "Are you having a good time dancing with the guys?"

"They're nice." She'd have a better time with him. "I saw you talking to Ty Savage. Did you mean what you said about being grateful to him?"

"Maybe. He's not too bad a guy." One corner of his mouth lifted. "For an asshole."

Her nervous laugh came out sounding a little breathy. "Did you see the ring he gave Faith Duffy?"

"Hard to miss that ring. It's like he thought that if he bought it big enough, she'd have to say yes."

"It'd be hard to say no to a ring like that."

"A big ring doesn't mean you'll stay married." He leaned his head back against the door and gazed at her from beneath lowered lids. "Believe me. I know."

He looked tired, his face a little drawn "Should I call the car service to come and pick you up?"

"No."

"It's not a problem."

"Stop. I'm not helpless."

"I know." She opened her purse and pulled out her cell. "But if—"

"I drove."

She looked up at him. "What?"

He raised one shoulder. "I drove."

"Your car?"

"What else?"

She dropped the phone back into her bag. "If you couldn't get a service to pick you up, you should have called me."

"Chelsea . . ." He scrubbed his face with his hands. "I've been driving for a month now."

"But . . ." She'd taken him to a doctor's appointment the afternoon before. "But I drove you yesterday."

"I know." He dropped his arms to his sides.

"I don't understand." Either she was crazy or he was. She chose to believe the latter. "You hate my driving."

"True, but I love the way your skirts slide up your thighs when you drive." He reached for her hand

and pulled her close. "What are you wearing under your dress?"

Maybe it was her, because she answered, "Nothing," and she knew better. Knew exactly that it would make his gaze all hot and intense as he stared down at her.

It did too. "Don't fuck with me."

"I'm not. I put on a thong but I could see the strap on my hip. So I had to take it off and go commando."

With his free hand, he opened the door behind him and pulled her into the stairwell.

"Mark!"

"Do you really think that you can tell me something like that, and I'll let you go off with Sam?" He backed her against the door and put his hands on both sides of her head. "That's not going to happen."

Her hands grasped his lapels and she looked up into his face. "I wasn't going to go anywhere with Sam or anyone."

"That's right." He lowered one hand and slid the strap of her dress down her arm. "You're coming with me."

Her palms slipped beneath his jacket and slid up his chest. "To do what?"

"Have sex. All night."

She liked to have sex all night. "You know that's a really bad idea. I work for you."

He shook his head and ran his hand up her arm to the side of her face. "No, you don't. I don't pay you."

"I get paid to work for you."

"And it's Saturday. You're not at work."

In her lust-filled head, that was good enough logic for her, and she rose onto the balls of her feet and kissed the side of his neck. "So, technically I'm not getting paid to do this."

A deep groan vibrated his throat as he slid a hand to the small of her back and lower to palm her behind. She sucked his warm, salty skin into her mouth and pulled the knot from his tie until the ends hung down both sides of his chest. "Or this." Her fingers worked the buttons at his neck until the top three lay open and exposed the hollow of his throat. "I want you, Mark Bressler." She ran her tongue up his neck. "I want to kiss you all over."

His fingers tangled in her hair, and he brought his mouth down onto hers. "Not until I kiss you first," he said through a hot breath. He kissed her hard and spread hot, aching passion across her flesh. It tightened her breasts and warmed her thighs. Instantly, the kiss turned into a ferocious feeding frenzy of need and greed and dominance. His hands were everywhere at once, pushing at the top of her dress until her breasts spilled out and her nipples grazed the front of his shirt. She felt every fibrous thread against the sensitive tips. One arm wrapped around her back, holding her up as she pressed into him. Into his hard chest and harder penis. She ground against him, feeling the length of his erection from her pelvis to her belly.

Mark shoved his warm hand beneath her dress and cupped her between her thighs. Heat spread to the core of her body, and her knees buckled. His arm tightened around her to keep her from falling. "You're wet."

"You're hard."

He rested his forehead against hers. "Let's do something about it."

"Here?"

He shook his head and took his hand from between her legs. "Meet me out front in five minutes."

She licked the corners of her mouth. "Where are we going?" Not that it mattered. She'd follow him anywhere he chose to take her.

"Home. My house."

She lowered her arms and shoved her skirt down her thighs. She supposed that made better sense than sex in a stairwell. "I came with my sister."

"You're leaving with me."

She bit her lip as she pulled her dress up over her breasts. "How do I look?"

One corner of his mouth lifted. "Turned on. Like you were about to get laid."

She smoothed her hair. "Better?"

"No." He tugged at the top of her dress, then put his hands on her breasts and adjusted her cleavage. He leaned back and looked at her. "You can't go out there like that."

She looked down at her nipples making two very obvious points in the front of her dress. She placed her palms over each and pressed inward.

Mark tugged the tie from around his neck and shoved it into his jacket pocket. "That's not going to help." He took off the jacket and hung it across her shoulders. "Five minutes." He grabbed the lapels and pulled them over her chest. "If you're not out front in five minutes, I'll come back to get you."

"I'll be there."

Chelsea tossed Mark's jacket on the island in the kitchen while he dug in a drawer and took out a box of condoms. She tugged the ends of his shirt from his wool trousers, and by the time they made it the short distance to the elevator, her shoes were off and his shirt lay on the floor. On the way up to the second floor, she unbuckled his belt and pulled it from the loops. His socks and shoes littered the hall to his bedroom, and he kissed her while he walked backward to the couch. He unzipped the back of her dress as she unzipped his pants. Their clothes hit the floor, and she slid one palm across his hard chest while her other hand dove beneath the elastic of his boxer briefs. Except for his underwear they were both naked. They stood so close, the tips of her breasts touched the hair on his chest.

Mark sucked in a breath and pulled back to look at her as she wrapped her palm around his hot, huge penis. A moment of concern lowered her brows as she rubbed her thumb along the bulging veins. It was one thing to wonder what it would be like to have sex with a man hung like a porn star. It was another to actually do it.

He tossed the box of condoms on the sofa, then he wrapped his hand around hers and moved it up and down his thick shaft. "You look worried."

"I am."

"I'll make it good."

She believed him and shoved his underwear down his legs. She knelt in front of him, licked the bead of clear liquid, and slid her tongue around the hot, bulbous head.

He groaned, and she looked up into his lust-heavy eyes. "Do you like that?"

"Yes."

"Want more?"

"God yes." She smiled and took as much of him as possible into her mouth. His head fell back and he tangled his fingers in her hair. She sucked him hard, cupping his testicles and caressing the sensitive vein beneath the head of his penis with her tongue. Within a few short moments, his semen flowed hot into her mouth and hit the back of her throat. She stayed with him until it was over. Until he reached for her and lifted her to her feet.

"Thank you," he said, and pulled her naked against his chest. He kissed her and held her against him as he sat with her on the couch. Her knees rested beside his thighs and she sat naked in his lap. He might have just found release, but she was still totally turned on and her hands slid over his shoulders and arms and neck. A horrifying thought entered her head, and she pulled back to look at him.

"Can you get it up again?"

He laughed. "Is that a question or a demand?"

"Both."

"Yeh. I think I can manage it." He slid his hands to her waist. "Stand up on the couch and straddle my face," he instructed.

"What?"

"It's my turn." His grasp tightened and he helped her to her feet. She sank a little into the leather. "Like that." He looked up at her as he leaned forward and kissed the inside of her thigh. "Put your foot on my shoulder." She did and he said, "I've been dreaming about doing this to you for weeks." He parted her flesh with his free hand and took her into his hot mouth.

"Ooh, Mark," she moaned. His tongue slid across her slick flesh and he gave her the most incredible oral sex of her life. He knew exactly what he was doing. He stayed at it, combining teasing, light touches and kisses like he was sucking the juice from a ripe peach. He kept at it until a wave of hot orgasm shook her body. She cried out, "Oh God, Mark." Not exactly a scream; then a deep, satisfied moan started at her toes and worked its way through her body. When it was through, her limbs felt weak, and she slowly slid downward. Mark's mouth slipped across her abdomen and stomach. He kissed her breasts and her cleavage. She slid to her knees, and with his hands free, he tore open the condom and rolled it down his long shaft. Hard again, he positioned himself between her thighs. She looked into his face as she sat. The first blunt stab widened her eyes. "I don't know if this is going to work."

He sucked in a deep breath. "Don't leave me." His hot gaze stared out at her from beneath his lowered lids. "Don't leave me now."

She lowered herself, sliding down. "I won't leave you." With each second, his gaze got even hotter.

"You're really tight."

"You're really big." Inch by inch, she continued, feeling stretched and completely impaled. He put his hands on her thighs and gently pushed her downward. She didn't feel pain, but she wasn't exactly comfortable.

He cupped her bottom in his palms. "You're so beautiful to me."

When he looked at her, his eyes all warm and velvet, she felt beautiful. He'd just given her one of the best orgasms of her life, and her heart squeezed in her chest. "Thank you."

"You ready?"

She nodded, and he lifted her up his long, thick shaft. It was a pity he had to wear a condom because she would have loved to feel hot flesh on hot flesh. Thick veins against slick vaginal walls. The bulbous head of his penis rubbed her G-spot and once again reawakened her passion. Slowly she moved up and down with him, finding a perfect rhythm. A little higher and a little faster with each stroke. She grabbed on to his shoulders and matched his rhythm, riding him hard. She tilted her head back and never wanted it to end, even as she raced to completion.

"Oh my God!" She rode him with mindless pleasure and complete abandon. On and on the pleasure
built. She might have called his name. She wasn't
sure as she rode up and up. Higher and hotter until
she hit a second peak more intense than the first.
Scalding heat constricted her inner muscles and
spread fire outward across her body. Every cell
caught fire, and she opened her mouth and silently
screamed as he continued to pump into her. Again
and again until his grasp on her behind tightened
and he stilled. The muscles in his arms and chest
turned to stone. The breath whooshed from his
lungs and he swore long and loud. The male equiva-
lent of a scream.

Chelsea smiled.

"Did I hurt you?"

"I'm okay." She did feel a bit raw, but so content
she didn't care. "Are you okay?"

Pure male cockiness turned up the corners of his
mouth. "Yeh. Your orgasm lasted a long time."

"Were you worried you couldn't outlast me?"

"No. I can outlast you." He shook his head and
slid his hands up her thighs to her waist.

She buried her face in his warm neck. "Can we do
that some more?"

He ran his hands up her bare back. "Honey, we're
going to do that all night long."

And they did. Three more times before Chelsea slipped from his bed and grabbed her dress from the floor. The sun rose through the slats in the blinds as she stepped into her dress. They'd drifted to sleep sometime around four. Sometime after Mark had made a hearty meal of frozen pizza and ice cream.

Chelsea reached for the zipper on the back of her dress and moved toward the door. She cast one last glance at the sleeping man tangled up in white sheets before she walked into the hall. Silent footsteps carried her down the spiral stairs and into the kitchen. She grabbed her shoes and her little purse and pulled out her cell phone. She called a cab and walked out of the house and into the fresh air.

There had been several times in her life when she'd suffered the walk of shame sex. When the impulses of the night before felt shameful in the harsh light of morning. When regret felt like a fifty-pound lump in her stomach.

Funny she didn't feel that way with Mark. She didn't feel ashamed. She should. Having sex with him wasn't right. Bad, and she probably would feel shame and regret. Later.

But right now . . . right now she just felt calm. Relaxed. Happy and totally wrung out.

Chapter Sixteen

 Chelsea carried her shoes into Bo's apartment, tiptoeing as quietly as possible.

"Where did you spend the night?"

Her shoes fell from her hands as she spun around. Jules stood in the kitchen, once again shirtless. "Christ," she gasped, and placed a hand on her heart. "What are you doing here?"

He shrugged. "Making coffee."

Coffee sounded good. "I'll be right back," she said, and ducked into her bedroom. She changed into a big hoodie and a pair of cutoff sweatpants. Her bed was still made, as if no one had slept in it. She moved across the hall and glanced into her sister's room. Bo was stretched across the yellow sheets, asleep and completely naked.

Chelsea moved into the kitchen and grabbed a mug. "So, tell me?" She poured herself a cup of coffee and glanced over at the man sitting at the table. "Are you going to make an honest woman out of my sister?"

He looked up from his newspaper. "Is Bressler going to make an honest woman out of you?"

"Who says I was with Mr. Bressler?" Lord, she hoped no one else figured it out.

"You left wearing his jacket."

Oh yeah. "How do you know it was his?"

"There were only two men there with charcoal Hugo Boss suits. Mark and Ty Savage."

God, leave it to Jules to notice something like that.

"I know you didn't go home with Ty," Jules continued, and returned his gaze to the sports page. "Besides, Bo told me you were driving him home."

"That doesn't mean I spent the night—you know—*spent* the night. Not like you and Bo." She sat across from him and took a sip of coffee. "That house has like six bedrooms." Then she told a huge whopper while keeping a totally straight face. "Mr. Bressler doesn't even really like me that much." Her brows lowered. Maybe it wasn't such a whopper. True, he'd liked her when she rode him like the mechanical bull at Gilley's. He'd seemed to like her in his jet tub and later in his bed.

"And you stayed in one of those?" He looked skeptical, while teetering on the edge of believing her.

She nodded just as the memory of their last time together entered her head. Good God, she'd never felt so wonderfully violated in her life. The man didn't ask permission to do anything. He just did it, and did it so well, he had her begging him not to stop. Her cheeks caught fire and she looked away.

"You're lying."

"Are you dating my sister now? Or is this a one-nighter?"

He frowned. "Don't change the subject."

She smiled and repeated her questions.

"I like Bo. A lot. I would never use her."

The statement was a pointed one, but the funny thing was, she didn't feel used. Maybe a little apprehensive and scared because she didn't know how Mark would treat her come Monday morning. But not used.

"When did you get home?" Bo asked as she walked from her bedroom tying a robe around her waist.

"A few minutes ago." Bo opened her mouth, and Chelsea held up one hand. "Mark has six bedrooms. I picked one." Which was true. She'd picked his.

"I thought he was Mr. Bressler," Jules reminded her.

Chelsea shrugged. Her attention was focused on her sister as Bo poured herself a cup of coffee. Bo slowly raised her gaze to Jules, and a little smile pushed up the corners of her lips. Jules saw it too and he returned her smile. Last night had been more than just sex for the two of them. More than mutual satisfaction.

Chelsea stood. Suddenly all the regret she thought she'd feel came crashing in on her, but it wasn't the regret she expected. She didn't regret spending the night with Mark Bressler. No, her regret was that he would never look at her like Jules looked at Bo.

"I'm going back to bed," she said, and made her way down the hall. The apprehension she'd felt a few moments ago bumped up a notch. What would she say to him Monday morning? And would he return to his usual MO and ignore her?

She didn't have to wait until Monday to find out. Mark called her at noon. She was sound asleep but she knew it was him before she opened her eyes. Not because she was psychic, but because of his special ringtone.

"Where are you?" he asked. The sound of his voice settled in her chest and made her feel kind of fuzzy and warm.

"I'm in bed."

"How long will it take you to get ready?"

She sat up. "To do what?"

"Drive to Issaquah."

"Why would I drive to Issaquah?"

"I want to look at that house up there. You're coming with me."

Typical of him not to even ask. "It's my day off."

"So?"

"So ask."

He sighed, and she could almost feel the touch of his breath on her ear. "Chelsea, would you *please* come with me to Issaquah?"

She swung her feet over the side of the bed. "To see the house I showed you last month?"

"Yes. Is it still on the market?"

"I don't know. Why didn't you say anything sooner?"

He laughed. " 'Cause I wanted you to show me more houses."

That really made no sense.

"Can you be ready in half an hour?"

She thought of her sister and Jules. "Give me an hour and meet me out front." She didn't want her sister *or* Jules to see her take off with the man she worked for, but she needn't have worried. By the time she got out of the shower, her sister and Jules were gone.

Chelsea dressed strictly for comfort in a blue ankle skirt and a peasant blouse. She pulled her hair back into a ponytail and slid her feet into a pair of jeweled flip-flops. As she shut the apartment door behind her, Mark's Mercedes pulled into the complex, gleaming beneath the afternoon sun. He parked in a space directly in front of Chelsea, and the car door swung open. One big hand grasped the frame and he stood. He moved toward her, back to wearing his usual white T-shirt and blue nylon jogging pants. His steps were a bit slower today.

"Are you okay?"

"Fine." His brows were drawn over his brown eyes like he was angry about something. Not like the time he'd threatened to kill her angry, but angry. Or maybe he was in pain.

"You look—" His mouth on hers cut off her breath in mid-sentence. Like a lot of thing he did to her last night, the kiss was a complete ravishment. Just as she was starting to get into it, he pulled back and said, "Don't ever sneak out of my house again."

She touched her moist bottom lip. "I didn't sneak."

"You snuck."

Was he really mad because she'd left in the middle of the night? "Are you upset because I didn't wake you up before I left?"

"I'm not upset." He glanced away. "I don't get upset."

But he was. "Sorry, I didn't mean to hurt your feelings."

He looked back at her and let out a frustrated breath. "I don't *get* hurt feelings. I'm not a girl."

That was such a ridiculous statement that she tried and failed not to smile. "I know you're not a girl. I think you proved it last night."

One corner of his mouth twitched. "You sore?"

"A little. I haven't worked out like that in a while."

He placed his hands on the sides of her face and looked into her eyes. "You're not some woman I picked up in a bar, Chelsea. You're not a one-night stand. Don't sneak out on me."

If she wasn't a one-nighter, what was she? "Okay."

He took her hand and moved to the passenger-side door. "I'm starving. Do you want to eat around here or in Issaquah?"

She turned and looked up at him. At the sun filtering through his hair. She might not be a one-night stand, but she wasn't his girlfriend either. She wasn't even in that really nebulous place where all relationships start. She worked for Mark. She couldn't *date* him. So, what was she doing getting into his car? "How far to Issaquah?"

"We were just there a few weeks ago."

"We've been to a lot of places in the past few weeks." She sat in the passenger seat and glanced up at him. "I can't keep them all straight." Then again, it was just a sandwich. A sandwich didn't mean anything. It was five bucks and she could pay that herself.

"It's about ten minutes." He shut the door and walked to the other side. "Or we can go with plan B," he said as he got in across from her. "Go to my house, order a pizza, and eat it in bed."

She laughed. "Was Issaquah just a ruse?"

"No, but we're going to end up at my house in bed anyway. Why waste time?" He put the Mercedes into reverse and backed out of the space.

She should probably be offended that he just assumed she'd fall into bed with him again. Maybe she should put up some resistance. Play a little harder to get. Or just resist temptation altogether. "Don't you want to see the house?"

"I can see it tomorrow with the Realtor." He looked across his shoulder at her, his eyes and voice a smoky caress. "The choice is yours."

"Plan B." She was weak. A sinner with no willpower to resist temptation.

He chuckled. "Good answer. You won't be sorry."

And she wasn't. They ate pizza in the leisure room and watched movies on the enormous television. Of course, he had just about every station.

"Even your television has the premium package," she said.

He chuckled and took her empty plate. "There's only one package you need to worry about," he said as he set the plate on the floor next to the chaise. He pulled her on top of him until her legs straddled his lap. She put her hands on his big chest and looked down into his deep brown eyes.

"I woke up wanting you again."

"We did it four times." Sheesh. She hadn't done it four times in one night since . . . maybe never.

He ran his warm hands up her thighs. "It wasn't enough. I want more. I want you." He brushed his thumbs across the silk center of her panties. Her flesh got hot and tightened in response. "Tell me you want me too."

She licked her suddenly dry lips and nodded.

He slid one thumb beneath her panties and touched her bare crotch. "Tell me."

It seemed important to him so she said, "I want you, Mark." She reached for the ends of her blouse and pulled it over her head.

"Why?" He slid his thumb across her slick core and she moaned out loud.

"Because you're good at making me want you." She lowered her face to his. "Because I need you."

She spent the rest of the afternoon needing him. She slid all over Mark's hard body, getting hot and sweaty. By the time she left, it was around ten that night, and she fell exhausted into her own bed. Bo had written a note saying that she was spending the night with Jules, and Chelsea didn't see her sister until they both left for work the next day. By the time she arrived at Mark's front door, apprehension once again sat heavy in her stomach. It was Monday morning, and the weekend she'd spent with Mark was suddenly real. She'd never wanted to be one of those women who had an affair with the celebrity she worked for, essentially her boss. She never wanted to be one of those women who was left with nothing but a broken heart and no job.

The front door to Mark's house was unlocked, and he sat in his office at the computer, typing something with two fingers. "That house in Issaquah has been dropped twenty thousand," he said without looking up. "Isn't that the one with the walk-in closet you liked?" He hit send and reached for his cane leaning against the desk.

"Yeah. It had all those revolving shoe racks." What did it matter if she liked it? "Are you okay? I haven't seen you use your cane in a few days."

"Some days are better than others." He stood and

walked toward her. "If you're worried, you can come upstairs and give me a rubdown." He pushed one side of her hair behind her ear.

"That isn't in my job description." She took a step back before she gave in to temptation and turned her face into his palm. "If I'm going to continue to work for you, we have to have boundaries." Maybe if there were rules, she wouldn't become a sad cliché.

He put one hand on his hip. "What boundaries?"

"No sex Monday through Friday."

"That's bullshit. That only leaves the weekends."

"Okay," she compromised. "No sex during working hours." And she meant it too. If she wanted to keep what little dignity she had left, she had to at least try and separate her working and personal relationship with Mark.

"I'll try to remember."

But he didn't. He didn't even try. It was up to her to be the strong one and maintain a distance. She had to remind him that sliding his hand to the small of her back or up her thigh wasn't work-appropriate. And touching her bottom during three-man hockey was definitely illegal contact. Not even when she fell on her butt. Later, after Derek left and the clock struck five, she let him kiss it better for her.

During that whole week, she didn't see very much

of her sister. But she wasn't surprised. That was how Bo operated. Whether it was a job or new boyfriend, she threw herself into it wholeheartedly. Most of the time her relationships ended in heartache. Chelsea had a good feeling about Jules, though. She had a feeling things would turn out all right. She wished she could say the same for herself.

She didn't know where her relationship with Mark would lead. It was so new and different and terrifying. Most terrifying of all, moving back to L.A. was losing its appeal. She didn't want to be one of those women who gave up her dreams for a man. Her head and her heart were at war, and she was terrified that her heart was winning the battle.

"I changed your ringtone," she told him as they lay in bed watching *Big Trouble in Little China*. For a hockey player he was surprisingly good at remembering dialogue.

He grabbed his phone off the nightstand and dialed. "Trouble" by Pink played from her purse.

"You're trouble," he said. "That's for sure."

"You're the trouble."

He picked up her hand and kissed her fingers. "You've been nothing but trouble since the day you showed up on my porch." Once again, she wondered where this relationship would lead.

The Saturday after the Stanley Cup party, Mark

surprised her with tickets to *Oklahoma!* and her heart won a bit more ground. "Do you like musicals?"

"Yeh."

What a liar.

After the play, he brought her to his house. Instead of taking her to bed, though, he took her hand and led her through the dark house. He opened the pocket doors to the formal living room—empty except for the Stanley Cup sitting on the floor in the middle of the white carpet. A bottle of Dom Pérignon lay in the top of the cup, surrounded by ice, while the crystal chandelier shot prisms of light across the shiny silver.

"Oh my God." Chelsea moved toward the three-foot trophy. "You took your turn after all."

"Yes."

She glanced about the empty room. "I thought there had to be a representative from the Hall of Fame with the cup at all times."

"Not at all times." He moved behind her and wrapped his long arms around her waist. "All the other guys took the cup to strip clubs or sports bars. Walker took it to the top of the Space Needle, and Daniel drove around with it in his convertible. Every guy who has ever dreamed of winning the cup dreams about what he's going to do with it. It's time I lived mine." He kissed the part in her hair. "If you wouldn't mind, I'd like to spray champagne on your naked body and make love to you in front of the cup."

"That's the dream you've always had?"

He shook his head, and his lips brushed the top of her head. "It's better than the dream I had."

She reached for the zipper on the back of her sundress. Her heart swelled so big that her chest ached, and in that moment, standing in that room, she couldn't remember one good reason why she would ever want to leave this man. Of all the people who deserved to share this moment with him, he wanted to share it with her.

The dress slipped to the floor, and she stood in front of him in her bra, panties, and four-inch snakeskin sandals.

"Leave the shoes on," he said as he grabbed the bottle of champagne and took off the cage. "They turn me on."

As far as she could tell, everything turned him on. "You're easy."

"And cheap too."

Hardly. She tossed her bra and underwear aside as he pushed the cork with his thumbs. "You're going to make the carpet wet and sticky."

"I'm planning on making you wet and sticky." With a soft pop the cork flew across the room and hit the closed drapes. A fine, gassy mist curled from the bottle's mouth and a stream of foam followed. He raised the bottle to his lips and took several long swallows. "Close your eyes."

She did, and a cold mist of champagne hit her chest. It smelled of rose petals. "That's cold," she complained.

"I'll warm you up in a minute." He lowered his mouth to her and kissed her as he poured the bottle over their heads. It ran over her closed eyes and the side of her face. The contrast of cold champagne and his hot mouth tightened her nipples, and desire pooled between her thighs. He tossed the empty bottle aside and ran his hands and mouth over her wet, sticky body.

His touch seemed different somehow. Lighter, and he lingered over each erogenous zone. He took his time, in no hurry to get the job done. Even when she tore at his clothes until he was as naked as she, he licked her shoulder and the side of her neck. He slid his mouth across her breasts to her belly, then he laid her down at the foot of the Stanley Cup. Prisms of light shot across her breasts and belly and the side of his face. He lifted his lips from her hip.

"Are you taking birth control?"

She knew why he asked, and the thought of hot skin on hot skin almost sent her over the edge. "I had my yearly exam and three-month Depo shot just before I moved up here. I'm clean as a virgin."

He smiled. "After my accident, I had every test on the planet. I'm clean, but I'm not quite a virgin." He moved until his face was just above hers. "Do you trust me?"

"Yes. Do you trust me?"

Instead of answering, he slid into her body, hot flesh against hot flesh. So good, she groaned. "Oh God."

He held her face between his palms and stared into her face. "You and the cup," he said. "Two of my biggest fantasies." He kissed the tip of her nose as he slowly moved his hips, driving into her and pushing her to the sweetest ecstasy of her life. Her whole body responded to his touch, catching fire and burning out of control. He drove into her, over and over. Hurling her toward climax. At the point of impact, her heart and soul shattered and she called out his name.

And when it was over, he took her hand and washed her in the shower. His touch was gentler than before. Gentler than it had ever been. "Thank you."

"Thank you." She dried his back and shoulders. "I'm just shocked you wanted to share this night with me."

"Who else?" He took the big fluffy towel from her

hands and wrapped it around her shoulders. "You stayed with me when I tried to make you go." He looked down into her eyes. "That means something to me."

"What?"

"I'm not sure. Maybe it means you're stubborn." He pushed a wet hunk of her hair behind her ear. "Or maybe that you like broken-down hockey players."

She should tell him about the ten-thousand bonus. His thumb brushed her jaw, and his eyes turned a rich velvet brown. "You're not broken down." Now. She should tell him now. She opened her mouth, and something else came out instead. "You needed me." And maybe she needed him just a little bit too.

"I still need you."

She closed her eyes against the pinch in the backs of her eyes and the pain in her chest. If she wasn't careful, she'd do the unthinkable. If she wasn't careful, she might fall in love with Mark Bressler. And that would be bad. She was leaving, and falling in love would be really bad. So bad she'd have to guard against it. And she did. Right up until the morning that he insisted on driving her to her doctor's appointment. He sat in the waiting room reading a golf magazine while she had her consultation with the plastic surgeon, and on the drive home, he waited for her to tell him what she'd learned.

"The doctor said I will probably lose sensitivity," she said as they drove across the floating bridge. Now that she knew more of the risks, she was a little scared.

"For how long?"

She shrugged. "Could last six to twelve months. Could be permanent." She'd known about the side effects and risks, but hearing them from the doctor had made them very real.

From behind his sunglasses, Mark looked across the car at her.

"I might not be able to nurse a child." She looked down at her hands clasped in her lap. Knowing all that, she still wanted to do it. She glanced up at his profile. "My family is going to freak out," she said, but what she really wanted to know was what Mark thought. She was too afraid to ask him. Too afraid he could get her to change her mind.

Silence stretched between them for several long moments before he said, "I love your body. You're beautiful just the way you are." He reached for her, and she fully expected him to tell her that he agreed with her family. "But if you're not happy with the size of your breasts, do something about it." He brushed his thumb across her knuckles. "Do what's going to make you happy."

That's when it happened. Her heart swelled up into her throat. The backs of her eyes burned, and she fell in love with Mark Bressler right there on the first exit to Medina. Fell in love with him so hard and fast it took her breath away. Fell in love even when she knew better.

The third Monday in August, Mark jumped in his Mercedes and headed to the Chinooks' head offices. They'd set up an appointment to talk about the assistant coach position, and he wasn't as adamant against it as he had been a few months ago. In fact, he was starting to warm to the idea. No harm in listening to what they had to say.

He pulled out of the driveway and headed toward downtown Seattle. He needed a job. Lying around and doing nothing was driving him insane. He needed something to do, other than wonder how he was going to change Chelsea's mind about her no-sex-at-work policy.

Which was bullshit. He'd only agreed because he figured he could change her mind. But she'd never budged from her position. Not the first week or the second week either. Not even when they'd been driving back from viewing a property in the Queen Anne district and he'd reached over and slid his hand up her bare thigh. He'd slipped his fingers inside her panties and she'd been slick and half ready. She'd let him touch her for a few brief moments before she'd pushed his hand away. Leaving *him* hard and fully ready. He'd fought an erection for the rest of the day, until, at five o'clock, she'd found him in the garage, putting away Derek's stick and a few pucks. "I'm off work now," she'd said, and practically launched herself at him. She'd torn at his pants. He'd bent her over the hood of the Mercedes, flipped up her little skirt, and entered her from behind. It had been down and dirty. Quick and raunchy.

And sweet.

But not nearly as sweet as the night she'd let him make love to her at the foot of the Stanley Cup. He'd had sex with a lot of women in his life. He'd had sex with her too, but that night had been different. He'd felt as if every cell in his body exploded. He'd felt blown apart, and when he'd come back together, he'd been changed. The way he looked at his life. And the way he looked at her.

He couldn't say that he was in love with Chelsea. The kind that came with a big diamond and wedding vows. He'd been in love like that before, but this felt different. This was easy, comfortable, like sliding into a warm pool of water as opposed to a jet tub.

No, he couldn't say that he loved her, but he did miss her when she left. Missed the sound of her voice and her clunky shoes on his tile floors.

He liked being with her. He liked talking to her and making her laugh. He liked the twists and turns of her mind and her sense of humor. He liked that she thought she was impulsive when she was clearly in control of everything around her. He liked the look in her eyes when she was determined to have her way. He especially liked the look in her eyes when she was determined to have her way with him.

No, he didn't *like* that about her. He *loved* that about her. He loved the way she touched him and kissed him and took control. He loved what she did with her hands and mouth and the breathy little sounds she made when he touched her. He loved looking into her face when he was deep inside her small body. The way the determination in her eyes grew heavy, drugged, as he drove into her. And he absolutely loved the tight contractions of her vaginal walls that squeezed and gripped him hard, pulling an orgasm from the pit of his soul.

When he thought back to the day she'd first arrived on his porch, he was glad that the stubborn determination that had once annoyed the hell out of him when he'd tried to get rid of her was the same determination that had made her stay. God knew she could probably get a better job. One that might pay better too.

He was not the man he used to be eight months ago. He was not a superstar hockey player. He didn't live large. Sportswriters were no longer interested in him, and multimillion-dollar endorsement offers had dried up. He was a broken-down former athlete who woke with sore muscles and needed a cane about half the time.

He drove into the parking garage and parked next to the elevator. Chelsea didn't seem to mind. She made him feel alive again. Like a man, but it was more than just sex. If that's all it was about, any woman would do. It was the way she looked at him. As if she didn't see his scars and broken life. She'd stuck with him when others had walked away. He didn't know why she'd stayed. He just thanked God that she was still in his life.

It had been two months since he'd been at the Key. Eight months since his last game. He'd scored a hat trick that night against the Penguins. He'd thought his life was golden. He'd been on top of the world.

He took the elevator to the second floor. Shit happened. Life changed. Time to move ahead and not wallow in the past. The doors opened, and Connie

Backus, manager in the benefits and compensation department, stood on the other side. He knew Connie from his numerous run-ins with her over the home health care workers.

"Hello, Mark."

He held the door open for her. "Hi, Connie."

"You look good," she told him, and flattened an armful of folders against her chest.

"Thank you. I finally feel good."

"I spoke with Chelsea Ross the other day. She said the two of you are getting along."

She could say that. "Everything is fine. Nothing to worry about."

"Good. We were a little concerned when we saw her wearing a man's jacket at the cup party a few weeks ago. We thought it might be yours."

He glanced at his watch. He was already two minutes late. "It was. She got cold. No big deal."

"Good." Connie stepped inside the elevator, and Mark lowered his hand. "We'd hate to think she was trying to earn that bonus money in other ways." Connie punched a button and laughed like they were in on some joke.

The doors started to close and he raised his hands and pushed them back open. "What bonus?"

Chapter Seventeen

Chelsea sat at Mark's desk, bored and answering e-mails while he was at some big meeting at the Chinooks' offices. He hadn't told her what the meeting was about, and she didn't have any idea when he'd return. She leaned her head back and glanced up at the different photographs and posters of him on the walls. Her gaze settled on the picture of him holding the puck with "500" written across it. A few days ago, he'd told her it was the puck that had scored the five hundredth goal of his career. She'd smiled like she'd understood the importance of that, and he laughed because she didn't have a clue.

"That's one of the things I like about you," he'd said. "You're not impressed by money and fame."

"Oh, I don't know." She'd thought about the bonus. She'd thought maybe she should tell him about it, but it didn't seem like the right time. Not while he was talking about her *not* being impressed with money. "I'd love to be so famous that movie roles are written just for me," she told him instead.

"That's different. That's being motivated by what you love to do, not by the money and fame that it might bring. I know a lot of guys who've chased money and fame when they should have been concentrating on playing better hockey."

She'd looked around his house. "You were never motivated by money?"

He'd shrugged. "Maybe a little in the beginning. But it was usually a mistake."

Money had motivated her in the beginning, but she couldn't call it a mistake. Not now. She'd fallen in love with him and there was no going back.

She rose to her feet and walked toward the photo. She moved through a sliver of light pouring through the closed drapes, and she raised a hand to the cool glass. She looked into Mark's smiling face and smiled herself.

Her fingers slid across the smooth surface, and her whole body felt alive, happy. There was no going back to those days when she thought he was a colossal tool. Too late. She loved everything about him.

She loved the sound of his voice and his laughter. She loved the way he smelled and the touch of his hand on her arm or the small of her back. She loved how she felt when he looked at her or simply walked into a room. She loved that his hard shell contained a soft heart.

She didn't know how he felt about her, though. Oh, she figured he liked her. Of all the people with whom he could have chosen to share his night with the cup, he'd chosen her. But like wasn't love. She knew he liked having sex with her, but sex wasn't a commitment.

She lowered her hand to her side. Fear knotted her stomach just below her happy heart. She was giving serious thought to changing her whole life for a man who *liked* her. She'd never changed for a man, and she ran through a mental list of all the reasons why staying in Seattle was a good plan. Reasons that had nothing to do with Mark.

She liked Seattle. She liked the feel of it and she liked the cooler weather. She liked being close to her sister and she liked the few local commercials she'd acted in. Maybe she'd try out again for a role in local theater.

Not *Oklahoma!* though. She couldn't sing, and Mark clearly hated musicals. She smiled, but her amusement was short-lived. She had to tell him about the bonus. It had been weighing on her mind, and she knew she had to tell him. Hopefully, once she explained it, it wouldn't be a big deal. The money had nothing to do with her feelings for Mark. She'd agreed to the bonus before she'd even met him. She'd fallen for him despite her attempts not to, but lately the money had begun to feel like a deep secret she was keeping from him.

Motion in the doorway caught her eye and she turned. Mark stood there watching her, one shoulder shoved against the frame, and her happy little heart swelled at the sight of him.

"I didn't hear you drive up."

He crossed his arms over his wide chest, and his gaze raked her from head to toe. "Ten thousand dollars is a lot of money. You're good, Chelsea. Maybe even worth it."

She didn't think he meant it as a compliment, and it felt liked she'd been stuck in the chest with a pin. "Are you talking about the bonus?"

"Yeh." He didn't look angry. Which was good. "I just had it explained to me."

"I was going to tell you." No, not angry. Just closed off like before, but she could explain. He'd understand. "I was just waiting for the right time."

"A good time would have been the day you showed up on my porch. Get it right out in the open.

Or if that just wasn't a good time, how about all the other times I assumed you were here because you wanted to be here? How about all the times I made an ass out of myself for thinking you're someone you're not?"

"I'm the same person today that I was yesterday."

"I don't know who you are."

"Yes you do." She moved toward him. She could explain. Make it all okay. She was good at making everything okay. "I should have told you. I wanted to, but I guess I was afraid you wouldn't understand."

"Oh, I understand. I understand that you think I'm a sucker."

She shook her head. "I've never thought that."

"I used to see ulterior motives from a mile off, but when you showed up, my life was such crap that I wasn't thinking straight. You used your body like a high-class hooker and I fell for it. I *was* a sucker."

Her feet came to a sudden halt in the middle of the room, and everything in her body stopped too. "What? I didn't use my body. It's not like that at all."

"It's exactly like that. You needed ten grand to get your surgery. I am just a means to get what you want." He straightened. "You didn't have to fuck me, Chelsea. You didn't have to go that far."

She gasped and shook her head. "That isn't why I

had sex with you. I tried not to, but . . ." She lifted a hand, palm up, then dropped it to her side. "I tried to keep it professional."

"You didn't try that damn hard."

She couldn't argue with that. She hadn't tried that hard. "In the beginning, I was here for the bonus. Ten thousand dollars is a lot of money. Maybe not to you, but it is to me." She pointed to her chest. "I didn't ask for the bonus. The Chinooks offered, and I jumped at the chance. I'm not going to apologize for that. In the beginning, I *did* stay for the money. You made my life difficult, but that's not why I slept with you and that's not why I'm still here."

"Then why are you still here?"

She looked at him standing there. Closed off to his anger and to her. She loved him. She loved him more than she'd ever loved another man. "Because I got to know you and you began to mean a lot to me." Her heart was breaking, and there was nothing she could do but tell him the truth. The terrifying truth. "I love you, Mark."

He laughed, but there was no pleasure in it. Then, finally, she saw some anger in his eyes. Cold, stony anger. "Nice touch, but I'm not a sucker. At least not today."

She'd just bared everything to him, and he didn't

believe her. How was that possible? Couldn't he see how much the truth hurt? "It's the truth. I didn't mean to fall in love with you, but I did."

"You expect me to believe that?" His jaw clenched. "Now? After everything?"

Anger and hurt and desperation coalesced in her stomach and chest and pinched the backs of her eyes. Tears pooled along her bottom lids, then slipped over her lashes. "It's true."

"The tears are a nice touch. You're a better actress than I thought."

"I'm not acting." She brushed the moisture from her cheek. The sick feeling in her stomach was far too real. He had to see that. She had to make him hear and believe her. "I love you." She pointed a finger at him. "You made me love you even when I knew it was a really bad idea. You made me love everything about you." She dropped her hand to her side as another tear rolled down her cheek. "You made me love you more than I've ever loved anyone in my whole life."

He shook his head. "Right."

"It's true. Being with you these past few months has meant a lot to me. Please, believe me."

"Even if I believed you, it doesn't matter."

It had to matter. She'd never pleaded with any other man. "I love you."

He looked into her eyes and pounded the last nail into her heart. "I don't love you."

The air left her lungs as if he'd hit her and she turned her face away. He didn't love her. She'd known he didn't, but hearing it from his own mouth hurt more than she'd ever imagined. "I knew you'd hurt me," she whispered through her pain. Raw pain and rage, at him and herself, swelled so big she couldn't hold it in. "I was right about you from the beginning. You're just another celebrity who thinks he can use people."

"Sweetheart, you used me to get your hands on ten thousand dollars."

"I told you it wasn't like that. I'm not a user." She looked back up at him. At angry brown eyes set in his face that she loved with her entire broken heart and aching soul. "But you are. You mess with people's lives, then move on with your own. You don't care. All you care about is getting what you want." Her hands curled into fists. She wouldn't hit him. No, but she wanted to. "You're no different from every other celebrity I've worked for. You're selfish and spoiled. I let myself think you were different." She swallowed hard, past the bitter lump in her throat. "I let myself forget who you really are. You're the man who insulted me the first day we met. You're just a colossal tool."

He laughed again. The same bitter laugh as before. "And you just said you love me."

The most agonizing part of it all was that she did love him. No matter that he didn't love her. She meant nothing to him. He'd pursued her, got her in bed, and now it was over. "And you always said you don't play unless you can win. Congratulations, Mark. You win. I lose." *Everything*.

He shrugged. "The Chinooks don't know you slept with me, and I won't be the one to tell them. You only have a few weeks until your contract is up and then the money is yours. You've earned it."

She turned back toward the desk and grabbed her purse. Her throat got tight, hot, and she pushed past him on her way out the door. The last thing she wanted to do was break down in front of him. The last thing she wanted to hear was more of his laughter.

Somehow she managed to make it to her car. Her hands shook as she shoved the key into the ignition. She half expected him to run after her and tell her to come back. That he believed her and he'd only said she meant nothing out of pain and anger. That they could work it out, but that was the gullible side. The side that had wanted to believe falling in love with Mark would work out in the end. The other side, the rational side, knew that he wasn't coming after her.

Knew she'd lost more than ten thousand dollars. She'd lost something more important than money. She'd lost her dignity and her heart.

Tears streamed down her face as she drove the short distance to Bo's apartment. Once there, she locked herself inside her room and let all her hurt and anger wash through her. By the time she heard Bo's key open the front door, her chest hurt from crying and her eyes were scratchy and red.

"Chels?" her sister called out.

Chelsea didn't want to see anyone, talk to anyone, but it was a small apartment and her sister would find her. "In here."

Bo stood in the doorway, took one look at her, and asked, "What's wrong? Did something happen?"

Chelsea didn't know where to begin.

"Did Mark Bressler do something to you?"

Leave it to her twin to narrow it down without Chelsea having to say a word. She looked at her sister, and a tear slipped from Chelsea's eye and dropped onto the pillow.

"What did he do?"

Nothing. Besides make her fall in love with him. She supposed she could make up a lie, but her sister would know, and Chelsea was too drained to think up anything believable. "I fell in love with him. I tried not to, but I did." She shook her head.

"He doesn't love me. In fact, he doesn't care about me at all."

Bo sat on the bed. Chelsea expected criticism. Waited for a lecture on how her impulsiveness always got her in trouble. How she never learned. Instead her twin sister, the other half of her soul, the dark to her light, climbed into bed and spooned her. Let the warmth of her body heat up the cold places. Her life was in pieces. An absolute mess. There wasn't a part of her that didn't love Mark, and she didn't know how she was going to get through the next few hours and days and weeks. She wanted the pain to go away. She just wanted to be numb.

But three days later, her emotions were still raw, and she couldn't seem to stop her tears from falling. Her life was in turmoil, and the thought of living in the same state as Mark, and perhaps seeing his face in a crowd, was unbearable. Yet at the same time, the thought of leaving Washington, and perhaps never seeing his face in a crowd, was just as unbearable.

She went through the motions of living. Of checking out help wanted ads. Mostly she ate junk food and watched junk TV.

"Georgeanne Kowalsky has a catering business," Jules told her over dinner Thursday night at a sports pub on Twelfth Street. Jules seemed to favor sports pubs, which was okay with Chelsea as long as he didn't start spouting stats. "At least she did a few years ago," he added. "I could call her and ask if she needs help."

"How much does it pay?" she asked as she dipped a fry into ketchup. She knew her sister and Jules had taken her to dinner to try and cheer her up. It really wasn't working, but at least the sports programming on the numerous flat-screen televisions filled any awkward silence.

"I'm not sure," he answered, and reached for his fork. "Probably more than you're making right now."

Which, of course, was zilch. She needed the money. She had enough for first and last month's rent, plus security deposit, on a studio apartment, but she needed more. Especially if she decided to move to Los Angeles.

"Maybe wear your Gaultier tunic for the interview," Jules suggested. "And brush your hair."

"I think you'd be great at it," Bo encouraged. She took a crouton off Jules's salad and popped it into her mouth. The two were already at the sharing food stage. She and Mark had never shared food. Licking champagne from each other's bodies didn't count.

"Maybe I can do some catering." As long as it had nothing to do with catering to celebrities and athletes. And as long as she didn't know what she was going to do with her life.

For the first time that she could ever recall, she didn't have a plan. Not even a vague one. She didn't feel a burning desire for anything. The feeling of numbness she'd craved had settled about her and she didn't have the energy to feel much of anything at all.

A commercial for athlete's foot splashed across several of the flat-screen televisions, and she dunked another fry. She wasn't going to get her breasts reduced. Something she'd always wanted, but she just really didn't care now. Her agent called with walk-on parts in local productions, but she turned them down. She just felt . . . drained. Like her life had gone from a thousand vibrant colors to two shades of gray. Blah and blah-er.

Across the table from her, Bo and Jules laughed at something that was clearly an inside joke between the two of them. He whispered something in her ear, and Bo ducked her face and smiled. Chelsea was glad for Bo. Glad that her twin seemed so happy and in love, but a part of her wished that could be Chelsea too. She reached for her fork, feeling an odd mix of emptiness and envy.

Over Jules's shoulder, a local news conference splashed across the screen. Chelsea glanced up as the television filled with the images of the Chinooks' general manager Darby Hogue, coach Larry

Nystrom, and Mark Bressler. Everything around her seemed to still, fall away as she stared up at the screen. The sound was off but the closed caption was on. Chelsea read the announcement that Mark had just signed on as the assistant coach to the Seattle Chinooks. He sat at a conference table wearing the charcoal suit and black dress shirt he'd picked out at Hugo Boss the day he'd threatened to have sex with her against the wall. The ends of his dark hair curled up around the bottom of a Chinooks' ball cap resting on his head. His brown eyes looked out from beneath the dark blue bill, and her empty soul drank him in like cool water. His face was a bit tanner than it had been a few days ago. Probably from coaching Derek without his hat.

Bressler: "I'm honored to be given this opportunity. I've worked with a lot of these people for eight years, and I look forward to standing behind the bench as we make another run at the cup this season," the caption read as he looked out at Chelsea from a dozen or so big-screen televisions.

Her heart squeezed and she set down the fork. Love and loss tore at her, and it felt like he was ripping her heart out all over again.

"What's wrong?" Bo asked, then turned and looked behind her. "Oh."

"He took the job," she said just above a whisper.

"Yeah. This morning."

On the screen, he reached forward and adjusted a microphone sitting on the table in front of him. His stiff middle finger pointed up as if he was flipping off the world. That same big, injured hand that had slid up her thigh and heated her up all over.

He'd accused her of having sex with him for the bonus money. He'd thrown her feelings for him back in her face like she was nothing, yet still her heart reacted to the sight of him. Still her body craved the touch of his hands.

"Are you okay?" Bo asked.

"Sure."

The one person who knew her as well as she knew herself wasn't fooled. Bo rose from her seat and moved beside Chelsea. "It will get better."

Tears blurred her vision, and she tore her gaze from Mark's image and looked into her sister's face. "He ripped my heart out, Bo. How will it ever get better?"

"You can get through this."

"How?"

She shook her head. "You just will. I promise."

Chelsea wasn't so sure, but Bo was trying so hard to convince her, Chelsea nodded. "Okay."

"What can I do?" Jules asked from across the table.

"You can go kick Mark Bressler's ass," Bo answered.

Chelsea glanced at Jules's face through her tears and almost laughed. He looked like a deer caught in the cross-hairs. "She's kidding." She didn't want Mark hurt. Not even now. Not even after he'd hurt *her* so badly she could hardly breathe past the pain.

He'd taken the coaching job, and if she stayed in Seattle, she'd have to see him on the news. Standing behind the bench yelling at people. How was she ever going to get over her feeling for him if there was a chance she would see him staring down at her from dozens of televisions?

Chelsea brushed her cheeks. She needed to get out of Seattle. It was the only way to get over Mark. "Could you call Georgeanne Kowalsky tomorrow?" She needed a job, maybe two. The sooner the better. The sooner she got enough money together, the sooner she could move past the pain and loss. The sooner she moved past the pain and loss, the sooner she could get her life back. A life that had nothing to do with Mark.

Chapter Eighteen

Mark lifted a corner of his cards and raised one finger. The blackjack dealer hit him with a queen of clubs and he folded. His luck was shit. Had been since he and the guys had arrived in Vegas Friday night. That had been two days ago, and he was already down eleven grand. Not to mention the couple of hundred he'd spent on shitty lap dances at Scores.

He sat at a table with Sam and Daniel inside the Players Cub in Mandalay Bay. His hip ached from the late hour and his head hurt from too much booze. This had been Sam's idea, of course. One last blow-out before Mark became the newest assistant coach. Before he was no longer one of the guys. Before he was officially part of the staff.

He felt good about his decision. Good about doing something other than sitting at home while life passed him by. If he couldn't shoot goals, calling shots from behind the bench was a good alternative. A few months ago, he'd been filled with so much anger he hadn't even wanted to consider a coaching position. Now, he looked forward to getting back into the game and making another run at the cup. Maybe getting his name on it twice.

"I'm out," he said, and picked up his chips.

Sam looked up from his cards. "It's early."

It was after midnight. "See you guys in the morning." He cashed in his chips and made his way out of the exclusive club and down the hall to the elevators. When Sam had called him Friday afternoon and mentioned that he and some of the guys were hitting Vegas, Mark had jumped at the chance to get out of town. He hadn't left Seattle since before the accident, and a trip to Sin City had sounded like a great plan. He figured he'd hang with the boys one last time, check out the strip clubs, and gamble. Surely two of his favorite pastimes would help take his mind off his problems.

Problem, rather. He had only one. Chelsea Ross.

Even as he made his way through the casino filled with people, he felt alone. A dark anger he hadn't felt in months filled his chest and lowered his brows. He'd fallen hard for her. Harder than he ever remembered falling for a woman. Harder than he'd even known was possible. She'd brought light and laughter into his life when there had been nothing but darkness and anger. She was like a comet streaking across the night sky, lighting it up for a few brief moments. Now all that darkness was back.

He pushed the button to the elevator and one behind him opened. He got inside and rode it up.

He'd fallen for her, and she'd been with him for money. She'd made him want her, made him believe she wanted him too. When the whole time she'd wanted money. And the really messed-up part was that he might have forgiven her for lying. Ten thousand dollars was a lot of money, and he knew why she needed it. Hell, he wanted her to have it, and he could have forgiven her just about anything just to have her light up his life for a while longer.

Anything but her last lie. She'd said she loved him, and something hot and angry and bitter had hit him hard. Right in the gut like a raging fist. He might not be the man he'd been eight months ago. He might have been a sucker for her sweet-smelling skin and soft hands, but he didn't like being played for a fool. God, did she really think she could lie right to his face and he was so desperate that he'd believe her?

He'd thought getting away with the guys would get Chelsea out of his head. He'd been wrong. She was front and center no matter what he did or how far he ran.

Once inside his room, he stripped to his boxers and climbed into bed. He stared up at the dark ceiling, trying and failing to get Chelsea out of his head.

You made me love you even when I knew it was a really bad idea. You made me love everything about you, she'd said as tears slid down her cheeks. *You made me love you more than I've ever loved anyone in my whole life.*

He'd wanted to believe her. He'd wanted to grab her up and press her into his chest until her lie became the truth. Until he smashed it and molded it into what he wanted. Until he believed it.

Mark reached for the remote on the nightstand and turned on the television. He flipped through the stations until it returned to the pay-per-view channel. He checked out the porn selection, but nothing sounded interesting. He arrowed across and hit the horror button. Up popped the latest movies and some "classics" like *Psycho, The Omen,* and *Slasher Camp.*

A brow rose up his forehead and he sat up straighter in bed. Who would have thought *Slasher Camp* was a "classic"? He pushed the select button and settled back against the pillows. The movie started off innocently enough. With counselors moving into the cabins and getting the camp ready for the season. About ten minutes into it, Chelsea stepped out of a school bus wearing cutoff shorts and a tiny tank top hacked off just above her navel. Her blond hair was pulled to the back of her head in a clip, and her blue eyes peered over the top of a pair of sunglasses. She'd been right. They'd hired her for her boobs, but it was her bottom in those shorts that drew his attention. A heavy weight settled in the pit of his stomach and his chest got tight.

"Hey, everyone," she called out as she dropped a duffel bag onto the ground. "Angel's here. It's time to party." She looked like a slut. Like a camp counselor slut. Like every teenage boy's fantasy. Like his fantasy too.

For the next ten minutes or so, Mark watched the counselors put away groceries and sweep out cabins, his attention completely focused on the few shots of Chelsea. He listened to the sound of her voice and laughter, and he watched her bottom in those shorts. Just the sight of her in a five-year-old horror flick twisted him into knots.

An actor with shaggy brown hair like a surfer and wearing a green Abercrombie shirt found an axe stuck in a wall. He pulled it out and placed it on a shelf next to the fire extinguisher. Then he stuck his hand in his pocket and pulled out a bag of weed. Mark remembered Chelsea telling him the bad boy was always the first to get it in a horror flick, and Mark figured Mr. Shaggy Hair Surfer would be the first to go. The camera panned to the window and what looked like someone in a mask watching from the forest.

At dusk, the scene changed to Chelsea standing at the end of a dock. The setting sun washed her body in gold as she shucked out of her shorts and whipped her top off. She wore a pair of white panties, and Mark got instantly hard. She jumped into the lake and swam about before heading to the shore. Water ran down her breasts and dripped from her chin as she walked up the beach. A male stepped into the shot, his back to the camera. She gasped, then smiled.

"You scared me," she said as she reached for Mr. Shaggy Hair Surfer. She kissed him long and hard and they slid to the sandy beach. The surfer touched Chelsea's back and behind and ran his hand up her thigh. Mark had an irrational urge to punch the kid in the head. To rip him apart. He felt sick as sounds of pleasure spilled from Chelsea's lips. Pleasure she found with someone else.

It was crazy. Chelsea didn't belong to him, but

even if she did, this was a movie, and those weren't the sounds she made when she had sex. He knew what she sounded like and that wasn't it. Her voice was breathier, lower during sex. She said, "Oh God" or "Oh my God" a lot. Sometimes, "Oh God, Mark!" And when she orgasmed, her moan came from some deeper, more satisfied place.

A huge, dirty hand grabbed a handful of the surfer's shaggy hair and cut off his head. Blood splashed all over Chelsea and she screamed. A bloodcurdling scream as she sat up and scooted backward into the woods. Mark remembered her telling him and the guys about this scene. He waited for the axe to cut her throat, and when it did, he looked away.

Mark Bressler, former captain of the Seattle Chinooks, had experienced more than his share of gore. He'd witnessed bones snap and blood gush. He'd seen razor-sharp skates slice flesh, and bodies clash with such force that he could actually hear the damage. For the most part, it had been just another day at the office. But this. He couldn't watch this. He couldn't watch anyone hurt Chelsea. Not even when he was still so mad at her it burned a hole in his stomach. Not even when he knew it was all fake. The axe. The blood. The scream.

She was an actress. She made it look real. As real as saying, "I love you."

He shut off the television, and the next morning he threw his clothes into a suitcase and took the first flight to Seattle. He felt more alone than when he'd arrived in Vegas. He grabbed the *In Flight* magazine and read about luxury condos on a golf course in Scottsdale. He thought of the houses he and Chelsea had looked at most recently. He needed to make a choice soon.

After the two-hour flight, he walked into his empty house, and his suitcase fell from his hand. The emptiness of the six-thousand-square-foot home pressed in on him. There was no one waiting for him. No light. No laughter. No one trying to boss him around. His life was complete crap. As bad as when he'd hit that patch of black ice and totaled everything. And just like that patch of invisible ice, his feelings for Chelsea had been surprising and painful.

The doorbell rang, and he didn't realize he'd half expected it to be Chelsea until he opened the door and stared into the face of a middle-aged woman with short, black hair and a pear-shaped behind. Within the space of three seconds, his heart sped up and came to a sudden halt.

"I'm Patty Egan. I'm your new home health care worker."

"Where's Chelsea?"

"Who? I don't know a Chelsea. The Chinooks' aftercare program contracted me through Life Force."

Life Force? "I don't need a nurse."

"I'm more than just a nurse." She handed him a stack of his mail.

Chelsea had been more than just an assistant. She'd been his lover. Somehow he didn't think he'd have the same problem with Patty, but he still wasn't about to have a nurse in his house and underfoot.

There had been a time in his life when he would have slammed the door in Patty's face and not really thought anything of it. Chelsea had called him a selfish dickhead. He'd like to think he wasn't selfish anymore. "Thanks, but no thanks," he said, and grabbed his mail. "I don't need you." He started to shut the door and added for good measure, "You have a nice day, though."

The doorbell rang again but he ignored it. He walked into his office and called Connie Backus. Someone must have found out about his relationship with Chelsea and fired her.

"Why is there a new home health care worker on my porch?"

"Sorry it took so long to get someone out there. But Chelsea Ross quitting on such short notice kind of left us in a bind."

The mail in his hand hit the desk. "Chelsea quit?"

"Last week. Tuesday I believe."

The day after she'd walked out of his life. "Did she give a reason?"

"She said something about moving back to L.A."

Chelsea stood with an icing bag in one hand, piping hearts on three dozen cupcakes. Some of the icing kind of squirted off one side and onto the table. Her luck had been going that way lately. One thing after another. A few days ago, she'd had a flat tire, and yesterday she'd lost her cell phone. The last time she remembered seeing it had been right before she'd jumped in the shower yesterday.

She'd worked for Georgeanne Kowalsky for three days now, and she could honestly say it wasn't bad. She'd certainly done worse. Holding the hair of a certain celebutard while she puked in an ice bucket came to mind.

She'd also applied for waitressing jobs at several different restaurants and bars. No sports pubs though. Nothing with televisions hanging on the walls.

Georgeanne stuck her head through one of the doors to the big kitchen. "Chelsea, there's someone here to see you."

"Who?"

"Me," Mark answered, and walked into the kitchen.

Chelsea's heart knocked against her ribs and she forgot to breathe.

"Are you going to be okay with him here?" Georgeanne asked.

No. Chelsea nodded and her boss left the kitchen.

"What are you doing here?"

"Searching for you?"

He was as tall and handsome as she remembered. Her chest caved in at the sight of him. She took a deep breath past all the pain and said, "We don't have anything to say to each other, Mark."

"I have a lot to say. All you have to do is listen."

"You can't order me around anymore."

He smiled a little as he moved past an industrial-sized mixer toward her. "Sweetheart, you were never good at taking orders. I'm *asking* you to listen."

"How did you find me?"

"Jules."

Jules knew the whole sordid story. "Jules told you?" The jerk. He had to know how much seeing Mark would hurt her. She was going to hurt *him* when she saw him tonight.

"I threatened to beat the living shit out of him if he didn't. For some reason he found that very funny."

Jules was kind of perverse that way. That's probably why he loved Bo.

He moved around the table toward her. "Why did you quit your job?"

She looked away. Away from the intensity in his brown eyes. She didn't have to ask what job. She shrugged. "I couldn't keep it. Not after everything."

He didn't say a word for several long moments. "I've put an offer on that house in the Queen Anne district. The one you liked."

"Oh." Had he driven all the way here just to tell her that?

"I accepted the assistant coach position."

"I know." She loved him, but seeing him was so bittersweet, her shredded heart felt like it was shredding all over again. "I have to go back to work now," she said, and turned toward the cupcakes.

"I lied to you."

She looked over her shoulder. "You didn't take the job with the Chinooks?"

"No. Yes." He shook his head. "I lied before that."

"About the house?"

"I lied when I told you that you mean nothing to me. I lied when I said I didn't love you."

"What?" She turned toward him. "Why?"

He shrugged. "Because I was stupid. Because I loved you and I was afraid you were just acting. Playing me for a fool, and I was mad because I didn't want to go back to my life before you showed up on my porch with your two-toned hair and orange jacket. I lied because I didn't think you could love me."

Of course she could love him. She couldn't help herself.

He took the icing bag from her hand and set it on the table. "The Chinooks sent another health care worker to my door this morning."

"Did you call her retarded?"

"No. I was very nice to her because of you." Somehow Chelsea doubted he'd been *very* nice. "I'm a better person since you came into my life," he continued. "I want to be better for you."

Just like Jerry Maguire, only Mark was hotter than Tom Cruise. Taller too.

"I love you and I'm sorry I didn't believe you when you said you love me." He reached into the pocket of his jeans and pulled out her missing cell phone.

"Where did you get that?"

"Jules stole it for me." He handed it to her, then pulled out his own cell and dialed. "I heard this song on the oldies radio station the other day and I can't get it out of my head." His cheeks turned a little pink as if he was embarrassed. "It's cheesy, but every time I call, you'll know how I feel about you." The face on her BlackBerry lit, then Glen Campbell sang about needing and wanting for all time.

She looked up as her heart swelled and tears

blurred her vision. "Jules downloaded this for you?"

"I did it. I had to buy the CD and record it on your phone. It took me a while."

She smiled at the thought of him trying to get all the lyrics just right. "I didn't know you could do this."

"I can do a lot of things, Chelsea." He slipped his phone into his pocket. "I can love you and make you happy, if you'll let me." He pulled out a ring. A *big diamond* ring.

She gasped. "Is that real?"

"Do you think I'd buy you a fake ring?"

She didn't know what to think. He was here. He loved her. He was shoving a four-carat diamond ring on her finger. This was all so unreal.

"You once said that it would be hard to say no to a big ring." He put the tips of his fingers beneath her chin and gently lifted her face. "Chelsea, I knew when you showed up on my porch that you were going to be trouble. You were bossy and annoying and you brought sunshine into a very dark time in my life. You saved me when I didn't even know I needed saving. I love you for that. I will always love you for that." He raised her hand to his lips and kissed the backs of her knuckles. "Please say you'll stay in my life and make trouble with me forever."

She nodded, and her big smile matched his

equally big grin. "Yes. Mark, I love you. These past few days without you have been horrible."

He pulled her against his chest, as if he never meant to let her go, and he lowered his mouth to her. The gentle kiss touched her soul, and when it ended, she slid her arms around his waist and laid her cheek against his hard chest. Beneath her ear she listened to the sound of his heart. Her eyes filled with tears and he kissed the part in her hair. "I know that you want to move back to L.A. and pursue your acting. I understand it's important to you. I have an alternative. You might call it plan B."

She smiled into the front of his white T-shirt. "What's plan B?"

"When you're not in a movie or acting in a commercial, you come to Seattle and be with me. During the off season I'll come and live with you in L.A."

"I don't think so." She shook her head and glanced up. The look in his eyes nearly broke her heart. "If I'm not here, who will make sure you don't backslide into your old cranky ways? Who will keep you in line and on your toes? Who will answer all your fan e-mails and play three-man hockey? Who will give Derek the stink eye?" He smiled, and she continued, "I have a plan C."

"What?"

"You once told me that you were only good at two

things. Hockey and sex. You sold yourself short." She rose on her toes and kissed his chin. "You're good at a lot of things, Mark. You're good at making me love you. I'm not going anywhere. I'm staying right here."

Mark ran his hands up her shoulders and neck and held her face in his hands. "With me."

She smiled. "Lucky you."

Former hockey star and all-around NHL badass Mark Bressler looked into Chelsea's blue eyes and chuckled. She was bossy and pushy and she made him damn happy to be alive. "Yeah," he said. "Lucky me."

And now a sneak peek at

Rachel Gibson's

next sexy title

Coming Spring 2011

From

**AVON
BOOKS**

Sam Leclaire was a good-looking son of a bitch. Everyone thought so. Everyone from sportswriters to soccer moms.

The girl wrapped up in his sheets thought so, too. Although she wasn't really a girl. She was a woman.

"I don't see why I can't go."

Sam glanced up from the knot in his tie and looked through the mirror at the supermodel in his bed. Her name was Veronica Del Toro, but she was known by just her first name. Like Tyra and Heidi and Giselle.

"Because I didn't know you were going to be in town," he explained for the tenth time. "Bringing a guest at this late date would be rude." Which wasn't the real reason.

"But I'm Veronica."

Now there. There was the real reason. She was rude and narcissistic. Not that he held that against anyone. He could be rude and narcissistic himself, but unlike the stories written about him, he really did know when to behave.

"I won't eat much."

Try not at all. That's one of the things that irritated him about Veronica. She never ate. She ordered food like she was starving, but she pushed it around her plate.

Sam slid up the knot and tilted his chin to one side as he buttoned down the collar. "I already called you a cab." Through the mirror he watched Veronica rise from his bed and walk toward him. She moved across his carpet as if she were on the catwalk. All long legs and arms and hardly a jiggle.

"When are you going to be back?" she asked as she wrapped her arms around his waist. She rested her chin on his shoulder and looked at him through dark brown eyes.

Sam tilted his head to one side and, as he buttoned the last collar point, he glanced at the clock on his nightstand. It was already half past six and the wedding started at seven. He really hadn't had time to meet Veronica. But she wasn't in town that often and she'd promised a quickie. He should have known better. "Late. When do you fly out?"

"In the morning." She sighed and slid her long hands up his dress shirt to his hard pecs. "I could wait."

He turned, and her palms slid to his waist. "I don't know when I'll get back. This thing could run real late." Although with the start of the regular season just around the corner, he doubted it. He pushed her dark hair behind her shoulder. "Call me the next time you're in Seattle."

"That could be months, and by then you'll be on the road playing hockey." She dropped her hands and moved toward the bed.

He watched her skinny behind as she stepped into her tiny panties. There were a lot of things to like about Veronica. He just hoped she didn't get all clingy on him. "We can always meet up on the road again."

"True." She reached for a black T-shirt, pulling it over her head before stepping into a pair of jeans. "But by then you'll have a black eye."

He grinned. "True." He grabbed his suit jacket and slid his arms inside. Last season he'd hooked up with her in Pittsburgh. That night against the Penguins, he'd scored a goal, spent four minutes in the sin bin for a double minor, and got his first major shiner of the season. Maybe she'd bring him the same sort of luck this year. He reached for his wallet and shoved it into the back pocket of his khaki trousers.

After Veronica slid her feet into a pair of pumps, they walked from the bedroom of Sam's downtown loft. Gray shadows hugged the scarce furnishings as misty sunlight cast dull patterns across the wood floor.

Sam held the front door open for Veronica, then locked it behind him. He moved down the hall and his thoughts turned to the game in less than a month against San Jose. The Sharks had been knocked out of the first round of the playoffs last season, but that didn't mean a guaranteed win for the Chinooks in this season's opener. Not by a long shot. The Sharks would be hungry and some of the Chinooks had partied a little too hard during the off season. Johan and Logan were each carrying ten extra pounds around the middle. Vlad was drinking like a sailor on leave and the organization had yet to officially name a new captain.

"I love weddings," Veronica said through a sigh as they moved to the elevator.

Everyone assumed Walker Brooks would be captain, but nothing had been announced.

The elevator doors opened and they stepped inside. "Don't you?"

"Don't I what?" He pushed the button to the lobby.

"Love weddings."

"Not particularly." Weddings were about as much fun as getting his cup rung.

They rode to the bottom floor in silence and Sam placed his hand in the small of Veronica's back as they walked across the lobby. Two heavy glass and stainless steel doors slid open and a yellow cab waited by the curb.

He kissed her good-bye, then said, "Call me the next time you're in town," as he shut the cab door.

Misty clouds clung to the Seattle skyline as Sam walked to the corner and headed two blocks toward Fourth Avenue and the Rainier Club. Life was good. Last season the Seattle Chinooks won the Stanley Cup and Sam's name would forever be inscribed on hockey's highest prize. The memory of holding the cup over his head as he skated in front of the home-town crowd brought a smile to his lips.

Within several moments, he caught sight of the old, exclusive club with its aged brick and carefully trimmed lawn that reeked of money. His professional life was on a high. Through blood, sweat, and hard work, he'd reached every goal he'd ever set for himself. He had more money then he'd ever thought he'd make in one lifetime and his personal life was pretty good, too. Women loved him and he loved them back. Probably a little too much sometimes.

He walked beneath the Rainier Club's black awning and a doorman greeted him. The inside of the prestigious club was so stuffy that he had a sudden urge to take off his shoes as when he'd been a kid and his mom got a new carpet. A few of the guys hung out at the bottom of a wide staircase looking a little uneasy, but otherwise good in their designer suits and summer tans. In two months, several of them would be sporting black eyes and a few stitches.

"Nice of you to make it," forward Daniel Holstrom said as he approached.

Harp music drifted down the stairs as Sam peeled back the cuff of his shirt and looked at his Rolex. "Ten minutes to spare," he said. "What are you all waiting for?"

"Frankie and Logan aren't here yet," goalie Marty Darche answered.

"Savage make it?" Sam asked, referring to the groom.

"I spotted him about ten minutes ago. First time I've ever seen him break a sweat off the ice. He's probably nervous that the bride has come to her senses and is halfway to Vashon."

Sam laughed as a shiny auburn ponytail and smooth profile caught his attention out of the corner of his eye. He turned. His laughter stopped. A woman moved across the lobby toward the front doors, talking into the tiny microphone in front of her mouth. A black sweater hugged her body and a little battery pack was clipped to her black pants. Sam's brows lowered and acid settled in the pit of his stomach. If there was one woman on the planet who hated his guts, it was the woman disappearing through the front doors.

Daniel put a hand on his shoulder. "Hey, Sam, isn't that your wife?"

Marty turned toward the front. "You have a wife?"

"Ex-wife." The acid chewed its way up toward Sam's esophagus. "She's my *ex*-wife."

Daniel laughed like he thought something was real funny. "Does being married for three days really count?"

Have you missed any
of these amazing romances
by Rachel Gibson?
Here's a glimpse into some
of her unforgettable Avon Books!

Welcome to Gospel, Idaho, where everyone knows that every sin known to heaven and earth is all California's fault. In TRUE CONFESSIONS, you'll see what happens when Californian Hope Spencer comes to town and falls for local sheriff Dylan Taber . . .

Usually, Dylan didn't mind helping in the search for missing backpackers. It got him out of the office and away from the paperwork he hated. But he'd been kept awake most of the night by Adam's puppy, and he wasn't looking forward to a nine-thousand-foot climb. He walked to the driver's side of the Blazer and shoved a hand inside the pocket of his tan pants. He pulled out the "cool" rock Adam had given him that morning and stuck it in his breast pocket. It wasn't even noon yet, and his cotton uniform was already stuck to his back. Shit.

"What in the hell is that?"

Dylan glanced across the top of the Chevy at Lewis, then turned his attention to the silver sports car driving toward him.

"He must have taken a wrong turn before he hit Sun Valley," Lewis guessed. "Must be lost."

In Gospel, where the color of a man's neck favored the color red and where pickup trucks and power rigs ruled the roads, a Porsche was about as inconspicuous as a gay rights parade marching toward the pearly gates.

"If he's lost, someone will tell him," Dylan said as he shoved his hand into his pants pocket once more and found his keys. "Sooner or later," he added. In the resort town of Sun Valley, a Porsche wasn't that rare a sight, but in the wilderness area, it was damn unusual. A lot of the roads in Gospel weren't even paved. And some of those that weren't had potholes the size of basketballs. If that little car took a wrong turn, it was bound to lose an oil pan or an axle.

The car rolled slowly past, its tinted windows concealing whoever was inside. Dylan dropped his gaze to the iridescent vanity license plate with the seven blue letters spelling out MZBHAVN. If that wasn't bad enough, splashed across the top of the plate like a neon kick-me sign was the word "California" painted in red. Dylan hoped like hell the car pulled an illegal U and headed right back out of town.

Instead, the Porsche pulled into a space in front of the Blazer and the engine died. The driver's door swung open. One turquoise, silver-toed Tony Lama hit the pavement and a slender bare arm reached out to grasp the top of the doorframe. Glimmers of light caught on a thin gold watch wrapped around a slim wrist. Then MZBHAVN stood, looking for all the world like she was stepping out of one of those women's glamour magazines that gave beauty tips.

"Holy shit," Lewis uttered.

In **NOT ANOTHER BAD DATE** Adele Harris asks the question, "What does a gal have to do to get a good date in this town?" She's had so many lousy dates, she's pretty sure she's cursed. And when she meets Zach Zemaitis, she hopes her luck's about to change... but is it?

K iss me, babe."

"No, really." Beneath the light of a sixty-watt bulb on her porch, Adele Harris placed a hand on the chest of her latest date. "I've had enough excitement for one night."

Investment banker and former nerd turned world-class jerk Sam King mistook the hand on his chest for a caress and took a step forward, backing Adele against the front door. Cool October air slipped across her cheeks and between the lapels of her coat, and she watched horrified as Sam lowered his face to her. "Baby, you don't know excitement until I fire you up with a kiss."

"I'll pass. I don't thi—urggg—" Sam smashed his lips against Adele's and silenced her protest. He shoved his tongue into her mouth and did some sort of weird swirly thing. Three quick circles to the left.

Three to the right. Repeat. She hadn't been kissed like that since Carl Wilson in the sixth grade.

She forced her free hand between them and shoved. "Stop!" she gasped as she reached into the small purse hanging from her shoulder and pulled out her keys. "Good night, Sam."

His jaw dropped and his brows lowered. "You're not inviting me in?"

"No." She turned and unlocked her front door.

"What the hell? I just spent a hundred and twenty bucks on dinner and I don't get laid?"

She pushed the door open and looked over her shoulder at the moron standing on her porch. The evening had started out okay, but had begun a downward descent with the salad course. "I'm not a prostitute. If you'd wanted a sure thing, you should have called an escort service."

"Women love me! I don't have to pay a prostitute," he protested a bit too much. "Women are dying to get some Sammy."

By the time the dinner plates had been cleared, the date had nosedived into the third level of hell, and for the past hour Adele had tried to be nice.

"Of course they are," she said, but failed to keep a bite of sarcasm from her voice. She stepped into her house and turned to face him.

"No wonder you're thirty-five and alone," he sneered. "You need to learn how to treat a man."

For the past hour she'd pretended interest in his narcissistic ramblings. His nonstop bragging and his presumption that he was quite the catch and she was *very* lucky. She tried to tell herself that it wasn't his fault. That lately she'd begun to suspect there was something about her that made men insane, but he'd just crossed the line. Poked at a very sore spot. "And *you* need to learn to kiss like a man," she said, and slammed the front door in his stunned face.

Maddie Dupree isn't in Truly, Idaho, seeking a husband, boyfriend, or anything in between. No, in TANGLED UP IN YOU she's determined to discover the untold story about the town's sordid past . . . and Mick Hennessy is part of that story.

The glowing white neon above Mort's Bar pulsed and vibrated and attracted the thirsty masses of Truly, Idaho, like a bug light. But Mort's was more than a beer magnet. More than just a place to drink cold Coors and get into a fight on Friday nights. Mort's had historical significance—kind of like the Alamo. While other establishments came and went in the small town, Mort's had always stayed the same.

Until about a year ago when the new owner had spruced the place up with gallons of Lysol and paint and had instituted a strict no-panty-tossing policy. Before that, throwing undies like a ring-toss up onto the row of antlers above the bar had been encouraged as a sort of indoor sporting event. Now, if a woman felt the urge to toss, she got tossed out on her bare ass.

Ah, the good old days.

Maddie Jones stood on the sidewalk in front of Mort's and stared up at the sign, completely immune to the subliminal lure that the light sent out through the impending darkness. An indistinguishable hum of voices and music leached through the cracks in the old building sandwiched between Ace Hardware and the Panda Restaurant.

A couple in jeans and tank tops brushed past Maddie. The door opened and the sound of voices and the unmistakable twang of country music spilled out onto Main Street. The door closed and Maddie remained standing outside. She adjusted the purse strap on her shoulder, then pulled up the zipper on her bulky blue sweater. She hadn't lived in Truly for twenty-nine years, and she'd forgotten how cool it got at night. Even in July.

Her hand lifted toward the old door, then dropped to her side. A surprising rush of apprehension raised the hair on the back of her neck and tilted her stomach. She'd done this dozens of times. So why the apprehension? Why now? she asked herself, even though she knew the answer. Because it was personal this time, and once she opened that door, once she took the first step, there was no going back.

If her friends could see her, standing there as if her feet were set in the concrete, they'd be shocked. She'd interviewed serial killers and cold-blooded murderers, but chatting up nut jobs with antisocial personality disorders was a piece of cake compared to what waited for her inside Mort's. Beyond the NO ONE UNDER 21 sign, her past waited for her, and as she'd learned recently, digging into other people's pasts was a hell of a lot easier than digging into her own.

"For God's sake," she muttered and reached for the door. She was a little disgusted with herself for being such a wimp and a weenie, and she squelched her apprehension under the heavy fist of her strong will. Nothing was going to happen that she did not want to happen. She was in control. As always.

TRUE LOVE AND OTHER DISASTERS'

Faith Duffy doesn't need the pro hockey team she just inherited, and she really doesn't need the loathsome team captain who comes with it. Ty Savage has lethal sex appeal . . . and Faith knows it would be disastrous to get involved with him. But as we all know, sometimes disaster is just waiting to happen . . .

*H*e stopped in front of her and held out his hand. "I'm sorry for your loss."

"Thank you." A slight frown creased her smooth forehead and her big green eyes looked up into his face. She was even more beautiful and looked much younger up close. She placed her hand in his; her skin was soft and her fingers a little cool. "You're the captain of Virgil's hockey team. He always spoke highly of you."

It was her hockey team now, and what she did with it was up for speculation. He'd heard she was going to sell it. He hoped that was true and that it happened soon.

Ty dropped her hand. "Virgil was a great guy." Which everyone knew was a stretch. Like a lot of extremely wealthy men used to getting their way,

Virgil could be a real son of a bitch. But Ty had gotten along with the old man because they'd had the same goal. "I enjoyed our long talks about hockey." Virgil might have been eighty-one, but his mind had been sharp and he'd known more about hockey than a lot of players. A smile curved her full kiss-me-baby lips. "Yes. He loved it."

She wore very little makeup, which surprised him given her former profession. He'd never met a Playmate who didn't love to paint her face. "If there is anything the guys and I can do to help you out, let me know," he said without much sincerity, but since he was the captain of the team, he figured he should offer.

"Thank you."

Virgil's only child stepped forward and whispered something in the Widow's ear. Ty had met Landon Duffy on several occasions and couldn't say that he liked him much. He was as ruthless and driven as Virgil, but without the charm that had made his father such a success.

The Widow's smile faltered and her shoulders straightened. Anger flashed in her green eyes. "Thank you for coming, Mr. Savage." Like a lot of Americans, she'd mispronounced his name. It wasn't savage, like in *beast*. It was pronounced Sah-vahge.

Ty watched her turn and walk away, and he wondered what Landon had said. Obviously, she hadn't liked it. His gaze slid down her blonde hair to her nicely rounded behind in the plain black dress that looked anything but plain. He wondered if Virgil's son had propositioned her. Not that it mattered. Ty had more important things to worry about. Namely, this Thursday's game in Vancouver when they'd take on the dual threat of the Sedin twins in the playoffs opener. Until three months ago, Ty had been captain of the Canucks, and he knew better than anyone to never underestimate the boys from Sweden. If they were on their game, they were a defenseman's worst nightmare.

"Have you seen the pictures?"

Ty removed his gaze from the Widow's departing ass and looked over his shoulder at his teammate, all-around shit-disturber, Sam Leclaire. "No." He didn't have to ask what pictures. He knew and had never been interested enough to search them out.

"Her boobs are real." Out of one corner of his mouth Sam added, "Not that I looked." He tried to appear innocent, but the black eye ruined it.

"Of course not."

"Do you think she can get us invited to the Playboy Mansion?"

"See ya tomorrow," Ty said through a laugh and moved toward the entry.